Holly Smale is the author of *Geek Girl*, *Model Misfit*, *Picture Perfect*, *All that Glitters*, *Head Over Heels* and Geek Girl novellas, *All Wrapped Up* and *Sunny Side Up*. She was unexpectedly spotted by a top London modelling agency at the age of fifteen and spent the following two years falling over on catwalks, going bright red and breaking things she couldn't afford to replace. By the time Holly had graduated from Bristol University with a BA in English Literature and an MA in Shakespeare she had given up modelling and set herself on the path to becoming a writer.

Geek Girl was the no. 1 bestselling young adult fiction title in the UK in 2013. It was shortlisted for several major awards and won the Teen and Young Adult category of the Waterstones Children's Book Prize. The series has been published in 26 languages all over the world. Holly is currently writing the sixth book in the *Geek Girl* series.

Follow Holly Smale on Twitter and Instagram:
@holsmale
www.facebook.com/geekgirlseries

*For Louise. Because everybody
needs a fairy godmother.*

GEEK GIRL

HEAD OVER HEELS

HOLLY SMALE

HarperCollins *Children's Books*

First published in Great Britain by HarperCollins *Children's Books* 2016
This edition published in 2016
HarperCollins *Children's Books* is a division of HarperCollins*Publishers* Ltd,
HarperCollins Publishers
1 London Bridge Street
London SE1 9GF

The HarperCollins *Children's Books* website address is: www.harpercollins.co.uk

1

Copyright © Holly Smale 2016

ISBN 978-0-00-796819-0

Holly Smale asserts the moral right to be identified as the author of this work.
All rights reserved.

Printed and bound by CPI Group (UK) Ltd, Croydon, CR0 4YY

MIX
Paper from
responsible sources
FSC˘ C007454

FSC™ is a non-profit international organisation established to promote
the responsible management of the world's forests. Products carrying the
FSC label are independently certified to assure consumers that they come
from forests that are managed to meet the social, economic and
ecological needs of present and future generations,
and other controlled sources.

Find out more about HarperCollins and the environment at
www.harpercollins.co.uk/green

head over heels: idiom

1   To be excited, and/or turn cartwheels
2   To fall in love
3   To become temporarily the wrong way up
4   To go at top speed
6   To fall over

ORIGIN: an inversion of fourteenth century expression *heels over head*, to literally turn upside down

1

My name is Harriet Manners, and I have friends.

I know I have friends because this is by far the busiest I've ever been.

Honestly, my calendar is *manic.*

Between group study sessions and movie nights, pizza-eating competitions and crossword round robins, it's all I can do to keep my epic new social life in some kind of order.

So now I've got two diaries: one to make sure I'm in the right place at the right time, the other for making sure everyone else is.

What can I say?

Winnie-the-Pooh was Friendship Ambassador in 1997: I have an awful lot to live up to.

The other reason I know I have friends is that I have a badge that says this in bright blue ink:

Team JINTH!

"Harriet," Nat said when I presented her with one. "Is this *totally* necessary?"

"Yes," I confirmed, pinning it to my Best Friend's coat. "We don't want our brand-new additions to feel left out, do we?"

Then I gave badges to Jasper, India and Toby.

Along with the key-rings and magnets I made on my laminating machine.

That's right: I am now in an official *gang*.

A clique, a posse, a fellowship.

A group of five happy kindred spirits, never to be parted. Just like the Famous Five or Scooby Doo, except one of us isn't a big brown dog.

And it's literally changed my life.

Studies have shown that people with a large network of friends tend to outlive their peers by up to twenty-two per cent, but I'm having so much fun I expect I'll last even longer.

It took sixteen years, but I finally found them.

People who genuinely want to know that the average London pigeon has 1.6 feet and the soil in your back garden is two million years old.

People who love discovering that a single sloth can be home to 980 beetles and that Martian sunsets are blue and then maybe trying to Google a picture.

I finally found *my* people.

Etymologically, the word happy comes from the Old Norse noun *happ*, which means *good luck or fortune*, and that's how I feel: as if everything is finally happening exactly as I've always wanted it to.

Because for the first time ever, I'm not on the outside looking in any more: I'm smack bang in the middle.

Part of a team and fitting in perfectly.

And I'm having the time of my life.

2

So where am I right now, you ask?

That's what you really want to know, isn't it: where a gang of this epic coolness – of this rare *synergy* – could possibly be spending most of their free time together.

Well, it's not the local launderette.

Those innocent days are behind me, I'm afraid.

I tried to keep them going, obviously.

In fact, for the first few weeks I even set up a circle of chairs next to my favourite drying machine and a tray of snacks on top of the coin dispenser, but India wasn't having any of it.

"Harriet," she said after our seventh game of 'Which Washing Machine Finishes First'. "We're sixth formers. Don't you think we should maybe hang out somewhere with… I don't know, less dirty underwear lying about?"

Honestly, I think she was just upset because her machine always finished last.

Some people are *super* competitive.

Anyway, after a lot of careful research and analysis I finally picked somewhere new: a cosy little cafe, less than fifteen minutes from my house.

And it's actually kind of perfect.

There are lanterns everywhere and bright velvet cushions and shelves with interesting books piled high. Little coloured fairy-lights are strung from the ceiling all year round, and newspapers featuring multiple crosswords are strewn across the tables: just begging to be filled *en masse*.

There's chocolate cake and ginger biscuits and every kind of coffee you could imagine: *espresso* and *macchiato*, *cappuccino* and *mochaccino*.

Basically, a lot of drinks with *o* on the end.

Team JINTH even has its very own special spot: a large blue sofa tucked in the corner with two red leather armchairs and a series of green vintage suitcases turned into a table, where we sit *all* of the time.

Unless other people are sitting there first, and then we have to sit somewhere else.

In short, the cafe is a strategic success.

Close enough for easy access, far enough to feel like a real escape. Glamorous, intimate, mature: the absolute height of sociable sophistication.

It's my new happiest place to be.

"The usual?" the barista says as I reach the counter, phone clutched tightly in my hand. "Or are we going to branch out and try something new and dangerous today?"

Without looking up, I type:

I'm here! :) What is your approximate ETA? Hxx

Then I shake my head and press SEND. "Just the same as normal, please."

There's a loud buzz.

"So an extra-large and chocolatey hot chocolate with too much foam it is, then."

"Yes, please. With extra powdered chocolate, in a round cup." I quickly type out another message. "So it looks like a real cappuccino and nobody can tell it hasn't got any coffee in it."

"A *Harriet-uccino*. Got it."

I know, I know.

Coffee may statistically be the most popular drink in the world, and in the UK we consume 70 million cups of it every day, but I tried it once and spent four hours talking to a pigeon.

Remember to wear your JINTH T-shirts for photo

opportunities! Hxx

There's another buzz.

Also don't forget the itineraries for tonight! Hxx

Apparently one in three teenagers send over three thousand text messages a month, and according to my last phone bill I am definitely heading towards that minority. (Although judging by my parents' reaction, you'd think I was already there.)

Being in a happily organised gang is a surprising amount of work.

There's another buzz, and the barista pauses from frothing up my milk to grab his phone out of his apron pocket and stare at it with one bright blue eye and one brown.

"You know, Harriet," Jasper says, "you're standing right in front of me. You could just *say* it."

I glance up in surprise.

His lightly tanned face is flushed by the steam, his dark blond hair has grown into a kind of scruffy mohican and his dark eyebrows are knitted together in their standard frown.

"But what if you forget? You might need it written down for later."

OK, there might be *another,* slightly less poetic, reason why we hang out here. Jasper's family owns this cafe, so he works here most evenings and every weekend and we usually get a discount or an extra sprinkle of chocolate.

If Jasper's in a good mood, that is. If he's in a grump, he gives us cinnamon.

"Take your *fake-uccino*," he sighs, shaking his head and passing it over the counter. "Burnt biscuit? I've screwed up another batch and need to get rid of them before Mum notices."

I beam at him: I *love* the burnt ones. "Yes, please."

"Such a little weirdo," he says, grabbing two from under the counter. "And what other documentation do I need to bring this evening? A passport? Some kind of visa? Do you have a fingerprinting machine for security purposes?"

Oh my goodness, that would be awesome.

Then I spot his smirk.

"Jasper King," I tell him airily, "I am very busy so if you're just going to be sarcastic, I have more important things to do."

He thinks about that for a few seconds. "I am literally always going to be sarcastic."

"In that case, I shall be over there, eating my biscuits." I stick my nose in the air. "Which I appreciate very much, by the way. Please send more over in due course."

Then, humming to myself, I take my hot chocolate contentedly over to my special section of the corner sofa.

I put little bits of typed-out, laminated paper on the rest of the seats to make sure they're officially reserved.

I take a huge gulp of my delicious *Harriet-uccino.*

And I sit down patiently to wait.

3

Unfortunately, we could be here some time.

Regardless of my gentle yet informative lectures about the importance of punctuality – and the street maps I drew for each of them individually – the rest of Team JINTH is almost always late.

Even though every single one of them lives closer to the cafe than I do.

So I may as well use this delay to update you on what *else* has been going on in the four months since you last saw me. Just try not to imagine me breaking up my biscuit and crumbling it into my hot chocolate at the same time, because that's not what I'm doing.

I'm not dropping three more sugar cubes in there either: that would be gross.

Or sprinkling extra chocolate on top.

Ahem.

1 Lower Sixth is going brilliantly. I am now Biology

16

Prefect, International Physics Ambassador and Director of Dinosaur Studies.

2 Those last two aren't real school positions: I gave them to myself.

3 According to my grades so far, I am acing my A Levels. Which is good, because 97.3% of accepted students at Cambridge University have A*AA, so I'm still on target.

4 I wrote Cambridge University a long letter letting them know this.

5 They have not written back.

6 My baby sister, Tabitha, has just started crawling, waving and clapping her hands every time she sees me.

7 Which is kind of a problem, because according to our baby book she's not supposed to be doing that for another two weeks.

8 Annabel's started working three days a week so that Dad can focus properly on his job hunt on the days he's not caring for Tabby.

9 Wilbur has returned from New York to take up his old position at Infinity Models agency.

10 I haven't done any modelling.

Well, none that I plan on telling you about right now, anyway.

I'm far too traumatised to go into it quite yet. All you need to know is I never want to hear the words "Paris Couture Fashion Week", "fluorescent swimming pool" or "giant rabbit head" ever again.

The humiliating nightmares are still recurring.

What else?

Nat and Theo broke up and she won a big fashion award at college – consequently she seems to spend even more time there, if that's possible; India was promoted from new girl to Head Girl – making her simultaneously cool and powerful; Jasper has done a lot of stomping around, covered in paint and scowling at everyone. (Everybody in my gang has a talent and that's his speciality.)

In fact, every person in my social circle appears to be on a similarly positive trajectory: the only way is up.

Literally, in Toby's case.

My ex-stalker has managed to grow another three

inches over the last two terms, and we're beginning to worry that – much like Alice in Wonderland – he's just going to keep eating things and shooting up vertically until he hits the ceiling.

And that's pretty much everything.

My entire life: neatly summarised in a series of beautifully organised bullet points and decisive sentences.

Except that's not what you want to know, is it?

You're sitting there, nodding – *yes, Harriet, lovely, Harriet, how interesting, Harriet* – but there's one burning question I haven't answered and you're not going to pay any attention until I do.

Trust me, I understand: that's how I feel about burning questions too.

So here it is.

I'm just sorry if it's not what you were hoping for, that's all.

Every time we fall in love, we statistically lose two good friends: reducing our average friendship group from five people to three.

So six months ago, I pushed a wooden box full of memories under my bed.

I opened the big box in my head.

I put love and romance inside and locked it up tightly.

Then I kept moving forward with the things that make me happy: into a neat, tidy and organised world with lots of extra space in my story now for other things. Like learning that polar bears can eat eighty-six penguins in one sitting and if you lift a kangaroo's tail it can't hop, or that outer space tastes of raspberries.

For spending time having fun with my gang.

So no, I don't have a boyfriend.

And no, I definitely don't want one.

Because there are approximately a hundred thousand billion cells in the human body, and for the first time in over fifteen months every single one of mine belongs to me again.

I think that's all you really need to know.

4

Anyway.

A lot can happen in fifteen seconds.

In just fifteen seconds, 69,000 tweets are posted and eighteen hours of YouTube videos are uploaded.

Every fifteen seconds, 615,000 Facebook statuses are updated, 51 million emails are written and 600,000 texts are sent.

Basically, a lot of socialising goes on.

Over the next quarter of a minute, I do my best to single-handedly boost those statistics.

With my phone mere centimetres from my face, I type as fast as I can: sending a group message letting everyone know it's unseasonably warm today so they probably don't need coats, and another asking if I should get their drinks in for them so they don't have to wait in line.

A text, asking where everyone is now.

Another, asking if they'd like a biscuit or slice of cake, then another just to let them know that I'm totally fine about the cancelled night-trip to the zoo last weekend.

A funny joke I just remembered about a duck.

Another about a whale.

An observation about an interesting squirrel I saw in a tree on the way here.

In fact, I'm texting so hard the only thing I *don't* do over the next fifteen seconds is look up or glance around the room.

Which means I'm just sending everyone an interesting fact about biscuits – it comes from the old French word *bescuit* which means 'twice cooked' – when a laugh comes completely out of nowhere.

And it takes a lot longer than it probably should to realise that although it doesn't belong to anyone in my friendship group, I still know it very well indeed.

Better than I'd like to.

"Well," a tall blonde girl says as I glance up, finger still paused on SEND, "if it isn't Harriet Manners."

And there – looming over me with an extremely confusing statement – is the one part of my life I failed to update you on: the single bullet point I completely left off.

Alexa.

5

I stare at my arch-nemesis blankly.

Apparently as soon as a young sea-squirt finds a rock to anchor itself to, it will eat its own brain because it doesn't really need one any more.

I think that's possibly what's happened to me.

This place is so safe and *so* comfortable – such a source of inner strength – I'm not really on my guard any longer.

Now my head is totally empty.

"What a charming surprise," Alexa continues with another laugh, blowing on her proper, caffeinated coffee. "I didn't realise you hung out here. Do you mind if I sit with you?"

Seriously: *again*?

Why does she always insist on sitting with me? The surface of the earth is 510 billion square metres. Can't she just – for *once* – pick one that isn't directly adjacent to mine?

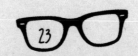

I watch as my bully of eleven years flicks the paper that says *Natalie Grey* on to the floor and sits down, propping her spiky high-heeled boots on the chair that says *Toby Pilgrim* and flinging her handbag on to *India Perez*.

So much for reservations.

"You know," she continues with a little smirk, "I wasn't sure about this place at first, but I think maybe it's kind of *growing* on me."

I nod vaguely. "Mmm."

"What are you drinking?" she asks curiously, staring into my cup. "*Go tea!*"

I blink a few times. My beverage is quite clearly not tea: it has fluffed-up milk on top and a ridiculous amount of chocolate sprinkles.

"Actually," I say, flushing slightly, "it's an extremely strong cappuccino. The caffeine molecule mimics the molecule *adenosine* and binds to natural receptors that would otherwise make you sleepy, thus keeping you – I mean *me* – super-awake."

Thanks to Jasper's drink-making skills, there's no way she can prove this is actually a kiddy-beverage. Thank goodness this time there are no pink mini-marshmallows floating on top.

"Please," Alexa takes another delicate sip and wiggles her eyebrows, "do tell me *mo'*."

I stare at her a little longer, totally bemused. Why does she sound like an American belle from the Deep South?

Then I decide I don't really care.

There's a spider in the United States called the *Loxosceles reclusa*. Its venom is so powerful it destroys flesh: chewing up cell membranes and cutting off the blood supply. Thousands of people every year used to be badly wounded by it.

They're not any more.

In 1984, scientists at Vanderbilt University in Nashville found the anti-venom that blocked the spider's venom and stopped it destroying anything.

There's a brilliant reason why I left Alexa off my list: she no longer matters. She doesn't make me cry and she doesn't make me hide under tables. After eleven years, I finally found the only thing in the world that could stop my bully hurting me.

Myself.

"No, thank you," I sigh tiredly, grabbing the crossword I left yesterday under the coffee table and studying that instead.

"Maybe we can *shave* it for later?"

"Sure," I say in a bored voice, writing EWER in four across: *boat or vessel*.

"It's so nice to see you finally *manning* up."

I nod and scribble ERINACEOUS in six down: *pertaining to a hedgehog.* "Uh-huh."

The door opens with a BANG.

"We'll really have to— OOMPH."

I glance up just in time to see a tornado of long black hair, blue coat and grey bag as Nat rips across the cafe with Toby and India close behind her.

And sits directly in Alexa's lap.

6

Nature is truly incredible.

When a red fire ant is threatened, pheromones are automatically released and every other member of its ant community will come rushing to the rescue.

Team JINTH must have a similar power.

The door is still swinging: that's how fast my entire battalion of friends has come charging in, swords drawn.

Metaphorically, obviously.

It's not 1675, and coffee shops are no longer the illegal hub of political uprisings.

"*Awwwww*," Nat says with a bright smile, lifting her feet to make herself as heavy as possible, "Alexa Roberts. You kept my seat warm for me. How *sweet*."

"It's warm?" India throws herself casually into the seat next to them and kicks off her purple suede boots. "Weird. I always assumed she'd be cold-blooded."

"That's ridiculous," Toby objects, perching on the coffee table wearing a T-shirt with a TARDIS drawn on

it that says TRUST ME, I'M THE DOCTOR. "All mammals have warm blood. Are we *JINTHA* now? Because we're going to need new baseball caps."

"*What the... how the...*" Alexa is worming her way out from beneath Nat and struggling to her feet, face purple, smirk completely gone. "GET THE HELL OFF ME, FREAK. You can't just go around *sitting* on people!"

"Oops," Nat shrugs with wide eyes. "The seat usually has my name on it. Or maybe you changed your name by deed poll because you're so desperate to be me."

"And Harriet didn't look like she was loving your company," India points out, propping her toes on the coffee table while her bright purple hair gleams under the fairy-lights. "It seemed like a good point to interrupt."

In fairness, I'd have probably been more entertained if I had a single clue what Alexa was talking about.

"This place is pathetically hipster anyway," Alexa snaps furiously, brushing her jeans down with a disgusted look on her face. "It's a destination for jokes like you to pretend you have real lives outside of academia. You can so *have* it."

HA. Told you it's super-cool in here.

Alexa sneers at me and I stare calmly back. Captain America has a shield made of *vibranium,* and it's completely indestructible. Hulk can smash it, Thor can hammer it, and nothing happens.

It feels like I finally have one too.

Smiling serenely, I lift my chin and give her my most regal expression. She absorbs it for a few seconds, clearly deeply impressed by my incredible majesty.

Then she bursts out laughing again.

"*Geek*," she says, shaking her head. "Laters, Manners. I *must dash*. This place is yours: I wouldn't want it anyway."

And – with a final flick of her hand – Alexa walks away.

7

Some battles in life you win, and some you lose.

I think it's obvious which one that was.

"Well," I grin broadly, triumphantly putting my crossword down on the table. "We definitely won that one, huh, guys."

Then I hold up my hand to high-five them all.

There's a silence.

"Uh, Harriet," India says, rubbing her top lip. "What are you drinking?"

Oh my God, why does everyone keep asking me that? *"It's coffee,"* I say a little too defensively. *"With caffeine molecules in it."*

Then I look to Nat for support, but her head is down, her shiny dark hair has fallen across her face and her shoulders are shaking.

"Did you know, Harriet," Toby says, putting a finger on his top lip, "that in Mayan times the cocoa bean was used as currency because it was more valuable than gold?"

I blink and look back at Nat. She's holding a finger up to her top lip now too.

OK: this is amazing.

We've obviously got some kind of gang *gesture*, even better than a high-five. My pals have become so utterly *in-sync and synergised,* we don't even need to talk about it first. That's how *in tune* we are with each other.

I beam and put my finger on my top lip too.

It seems a little inappropriate – especially in light of the Second World War – but who am I to question our clique motives?

This is what I love so much about us.

We work seamlessly together: like a prickle of porcupines, or a dray of squirrels, a journey of giraffes or a band of mongoo—

"Hey, genius," Jasper says, suddenly appearing from the kitchen with a tray full of clean mugs, "you've got chocolate all over your face."

Then he puts the tray down on the counter and disappears again.

I blink at the space Jasper was just standing in.

There's a mushroom called the *Omphalotus olearius* that gives off a glow so bright it's possible to read a book at night by its light. My cheeks are suddenly so luminous,

I could power an entire nocturnal library.

Growing on me. Goatee. Mo'. Shave it for later. Manning up.

Must dash. Mustdash. Moustache.

Oh my God, Alexa didn't think my expression was regal and majestic at all.

Unless she assumed I'm Abraham Lincoln.

Still shaking with suppressed giggles, Nat holds a hand-mirror up and sure enough: there's a thick dark brown line on my upper lip and a large poo-coloured streak on my chin.

Sugar cookies.

"You know," Toby says loyally as I bury my head in my arms with a humiliated groan, "beards actually make you 63% more likely to win a staring contest. No wonder Alexa left so quickly, Harriet."

And that does it.

With an explosion of giggles, India and Nat collapse on the sofa and I remember again why I tend to hang out in places away from the public eye.

Maybe I didn't win that particular battle after all.

8

Statistically, we each go through 396 friends in a lifetime and only keep 36 of them.

Maybe I should just keep looking.

I bet the other 392 wouldn't spend eight whole minutes laughing at my foamy facial hair.

By the time everyone has stopped giggling – and I'm wiped clean with a series of damp cloths – normality has finally resumed.

Nat's sipping her coconut milk latte; India's sprawled across the sofa with her second espresso and Toby's ploughing through a glass of hot milk. Jasper pops over occasionally to contribute another burnt biscuit or sardonic comment.

And I've spread my documents across the table.

Tonight is the first ever Team JINTH sleepover and I am the inaugural host. And I don't want to sound vain, but I have arranged *everything*.

33

I've organised which games we'll play and which films we'll watch and what kind of food we're going to eat. I've written a How-Well-Do-We-Know-Each-Other quiz and a *Are We Really Having Fun?* questionnaire so we'll know how to improve next time.

I've even drawn a diagram of where on the floor we'll sleep.

It's going to be *amazing*.

"He did *what*?" Nat splutters into her coffee. "*No.*"

"He *did,*" India insists, grinning. "Halfway through the date, he put his leg on the table. *Plop.* Then he said 'I've been told I have very handsome shins'."

Nat explodes with laughter.

"The tibia *is* the second longest bone in the body," Toby says, nodding. "He may have had a point."

"So…" Nat sits forward. "What did you do?"

"I told him to get his flaming foot out of my dinner before I ate it and then I said I'd call him."

"*Ooooooh. Cold.*"

"Cold call him?" Toby says in confusion. "Like a telesales person? Sometimes they ring us about windows even though we clearly have eight already."

"When somebody says they'll *call* you, it means they won't call you. Or they'd have been more specific."

"Yup. It's dating speak for *this is over now please go*

away and never speak to me again."

"Aaaaah," Toby nods. "I'm afraid I've never been rejected by a girl so I wouldn't know."

Nat blinks at him in silence.

"*Anyway*," I say, plopping my Filofax on the table. "Gang. About tonight. The itinerary is looking shipshape, but I just need to run through a few extra components. I've got Telling Each Other Secrets down at 9pm, is that OK?"

"Umm," Nat says, putting her coffee down, "actually, Harriet, about that…"

"Secrets at nine?" Toby says, pulling out a TEAM JINTH SLEEPOVER notepad. "Are you sure? I've got it down at 10pm. Just after the Pillow-Fight at 9:35."

I frown and check my notes. "I've pencilled it in wrong. Thanks, Tobes."

It's been surprisingly useful having Toby as my second-in-command. It's just too easy to forget what fun you're supposed to be having and when.

"Harriet?" Nat says. "Hang on…"

"I've also bought the snacks already." I check the list. "We just need to make sure we stick to salted after 11pm or we're going to crash by midnight."

"Seriously?" India says, lifting her eyebrows into dark ticks. "Are you regulating our blood sugar levels?"

"Of course not," I laugh. "Although I think there *is* a kit you can buy from pharmacies. Maybe I should swing past on my way back h—"

"Harriet," Nat says, prodding me. "*Listen.*"

"*Natalie,*" I grin. "Don't worry! I looked up beautifying face masks on the internet and made one out of avocado, lemon and olive oil."

"That's not..." Nat rubs a hand over her face. "We have a problem."

"Personalised bedding," Toby whispers. "I *told* you we needed monogrammed pillows."

Nat crosses her eyes at him.

"I can't make it tonight, H," she says slowly. "I'm so sorry. I know you've organised... everything, but there's a textiles exam on Monday and I'm just not ready for it."

"Oh thank *God*," India sighs. "I've got a Head Girl presentation to prepare for lower school so I can't come either."

I stare at Nat and India in shock.

Human brains are 10 per cent smaller than they were 20,000 years ago, and I can actually feel mine reducing.

"But you're half the sleepover," I point out stupidly. "I can't have it without you. It would just be..." I glance pointedly at Toby and Jasper.

Enough said.

"Subtle as always," Jasper says from where he's been cleaning the table next to us. "Guess I'd better keep my salsa and cheddar cheese face mask for myself, then."

Toby turns to me with lit-up, hopeful eyes.

"Not going to happen," I say quickly. Second-in-command is one thing: sleepover-for-two is quite another.

Then I collapse back into my seat.

I don't believe this. All that effort for *nothing*?

Ugh. I really wish people would let me know when they're editing my plans: this is my *life* they're rearranging.

Quickly, I force myself to rally.

"Next weekend?" I say, flicking through my Filofax as Nat drains the last of her coffee and stands up. "The weekend after? Half term? Easter holidays? Bank holiday?"

India opens her mouth and shuts it again.

"Sure," my best friend says, swinging her handbag over her shoulder and pecking me on the cheek. "We'll sort something out."

9

They don't sort something out at all.

It's now mid-March – two entire weeks later – and between exams and revision, jobs and dates, we've only *just* managed to pin down a time that the five of us can actually do.

And it's right now.

Frankly, I don't think people really appreciate how much *notice* is needed to throw a decent sleepover, because I just received this:

J got night off work last minute and I'm out of college early! Drag out the sleeping bags – it's on! Meet at cafe! Nat xx

And now I'm having a meltdown.

Biologists recently found 300 different species living among the debris floating in the ocean, including puffins, turtles, seals, whales and penguins: all of which have to

wade through mountains of human detritus just to get to bed at night.

I know exactly how they feel, because that's what my bedroom currently looks like.

Books are leaning in mountains against walls, draft essays are scattered, practice equations are crumpled. Paper is pinned over every wall: Excel sheets, schedules, timetables, Post-its.

My wastepaper basket looks ready to explode.

Ditto my dirty laundry.

A bowl of half-eaten tomato soup sits on my dressing table and I'm pretty sure my dog is in the room somewhere too but I couldn't swear to it.

Also possibly Annabel's cat.

The only difference between me and the poor puffins is: this mess is mine, which means it's my responsibility to tidy it up.

In *nine minutes flat.*

"Harriet?" Annabel says as I charge across the room, pick up an armful of laundry and throw it into the bottom of my wardrobe. "What on *earth* are you doing?"

She appears in my doorway with Tabby on her hip just in time to see me ram the wardrobe doors shut with my shoulder and stick a biro through the front handles.

It's probably a good thing she didn't catch me using the vacuum cleaner to pick up jumpers.

Or shouting "*Scourgify!*" at the sock drawer.

"Cleaning my bedroom," I say, grabbing a handful of textbooks and stuffing them on to an already exploding bookshelf. "Did you know that the average desk has 400 times more bacteria than a toilet seat?"

Then I look cautiously at mine.

I think I'm safe: it's coming up to exam time and there's so much paper on it I haven't actually seen the wood in months.

"You're *cleaning your bedroom*?" Annabel lifts one eyebrow. "Goodness. No wonder I was so confused. Tabitha, regard this historic event carefully. It may never happen again."

My sister laughs and waves Dunky, her favourite grey toy donkey, at me.

So I blow her an affectionate kiss.

The minute she's old enough, I'm going to have to explain the concept of slander. I've tidied my bedroom at least twice this year, so Annabel's insinuation is *very* unfair.

"Everything needs to be perfect," I explain, grabbing Winnie-the-Pooh off my bed. "It's not every day we have people stay over, is it?"

Then I give Winnie a kiss and put him in the box on top of my wardrobe. I don't want my friends thinking I still spend every night sleeping with a cuddly bear.

Even though he's the best and I totally do.

"I'm very impressed," Annabel smiles. "This is incredibly thoughtful of you, sweetheart."

I nod, quickly lobbing the 'WELCOME!!!' banner across the door. "It's important to make the people you love feel wanted in your home."

"It is. I'm so glad you're being mature about this, Harriet."

I glow with pride. She's right: I really *am*.

"It's going to be so much fun," I tell her excitedly, kicking my roller-trainers under the bed. "We're going to spend *the whole night* examining my book of Interesting Animal Facts and quizzing each other on them. I've made a Q and A especially."

Annabel frowns. "Well... not the *whole* night. She'll need to get some sleep."

Good point. Nat *does* get grumpy when she's tired. "OK, we'll probably be worn out by the choreographed dance routines anyway."

"Choreographed *dance* routines?"

"Don't worry. If there isn't space in here we can move the break-dancing to the living room."

"*Break-dancing*?" There's a pause while Annabel shifts Tabs to her other hip. "Sweetheart, it's very kind of you to arrange everything so carefully, but sixty-eight really isn't as young as you think it is."

I pause from randomly flicking a duster at the shelves and quickly do the maths in my head. Jasper and India are seventeen, but Nat and Toby are still sixteen.

So 17 + 17 + 16 + 16 =

"I think it's sixty-six," I correct as politely as possible.

"Sixty-eight, sweetheart."

"Sixty-six. You've inaccurately added a couple of birthdays."

"Harriet," Annabel laughs, heading back towards the hallway, "I appreciate your enthusiasm for both maths and human development, but I know how old my mother is."

I turn to stare at her blankly – what has *that* got to do with anything? – and that's when I hear it. A familiar *chug-chug-chug*. A *sputter-sputter-sputter*. A *thud-thud-thud*.

The sound of an ancient pink VW Beetle, reversing up the driveway.

Apparently the human brain absorbs eleven million bits of information every second, but we only notice forty of them.

Right now you can make that just one.

There's a loud *crunch*.

"Yoooohooooo!" a familiar voice calls as I run to my bedroom window and fling it wide open. "Kittens, I'm here early! Goodness, that's a funny place to put a hydrangea."

And there – beaming at us from out of the car window – is my hippy, nomadic grandmother.

Bunty.

10

Do you want to know a fascinating fact about the salamander? It can have its brain removed, cut into slices, shuffled like cards, put back in and yet still function as normal.

The same clearly can't be said for me.

I didn't include Bunty in my earlier summary because I had no idea what to tell you. Last time I heard from my step-grandmother, she was camped out in a llama sanctuary in Nepal. Before that, she was trying to break into Tibet without a permit.

A couple of months before that, I got a postcard from Bolivia saying

I'm actually in Peru, darlings, but don't tell anyone! Especially not the government ;)

Either way, she was anywhere but *here*.

Blinking, I watch my grandma hit the brakes with a loud squeak and then start cheerfully backing into our hedge. My chopped-up brain feels like it's desperately trying to fit itself back together again.

Oh my God. Annabel wasn't talking about my Team JINTH sleepover.

She was talking about *Bunty*.

No wonder there was such alarm about the dancing: it could literally break my grandmother.

"Harriet," Annabel frowns, pausing in the hallway as she watches me work this all out, "this shouldn't be a surprise. I've been reminding you about this visit for the last two weeks." She sighs. "I *knew* I should have made you put that phone down."

I stare at her, tiny bits of brain slowly dissolving into sludge. "Bunty's staying with us *now*?"

"Yes, *now*, Harriet." Annabel glances out of the window to where my grandma has begun three-point-turning across the lawn. "Although she wasn't supposed to be here until later tonight."

"But… I don't understand. Where is she going to sleep?"

"You're giving her your bedroom. I assumed that was what you were tidying up for."

My eyes shoot wide.

I love my grandmother, but this is my sanctuary. My refuge. *She's going to rearrange all my bookshelves.* "But I'm having a massive and seminal sleepover tonight. Where is everyone going to *go*?"

"You'll just have to postpone it for a while, Harriet," Annabel says calmly. "I'm very sorry."

"But... I can't postpone again. Everything's *arranged*."

"Then rearrange it."

There's the sound of a car door being shut outside, and flip-floppy footsteps crunching up the gravel. Annabel carefully shifts a gurgling Tabby and starts heading down the stairs.

In a panic, I race after them.

Quick, Harriet. Do something. Save the Team JINTH Sleepover Plan. "But can't she just sleep on the sofa like she did when Tabitha was born?"

"No, Harriet." There's a knock on the front door. "She's staying longer this time. I... don't know how long for. She needs a real bed."

"And I *don't*? I have important *exams* coming up, Annabel. Homework. Coursework. *Essential biology experiments*."

If in doubt, always fall back on academia.

"Chickens?" a bright voice calls through the letterbox.

"You don't have another birdhouse, do you? I think I've broken this one. They may need to temporarily squat in a tree."

"Just one second, Mum!"

"But…"

"*Harriet,*" Annabel whispers sharply, spinning round. Her face is so firm and so lawyer-y, my mouth automatically closes with a *snap.* "Stop saying *but.* This is not up for discussion, so just *try* and be a grown-up about it. Please?"

I blink. Nobody wins an argument against Annabel. Ever. I bet she can make grown judges cry.

"Thank you, darling," she says more gently, giving my shoulder a quick squeeze. "I truly appreciate it."

And the front door swings open.

‖

OK: *try and be a grown-up about it*?

What is *that* supposed to mean?

I'm sixteen and a half years old, thank you very much. If I lived in Cuba, Turkmenistan, Kyrgyzstan or Scotland, I'd be a legal adult already. In fact, in American Samoa I've been one for two whole years.

Maybe I should just move there.

I squint at the tanned figure, shining in the doorway. My grandmother is backlit by sunshine, giving her the appearance of a stained-glass window. Her hair is glowing bright pink, blue sequins are glinting all over her floor-length orange dress, a tasselled green pashmina is dangling across her shoulders and there are approximately fifteen daisies wound randomly through her hair.

And at least one caterpillar.

It's heading quietly but determinedly towards her left

ear as if it's been living on her head for quite some time.

"Darlings!" Bunty beams, holding her shimmering arms out wide. "My three favourite girls in the whole wide world, come and give me your best cuddles."

I hop forward and give her a hug.

Last time I saw my grandmother was for about five minutes after our return from New York last year, and I've genuinely missed her. It's not Bunty's fault that we clearly need a bigger house.

Or a more comfortable sofa.

"Harriet, darling, your aura is *glorious* at the moment," she says, holding me at arm's length and assessing me. "It's the most *beautiful* shade of yellow, with a few splashes of orange." She widens her eyes. "And *gold*. Golly, that's new. How wonderful."

She turns to survey my sister.

"Still a gorgeous red with a hint of bright pink," she says approvingly, touching the end of Tabitha's nose. "That's my little maverick."

Then Bunty puts her hands gently on either side of Annabel's face and studies her for a few seconds. "Pale blue, darling," she says. "We'll need to do something about that."

Annabel smiles faintly. "We will."

"Let me see what I've got." Bunty starts rummaging

through her patchwork satchel, then pulls out a feather and incense cone. "A Native American smudge kit should do the trick. The cedar smoke will clean any negative energy out in a jiffy."

"But where will it *go*?" Dad says, wandering in from the garden shed, where he's been preparing for his next job interview. "Don't give it to me, Bunty Brown. I'm already trying to find work in an industry that sells things to people who don't need them."

"You'll definitely want to use a bigger feather in that case, Richard," she smiles affectionately. "I may need to hunt down an eagle."

"Or an albatross," Dad grins.

"Actually," I interrupt as they hug, "the ostrich is the biggest bird in the world but the Great Argus pheasant has the longest feathers. They're in its tail."

They laugh, even though that's a totally accurate fact that they obviously didn't know already.

"Chickpeas, I promise I won't get in the way," Bunty says, dragging a brightly coloured carpetbag through the door. "I was en route to a Jivamukti yoga retreat in Mongolia and I thought: why not say hello?"

"Give me that." Annabel picks up the bag. "You're not in the way, Mum. In fact, Harriet's tidied her room for you especially. Haven't you, Harriet?"

She gives me a sharp look that says: *haven't you, Harriet,* so I nod as convincingly as I can.

"Don't be silly billies," Bunty says breezily. "I'm taking the sofa in the living room as usual and I won't hear another word about it."

"But—"

"*But* is a word, Annabel. Harriet's sixteen and she needs her own space. Western beds are terribly bad for the spine anyway."

My stepmother opens her mouth to object again, then shuts it with a *snap*.

Huh. Maybe she doesn't win against *everybody*.

"Plus," Bunty continues with a little wink at me, "my mystical talents are telling me my beautiful granddaughter has something lovely planned with her friends for this evening. Am I right?"

I stare at her in amazement.

How does she… What did she… How on earth can she possibly…

Oh.

I still have the Team JINTH Sleepover Plan gripped tightly against my chest.

A wave of gratitude washes over me.

"Oh thank you thank you *thank you.*" I throw my arms around her. She smells of pine needles and blueberries.

"You're the best grandma in the whole world."

"I'm definitely one of them," she laughs. "I've checked. Now, darling, go and have fun with your friends."

12

Scientists say that if you added up all the adrenaline inside everyone in England, it would weigh less than three ounces. To put it into perspective, that's the equivalent of a very small armadillo, an extremely large tarantula or three average house mice.

I'm so excited, I must be using at least half of it.

Buzzing with happiness, I grab my satchel, slam my trainers on and say a brief goodbye to Tabby and Bunty. With a small effort I manage to ignore Annabel's I'm-Disappointed-In-You expression and the Talk-To-Her eyes she's subtly making at Dad.

Then I fly out of the house, imaginary wings at my feet.

I know that *logically* it makes no sense to meet the team at the cafe only to turn around and bring them all straight back here, but that's what I'm doing so deal with it.

It's my first ever gang sleepover. Not including the disastrous party I threw last year, it's the first time I've

ever hosted *anything* that isn't just Nat and me.

Tonight is going to blow everyone *away*.

Beaming, I skip down the road.

I quickly pick up a few interesting leaves for Jasper's art assignment, a pretty purple flower for India, a piece of interesting wood for Nat (she's doing a design project on sustainability) and a small pebble for Toby (no particular reason except I didn't want him to feel left out).

And I've just reached the cafe when my pocket starts vibrating. A millisecond later, Bibbidi-Bobbidi-Boo begins playing loudly.

Sugar cookies.

Hesitating, I peer through the window.

The gang's in there already, sitting in our normal spot, drinks in front of them. Nat's looking at the front of an envelope, Toby's drawing a diagram of something and Indi's staring at her phone. Her socked feet propped on the table. Thanks to my fight with Annabel, I'm late.

My phone's still ringing and – when I drag it out reluctantly – FAIRY GODMOTHER is flashing on the screen.

This might be important.

Or it might not be. With Wilbur it's sometimes difficult to tell.

Quickly, I rap loudly on the cafe window.

I'm here! I mouth as they look up simultaneously.

Don't do anything interesting without me!

My friends stare at me through the glass.

Just like that! I mouth gratefully, giving them a thumbs up. *I'll be just one minute!*

Then I turn around to take the call.

13

Honestly, it's been great having Wilbur back from New York.

Just not necessarily as an agent.

Since the Paris debacle, the phone hasn't exactly been ringing off the hook for my professional services. In fact, last time Wilbur called me it was four nights ago to give him advice on ordering pizza.

I suggested tuna and pineapple: it was a great success.

"Hello?" I say distractedly. Through the window I can see Nat rubbing her eyes and India shaking her head.

What was that? What did I just miss?

"Happy Friday, baby-baby-buffalo! How are you today, milk-muffin? Are you just *bubbling* under the unseasonal sun?"

Nat opens the envelope and says something and Jasper emerges from the kitchen, glances momentarily at the group and then narrows his eyes and looks around the cafe.

I rap on the window again and wave.

He gives a rare grin and points at the full brown paper bag in his hand.

Ooh, yay. More burnt biscuits.

"Hello?" Wilbur says, tapping his phone. "Mini butterball? Are you still there or are you focusing on sprouting freckles like a little duck's egg?"

Whoops. *Focus, Harriet.*

"Sorry." I face the other way so I can concentrate properly. "I'm here. What's up?"

"Speaking of *up*, have you seen the gif of you doing the rounds on email yet, my little fish flake? You are utterly *hilairical*."

An abrupt memory flashes: strobe lights, a moving floor, a sudden splash of water. I clear my throat in embarrassment.

Nope. Still not going to think about it.

"It was *six weeks ago*," I say defensively. "The fashion industry needs to get over it already. Have they got nothing better to do?"

"Not really," Wilbur admits. "There's a bit of a lull between the spring and summer collections. You're filling the gap nicely."

My phone beeps and I glance at the screen.

"Huh. That's weird. Stephanie is calling me too. She

hasn't spoken to me since Paris."

"Hmm? Oh, just cancel that, pumpkin. She's just trying to make people buy her new velvet hairband range."

Then Wilbur clears his throat loudly.

"*Anyway*. The reason I'm ringing you today, Harriet, is for a very special, once-in-a-lifetime opportunity…"

I squint a bit harder through the window: India's started pulling her purple boots back on.

"For a limited time only, you *too* can be a part of a group of select and elite members of the fashion industry…"

Now Toby's putting his folder in his backpack.

"…a *plethora* of talents from every corner of the globe…"

Nat's getting her coat. Are we leaving already?

"…from Niue to Nauru…"

"Huh? Wilbur, what are you talking about? Niue and Nauru? They're both islands in the Pacific Ocean. That's not every corner of the globe. It's just one corner."

"*Dingo-bats,*" he sighs. "Never mind."

There's a short silence, then Wilbur coughs. "What I'm trying to say is… Harriet, will you come with me?"

"To the South Pacific?"

"To the new modelling agency I've just set up."

And he's suddenly got my full attention.

"You've left Infinity? But…" *Again* sounds a bit rude. "Didn't you just go back to working there?"

"Darling moo, who wants to polish the crown when you can wear the tiara?"

I have no idea what that means.

"Everything's ready," he continues quickly. "I have the *best* contacts, and all my top models and designers are signed so it's really no big deal if you don't want to…"

"Wilbur," I smile, looking back through the window, "of course I want to. I'll come with you."

"You will?"

"Yes! You're my fairy godmother. Where you go, I go." Also I kind of get the sense that after Paris my time at Infinity Models is as good as over. And I really hate Stephanie, but that's just an unexpected bonus.

Wilbur lets out an enormous happy sigh. "Harriet Manners, you are the pompom on my jaunty beret. Has anybody ever told you that?"

I laugh. "Probably not. So what's the plan?"

"I just have a few more duckies to line up and then I'll give you a tinkle?"

I nod and start heading towards the cafe doors.

"I'm your girl, Wilbur. Just tell me what I have to do."

14

Now, I'm not famous for my ability to read people.

In the past, there has certainly been the *odd* occasion where I've *possibly* missed a hint here or a gesture there or an outright statement kind of everywhere.

But not this time.

As I skip into the cafe, my friends' urgency is unmistakable. Bags are being slung on, coats grabbed, coffees slurped and cake polished off.

And I think we all know why.

They clearly want to get the party started as quickly as possible.

Wow, these guys are *keen.*

"Gang!" I smile, taking my normal seat. "Chill out! There's *plenty* of time to get to my house. The Sleepover festivities don't commence for another –" I glance at my watch – "nineteen minutes at *least."*

I pick up my slightly cold Harriet-uccino from the table. "Although admittedly a few extra minutes wouldn't

hurt anyone," I add, gulping some down and standing back up. "We could do with another run-through of the plans."

Then there's a silence.

A silence so long you could use it as a tree-swing, should you be capable of swinging from silences.

"Do you want to tell her," India says to Nat, "or shall I?"

I blink at them. "Tell me what?"

"Umm, Harriet," Nat says quickly, going pink around the ears and brandishing the paper at me, "I've just opened my last essay. I got a C. I'm going to have to put some more work in, like yesterday."

"And my mum's texted," India grimaces, quickly flipping up her phone. "She doesn't want me staying out so close to exams."

"I could really use the extra time to get some painting done," Jasper says, grabbing his big black A Level art folder from behind the counter, "if everyone else is going to be working."

We automatically turn and look at Toby.

"Has anyone seen my new Dr Who Sonic Screwdriver with LED Flashlight?" he says, holding it up. "It's really useful for confusing cats."

"So what are you saying?" A hot fizzing is starting at

the base of my stomach, as if somebody's just combined vinegar with baking soda. "Are you cancelling on me again?"

"Not *cancelling*," Nat says, flushing a little harder and fiddling with the paper. "Just... *delaying*."

"Again?" I say, stomach still fizzing.

"It's only the second time."

"You're cancelling my sleepover AGAIN?"

"Our sleepover," India says, frowning. "It's *our* sleepover, Harriet."

"That's what I said," I snap, crossing my arms.

I can't believe this.

Why can't my friends organise their spare time properly like I have? I've got exams coming up too, and you don't see *me* panicking and changing plans at the last minute.

Mainly because I've been revising in reasonable chunks every single night for the last six months and my carefully calculated schedule is working perfectly.

But still: *preparation*.

"Harriet," Nat says tiredly, putting the paper back in her stuffed handbag and rubbing her eyes again. "What do you think I'd rather do? Examine the thread count of different fabrics or watch romcoms with you guys?"

"Wait," Jasper says in alarm, "we were going to

watch romcoms? When was this covered?"

"Oooh!" Toby says, sticking his hand up. "I know this one! Ask me! Ask me!"

And – just like that – my sulkiness pops.

I'm not being very fair, am I?

Everyone's genuinely busy working and revising and obviously they don't *want* to not have fun tonight.

I'm just disappointed, that's all.

Then I look closer at my normally happy gang and something in my chest twinges. The skin around Nat's eyes is darker than normal; Jasper's scowl is deeper and there's a smudge of orange paint near his ear. India's got black roots for the first time since I've known her.

Toby looks well rested and calm, but I suspect he has a similar schedule to mine.

A group at the University of Virginia studied twenty-two different people who were under threat of receiving an electrical shock to either themselves, a close friend or a stranger.

It turns out the brain activity of a person in danger is indistinguishable from the brain activity of a person when someone they love is in danger instead.

My friends are tired, stressed and anxious.

These are my people and if they're not happy, I'm not happy either.

Something needs to be done.

"OK," I say, thinking fast. "How about I sort out a little food fest for when you've got half an hour free?"

"That would be great," India smiles broadly. "Thanks, Harriet."

"You're ace," Nat says, giving me a hug.

"Hang on." Jasper looks up from his art folder. "You're not going to turn us into fajitas or burritos, are you, Harriet-uccino? I *knew* those guacamole face masks you had planned were leading to something."

I stick my tongue out at him.

"Don't worry, guys," I say reassuringly, putting my Team JINTH Sleepover folder away. "I've got this."

After all, isn't that what friends are for?

15

Recently, ecologists set up cameras on the Indonesian island of Borneo in order to evaluate the environmental impact of logging in the Wehea Forest.

To their surprise, they found that – rather than swinging from trees – the orang-utans decided to use the felled timber as roads, save energy and just walk to where they were going instead.

The moral of the story is: it's important to *adapt*.

And also – let's be honest – avoid unnecessary exercise at all costs.

By the time I get home, I've already started mentally working through a new plan. I can't let my friends lose their happy glow. So there's no time for a sleepover any more: that's OK. I'm flexible. Supple. Capable of changing direction at will; of dipping and swerving through life like a swallow or a swift or a house martin.

Or maybe some kind of nimble pigeon.

I'm going to make my friends the best Team JINTH Picnic of All Time.

It's going to be a quick, breezy, casual picnic in the park: the kind of picnic that provides physical, mental and spiritual sustenance *fast* when you need a proper break.

The kind of picnic that screams 'happiness' at the top of its lungs. Because, let's face it, nothing says joy and relaxation like a full stomach and personalised biscuits.

All I need now is a suitable theme.

Maybe a few decent recipes. A couple of drink options. Possibly bunting. It wouldn't hurt to work out exactly where to position us to maximize sunshine and protection from the wind, either.

I'm pretty sure there's room for the five of us on the roundabout, but maybe I should measure it first just to—

"Harriet?" Annabel says as I burst through the front door with a *bang* and start pounding straight up the stairs.

"Can't stop!" I call cheerfully over my shoulder. "Super busy!"

Taking into account preparation time and the actual picnic itself, I'm going to have to rearrange my week's revision plan.

This is exactly why it's so handy to have it saved as a spreadsheet. A few quick presses of a button and a new colour-code, and I'll have a brand-new, highly flexible schedule with space for spontaneous, spur-of-the-moment activities like picnics.

"Harriet!" Annabel says a lot more loudly. "Just wait a second!"

I pause at the top of the stairs.

Then I glance down and blink: something's changed. "Is there... How the..." I sniff the air. "What's that *smell*?"

Wait: is Annabel wearing an *apron*? I didn't even know we had one. Both of my parents think that warming up a stale croissant qualifies them for MasterChef.

"I'm 'cooking'," my stepmother confirms, inexplicably making quotation marks with her fingers. "'Broadening my skill set', 'sustaining the family', 'providing nutrition, vitamins and minerals for my loved ones' and so on."

That's a lot of air-quotations for statements that probably should be said without irony.

"You're *cooking*?" I repeat in amazement. "No *wonder* I was confused. Tabitha, mark this historic occasion. It may never happen again."

Then I raise my eyebrows pointedly.

"I probably deserved that," Annabel smiles. "Even though your father has actually taken Tabitha out for a walk so I'm not entirely sure who you're talking to."

There's a soft jingling sound and Bunty pokes her pink

head through the living-room door. "What do you think, darling? Apparently I can fit more souvenirs in my car boot than I thought."

She waves a ring-clad hand around.

The living room looks like an enormous butterfly just went bang: brightly coloured printed blankets, dream-catchers, crystals, bells and cushions are everywhere. Lamps are switched on in every corner and new plants sit in pots. Crystals are spread on every surface.

Huh. That was fast.

"This is for you," Bunty says, handing me two small brass cymbals on a long piece of leather. "They're Buddhist *Tingsha Chimes* from Tibet. The sound is immediately calming. Try it."

I obediently hit them together. The air is filled with a sweet, high, long note that fades slowly into nothing.

Nope. Didn't work: still busy.

"How about we all have a cup of tea?" Annabel says brightly. "The kettle's just boiled."

"Yes, please!" I say gratefully, turning round and heading across the hallway. "You can leave it outside my door!"

"Harriet, that's not what I m—"

"Thank you!" I shout.

And with a firm *click* I close my bedroom door behind me.

16

The next few days are manic.

Sitting on my bed, surrounded by bright textbooks like a bird in a shiny and informative nest, I plough through as much schoolwork as possible.

I study compositions of various amino acids: alanine, cysteine and valine. I memorise the tertiary structure of ribonuclease molecules, and precisely how the polypeptide is folded.

Given that $y = x5 - 3x2 + x + 5$, I find *dy/dx* and *d2y/dx2;* I factorise $x2 - 4x - 12$ and sketch the corresponding graph. I learn the baryon numbers of quarks and antiquarks, and the properties of leptons and antiparticles.

(I finally know what they are, by the way. No thanks to a certain American governess.)

I even discover that there are as many bacteria in two servings of yoghurt as there are people on earth.

Then promptly abandon breakfast.

And – during my breaks – I make a JINTH Picnic Pack.

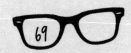

There's a menu and personalised paper crockery, napkins and music. I've even got mini sparklers just in case it gets dark and we want the calming, happiness-inducing party to continue.

This fun is going to be *off the chart,* while also being very much on it.

Every now and then Annabel and Bunty try to distract me – do I need my chakras cleansing? Why don't I eat with them for once instead of on the floor of my bedroom? – but I cannot be moved.

Even school can't divert my focus.

As India, Toby and Jasper disappear to their various billion extra-curricular activities, I hunker down with neat notes in the corner of the common room and study.

By Tuesday afternoon, I've completed an entire week's worth of revision. Which means I'm now available for any kind of spontaneous social occasion that might pop up.

Whenever that might be.

Although it's been 71 hours and I still haven't heard anything, so maybe my hints have been too subtle.

Hey team JINTH! Weather forecast for Wednesday is good! ;) Hxx

Partly cloudy with bursts of sunshine on Thursday!

Wind only 11mph! ;) Hxx

Humidity on Friday 73% so cover your sandwiches! ;) Hxx

Finally – at 4:30pm, just as I'm arriving home from school – I get a reply.

OK Harriet! Park at 5? Nat x

Quickly, I calculate the timings.

Ten minutes to prepare, five minutes to pack and get dressed, five minutes to run to the park, five minutes to recover from running to the park.

That leaves me a few minutes to set up the picnic and that's all I really need. Time to officially Get Happy, Team JINTH.

They are going to be *blown away*.

"Gosh," Bunty says, appearing in the kitchen doorway as I'm quickly shoving together the JINTH sandwiches. "They look *terribly* creative, darling."

Jam, Nutella, Tuna and Ham.

Admittedly I struggled with the *I* and settled for Iceberg lettuce but they can always pick it out.

"These sandwiches have a very wide range of

nutrients," I inform her, tucking them into a Tupperware box. "Vitamin A, calcium, protein."

Not to mention saturated fat, but never mind.

"Delicious," my grandmother beams, leaning against the doorway. "You're such a busy little bee these days, darling. *Buzz buzz buzz*."

I nod, chucking in a large packet of crisps. "There's just *so* much to do."

"I can see that," Bunty laughs. "Just –" she puts a heavily turquoise-ringed hand on my arm – "leave a little room in the garden for the fairies to dance."

I blink at her. *Oooh. Dancing*.

Turning around, I quickly grab the break-dancing manual from the kitchen table. There should be *plenty* of room for that in the park.

"I'm so glad you seem happier now," Bunty continues more gently as I swing the enormous basket over one shoulder. "Tell me, after all those letters did you ever decide to get hold of N—"

"Napkins," I say quickly, grabbing a handful. "Yup, got some. Thank you!"

I kiss her briskly on the cheek.

Then I swing my satchel over the other shoulder and charge towards the front door.

"Harriet?" Annabel appears at the bottom of the

stairs with a damp, flushed Tabitha straight out of the bath. "I'm making some kind of Peruvian chicken stew from a recipe Mum brought back. Would you like some?"

"Yes, please!" I call over my shoulder. "Leave some in the fridge and I'll heat it up later!"

Let the fun times begin.

17

This is why it *always* pays to prepare.

With just seventy-three seconds to spare, I quickly spread out my picnic blanket and distribute the JINTH branded plastic cups and paper plates; hang bunting from the overhead tree – one letter on each flag – and slot my iPod with carefully selected playlist into the speakers.

Skilfully, I set out Monopoly and do my best to ignore a young couple wandering past: giggling, holding hands and snuggled up inside the boy's coat.

It's not *that* cold.

By the time I hear footsteps on the path, I'm as ready as I'm ever going to be.

Which, for the record, is *very ready*.

"No *way*," Nat's saying loudly. "Christopher and *Ananya* are going out?"

"*Right*?" India's voice is clear as a bell. "*Christopher.* The dude still thinks he's Hamlet, for God's sake. He turned up to their first date wearing a freaking beret."

"Ugh. He kissed me once, you know. I nearly removed his lips for him."

"Connecting at the mouth actually helps humans to exchange unconscious biological information about each other. He was probably just trying to work out if your immune system was different from his."

I can't see them yet, but that's obviously Toby.

"Look at that orange and red sky. It looks like something from a Turner painting."

And that's Jasper.

"Well," Nat continues sharply. *Come on come on come on hurry up...* "After what happened last year, I think they probably deserve each oth—"

They finally reach the opening to the park. My goodness, they walk slowly.

That took *forever.*

"Ta*da*!" I shout in excitement, jumping up with my arms spread out and my hands waving. "Welcome to Picnic JINTH, friends! Come over! Settle down! We have everything your hearts could possibly desire!"

There's a stunned silence.

"*Look*!" I prompt, dragging India and Nat by the hand towards the blanket. "I made a special Scrabble game! We can only use J, I, N, T, H and the rest of the vowels, but you'd be shocked at how many options there are."

"AUNTIE and ATONE are just two of them," Toby says, sitting on the blanket.

"We also have JINTH napkins!" I say, pulling them out in a triumphant fan shape.

"Genius!" Toby shouts, clapping his hands.

"And JINTH biscuits!"

"Visionary!"

OK, I need someone other than Toby to be impressed now: India, Jasper and Nat are still staring at the blanket in silence.

"Sit down!" I say quickly, gesturing. "Make yourselves at home! Eat! Drink! Be Happy!"

I'm starting to sound like a novelty tea towel.

"Blimey, Harriet," Jasper says, running a hand through his hair and lowering himself on to the floor. "You don't do things by halves, do you."

"This is… above and beyond," India says, pulling out a plastic carrier bag. "I brought… uh. Three quarters of a pack of Jammie Dodgers."

She slides them on to a plate in obvious embarrassment.

"There was really no need for this, Harriet," Nat says gently, perching down and offering a small packet of cheese straws.

"Don't be silly!" I say cheerfully, handing out cups of lemonade. "We can share, that's what a *team* does!

Now, sit down and relax. What were you just saying about Christopher? Oh my goodness, remember that time we were on stage together and Alexa…"

My pocket suddenly starts vibrating.

A fraction of a second later, Bibbidi-Bobbidi-Boo starts playing.

"Uh," I continue smoothly when it stops ten seconds later, clearing my throat, "when Alexa started playing animal noises and—"

The Fairy Godmother tune starts again.

Jasper, India and Nat are staring curiously at my pocket. Toby's blowing on his little Monopoly dog and rubbing it on his jumper sleeve.

"You should answer your phone, Harriet," India says finally.

"Yup," Jasper says with arched eyebrows. "It might be a little old lady in a blue hooded cloak with a wand, a pumpkin and a couple of lizards."

I swallow. Please no.

Not now. Literally any other time you like: just not now.

Raising my eyes to the skies, I send a silent, furtive prayer out into the Universe, grab my phone and turn the other way. "Hello, Wilbur?"

The Universe clearly wasn't listening.

"Prepare the unicorns, bunny. It's time."

18

Time doesn't actually exist.

Even a second isn't what we think it is: it's officially the duration of 9,192,631,770 periods of the radiation corresponding to the transition between the two hyperfine levels of the ground state of the caesium-133 atom.

And unicorns aren't exactly roaming the streets either, so technically Wilbur is making no sense whatsoever.

But I know exactly what he means.

I just can't quite bring myself to believe it.

I stare at my beautiful team picnic, heart sinking. "Th-there's a job this evening?"

"No, a big casting in London." I can barely hear Wilbur over the clattering noise in the background. "I only just found out, olive-pip, but if you leave right away you can make it."

I glance back at my friends, now peeling open the sandwiches and peering curiously at their contents. "And

there's no way we can postpone?"

"I'm afraid not, monkey." The noise in the background is getting even louder. "They're sending the details over, so I'll email them straight through."

In a panic, I quickly race through my options.

There aren't any.

I made a promise to Wilbur that I'd help out with his new agency, and I should stick to it: regardless of how little I actually want to. I start dejectedly buckling my satchel back up.

What were the chances of this happening?

One in 228, that's what.

I've been modelling for fifteen months – 547 days – and in that time I've done just *two* official castings. One with Yuka and one with an American magazine. I had a statistically higher chance of winning a cash prize with Premium Bonds than getting this call right now.

Maybe I should think about investing.

"Sure," I sigh, standing up. "I'll get there as soon as I can."

"Just remember your book, poppet. That's super important."

I nod. "Got it."

"Fantasmico," Wilbur breathes. "And baby-baby-panda? *Thank you.*"

I put the phone down and look sadly at the gloriousness in front of me. My wonderful, carefully planned picnic, completely ruined.

Unless…

"I have to go to London," I say, looking at my watch. "But I can be here again in… an hour, maximum?"

Then I glance up at them hopefully.

"That's not a question, Harriet," Toby points out. "You've put a question mark on the end, but it's actually a statement."

I look beseechingly at Nat. *She* understands my subtle rhetoric. "Umm," she says after a few beats, glancing around the park. "Sure. I guess we can wait."

"We won't start playing Scrabble until you return," Toby agrees.

"And we'll try as *hard* as we can not to eat the meat-chocolate-fish-salad sandwiches," Jasper says, lifting his eyebrows. "But I can't promise anything: we're only human."

India's jabbing her purple heel into the mud in silence. She's clearly even more disappointed by this crushing news than I am, poor thing.

The happiness factor is depleting by the second.

"Don't worry!" I say, patting her arm. "I'll be back before you know it and then you'll have so much fun, just wait and see! Team JINTH forever!"

Quickly, I type a quick text to Dad:

Just going to London for Wilbur! Won't be long! Hxx

And I start running.

19

In some Micronesian cultures, they believe that sweat is a warrior's *essence*.

I won't go into unnecessary details.

Suffice to say, by the time I reach the address Wilbur texted me, in the middle of Soho, I've jogged so enthusiastically there's Extract of Harriet pouring down the middle of my forehead.

And my back, my knees... the soles of my feet.

I'm basically in the final death throes of the Wicked Witch of the West, and I'm melting all over the reception desk.

Quickly, I wipe it off with my jumper sleeve and try my best to inhale without sounding like a broken vacuum cleaner.

Then I ping the bell and glance around the empty atrium.

This building is utterly enormous.

The furniture's white leather, the walls are entirely

exposed grey brick, and there's glass, green plants and gravel everywhere, like some kind of giant terrarium made for humans.

"Hello?" I call out urgently, dinging the little bell again. My voice bounces around the room like a ball. "Is anybody there?"

The only sound is another bead of sweat dripping on to the glass desk with a tiny *plip.*

Oh my God: I must have missed the casting.

Who are we even kidding? The fastest mile ever run by a woman is four minutes, twelve seconds, and I don't think I'm in danger of beating that record any time soon.

At one point of my journey I ended up air-vomiting against a lamp-post.

I scan the room again: still nothing.

Then I spot a paper sign stuck on a door, with this written on it in black marker:

MODELS—>

Heart still hammering, I rip my bulky coat off. I unwind my long, sticky red scarf, throw it over my shoulder and rearrange my sweaty T-shirt.

Then I start trotting down the corridor.

It feels like it goes on for miles – like one of my

horrible cross-country nightmares – but with a final burst of exertion I finally reach a door with CASTINGS written on it.

Panting, I stop with a wave of relief.

And also a wave of nausea: I'm really not built for this much physical activity.

"I'm here!" I breathe, rapping sharply on the door and wiping several drips from my forehead. *Please. Please don't have gone already.* "Don't worry, I'm here!"

"Now just hang on a—" somebody says.

But it's too late: there's nowhere to hang on *to*.

With a final wobble my exhausted legs give way: throwing my entire weight against the door.

It opens with a *click*.

And – with a tiny squeak of horror – I fall face down into the world of fashion.

20

There are probably better ways to enter a room.

On horseback, for instance.

Riding an enormous motorbike or standing on the gold wings of a flaming chariot. Cartwheeling or back-flipping; balanced precariously on the spine of two dragons, while simultaneously blowing a bugle.

All of which would have been more subtle than shouting OOMPH and smashing out into a star-shape with my face pressed firmly against the floorboards.

The door swings behind me with a *bang*.

None of an octopus's limbs know what the others are doing: I think the same can clearly be said for mine.

"S-sorry," I say, struggling upright with an embarrassed laugh and tucking a strand of soggy hair behind my ear. "Th-there are thirteen muscles in each leg and I think one of mine decided to give u—"

I falter to a stop.

I've fallen into yet another big, grey room with huge

windows, a long white table and white seats. Colourful prints hang in frames along the walls, the table is covered in little plates and glasses, and there are nine serious-looking people: most of whom are wearing dark suits and ties and smart dresses.

And every single one of them is eating a sandwich.

Or trying to, anyway.

My explosion through the door seems to have interrupted that process somewhat.

"Umm…" I stutter as they pause mid-chew. "Sorry, is this not the modelling audition?"

"It's *going* to be," the only man wearing denim says, putting a ham baguette down. "Right now it's our late lunch."

I don't believe this. Did I just run straight from one picnic to another, like some kind of crazed teddy bear?

"Oh."

"Yes, *oh*." The man eyes me coldly. "Do you usually come bursting into private meeting rooms without waiting to be invited?"

"N-no."

"Good to hear. Well, feel free to burst out again. You can return at the allocated time, with the other, less horizontal models."

Then Denim Man stuffs the baguette in his mouth, rips

a bite off and turns towards the lady sitting next to him.

I clear my throat carefully.

"What… time would that be?" I glance quickly at my watch. "More specifically?"

"Do you have somewhere you'd prefer to be?"

My cheeks were already hot enough to generate their own electricity, but it feels like they're about to vibrate off my face. Some deep survival instinct is telling me to be extremely careful.

Yes. "N-no."

His frown deepens. "OK, tell you what. As you're obviously so *keen* to jump the queue and present yourself before everyone else, why don't you just go right ahead."

"E-excuse me?"

Denim Man glances at the rest of the group. They've put down their wraps and baguettes and are staring at me the way my class stared at the chimpanzee flinging poop around at the zoo on our biology field trip.

Except with considerably less amusement.

"You have three minutes, whoever you are. This is your big chance to wow us. Starting from –" he looks at his watch – "*now*."

21

The Guinness world record for consecutive push-ups in the precise time I've been allocated is four hundred and twenty. There's something aggressive and army-like about this man's tone that makes me wonder if I'm expected to drop to the floor and beat it.

Instead, I put my satchel cautiously next to my feet in an attempt to stabilise me and/or anchor me to the ground.

Then I take a deep breath.

You can do this, Harriet. You're an experienced model now. A paragon of knowledge, a shining example of professionalism and expertise.

"Hello, everyone," I say, inexplicably curtsying with my fingers holding out the bottom of my T-shirt. "I am Harriet, the fashion model."

Brilliant. Now I sound like one of those creepy dolls you can make say things by pulling a string at the back of their heads.

"From which agency?"

I stare blankly at the lady who just asked that. Which *agency*? I never actually thought to ask. "Ah… Baby Baby Panda and… Associates?"

"Ridiculous name," Denim Man snaps. "Book?"

Quickly, I bend down and grab it out of my satchel, then plop it on the desk in front of them.

They all lean over to look. "What *is* this?"

"*Crime and Punishment* by Dostoyevsky," I explain politely, even though it's written right there on the cover. "It's not as good as *Notes From The Underground*, but still perfectly captures the human condition at its most raw and vulnerable."

Denim Man sighs. "Are you trying to be cute?"

Obviously I am. Isn't that what's expected at a modelling casting?

"Your *book*," the woman explains patiently. "Your modelling portfolio? With modelling photos? So we can see what modelling work you've done?"

My cheeks flush even harder. Now I'm not in a distracted rush, *I realise* that Wilbur didn't mean *bring a translation of a Russian classic with you*.

I should at least have brought *The Idiot*.

It would have been more appropriate.

"My portfolio's at home," I confess after a pause.

"Under my bed." Thanks to my fiasco in Paris, it's been collecting spiderwebs and dust bunnies for quite some time.

"Right." Denim Man leans back against his chair and folds his arms. "So *why* do you think you're right for this particular job? What do you have to offer us that no other model has?"

This feels like my first ever casting with Yuka Ito, over a year ago. Except I'm even less prepared and making even more of a fool of myself, and I didn't even realise that was possible.

Isn't it supposed to work the other way round? Shouldn't I be considerably better at this by now?

Or at least a *tiny* bit improved?

"Ah..." On the way here I had more than half an hour of sitting on a train, making animal shapes out of clouds. *Why didn't I check my emails?* "You're very good... uh. Fashion people. Your clothes are really..." *What?* "Sewn... neatly."

"This isn't a fashion agency." My audience looks at each other. "Do you even know where you are?"

Another wave of shame washes over me.

"N-not in *detail*." Oh my God, at the very least I could have paused to look at the sign on the outside of the building. What is *wrong* with me?

Please don't anybody answer that.

My phone beeps. "Umm," I say, grabbing for it with a slippery hand and unsuccessfully trying to switch it to silent. "S-sorry."

It beeps again and I stab at it again. "Sorry."

A third time: ditto.

Most British people will apologise more than two million times in their lives. I suspect I'm going to run out in the next ten seconds.

In a final act of desperation, I wrap it in my scarf and throw it to the bottom of my bag.

"And is this your best effort?" The casually dressed man has stood up with his arms still folded. "This is you, bringing your A game?"

Step it up quickly, Harriet.

"I've done lots of jobs," I say quickly. "I was the face of Yuka Ito, I shot a big campaign for Baylee, I've been to Japan and Russia and Morocco... and..." *Don't mention Paris don't mention Paris...* "And I did a really cool magazine in New York last year."

"I *knew* I recognised you!" an American lady cries, throwing her hands up. "You were wearing a sack and covered in mud!"

That is not the image I was trying to prompt.

Mr Denim frowns. "You *are* familiar, but... there's

something I can't quite place... about... the... hair..."

He frowns at the top of my head and that's when it hits me. Like a pile of heavy bricks, slowly tumbling down on top of my head. *Clunk.* Then another two: *clunk clunk.*

Clunk, clunk, clunk.

Clunk clunk clunk clunk clunk clunk clunk–

Until it feels like there's a whole wall of realisation lying on top of me and I have no idea how I'm ever going to get up again.

The brightly coloured prints. The central Soho location. The vast reception. The dark formal suits, and one person inexplicably wearing casual clothes. The *exposed grey brick walls.*

This isn't... It can't be...

Statistically, there's just no way that this could be...

"Harriet *Manners*?" the man says, reaching the same realisation at exactly the same time. "As in, *daughter of Richard*?"

And – with a final *clunk* – any remaining chance I had of getting this job flies straight out the window.

22

Here's an interesting fact about the duck-billed platypus: it doesn't have a stomach.

I know exactly how it feels.

In case you've forgotten: fifteen months ago my life wasn't the only one that changed for good. On the exact day that I was scouted for modelling, Dad was fired as Head Copywriter for a big London advertising agency for telling an important client to go and French Connection themselves in the middle of their reception.

And that's where I am now.

Which means – judging by the denim – the angry man is almost definitely Dad's old boss, Peter Trout: Creative Director and Head Honcho.

Pufferfish look cuddly but their spines contain tetrodotoxin: a poison so deadly it can kill you with a single prick.

93

I didn't know trout could too.

"So," Peter says, folding his arms. "*You're* Harriet Manners. That explains a lot."

I blink. "Does it?"

"Clearly being an uncontrollable maverick with no regard for rules, regulations or general codes of conduct runs in the family."

OK, that's really quite rude.

Also, I'm an extremely well-behaved, reliable and law-abiding citizen, so this man clearly doesn't know me at all.

"Actually, that's not entirely—"

"Oh!" the American lady exclaims again. "*You* were the girl who sat down on the catwalk in the middle of a fashion show in Russia last year! I saw that in the paper!"

"And we heard about Yuka's last model," the woman next to her adds. "Didn't you ruin a couture dress with octopus ink? It was the *talk* of fashion week last year."

"Don't you tend to *faint* on camera?"

I open my mouth to object against these horrible, unkind accusations, then realise they're completely accurate and promptly shut it again.

The whole group has started loudly whispering at each other. "She's *not* the girl in the Paris…"

"You got that email too?"

"It's hard to tell without the giant ears, obviously."

In the meantime, Peter Trout is regarding me with a vague air of satisfaction. I hate to admit it, but the evidence is rapidly mounting.

It's horrifying.

I'd built an entire identity on being the second most sensible Manners after Annabel, but that clearly isn't the case.

I'm rapidly slipping to less savvy than my dog.

"And now you show up to *my* agency," he snaps, "all '*don't worry I'm here!*' as if your reputation precedes you. Well, missy: it clearly does. And not in a good way."

My cheeks are burning. "But—"

"This industry doesn't need any more special little snowflakes who think the rules don't apply to them, young lady. As your father proved, we already have enough."

I stare at him, dumbfounded.

Every winter in the US alone, at least *one septillion* ice crystals fall from the sky. There are literally very few things on this planet less special than a snowflake.

Also, I'd like to make the point that he's the only one in the room not wearing a suit.

His irritation is visibly rising.

"Frankly, your uncontrollable father cost this agency

thousands of pounds. And now you have the *audacity* to break into *my* company, *my* lunch, in front of *my* clients, dripping with sweat, jumping the queue, giggling, phone ringing, wearing whatever *that* is…"

"A home-made JINTH T-shirt and dungarees."

"…no portfolio, unregistered agency, no idea what you're doing or what time you should arrive or why you're here or what job it is you're even trying to get."

His argument is undeniably strong.

"But I—"

"And we're… what, exactly? Supposed to be won over by your eccentricities? Charmed by your quirks? Besotted with your totally unprofessional attitude and lack of respect for this industry and everybody in it?"

I'm so hot with shame there's a chance I'll combust and they'll have to identify me from the name written on the inside front cover of my Russian literature.

Swallowing, I lift my chin. "I'm very sorry, Sir. I didn't mean it."

"From what I can tell, model Harriet Manners, you never seem to *mean* anything."

I'm completely speechless.

"So I suggest," he says, sitting back in his chair and making a triangle with his fingertips, "that you stumble out of the modelling industry and leave room for somebody who actually *wants* to be there."

Mr Trout picks up the last mouthful of his baguette and points with it at the door.

"*Now* you can go."

23

Experience is apparently genetic.

Scientists discovered that the knowledge one mouse acquires is passed on to future generations, buried deep in their DNA: which means a lesson learnt by a parent can permanently alter the behaviour of its children.

This clearly doesn't work for the Manners family.

Neither Dad nor I have learnt *anything*.

Staring at the floor, I manage to scoot out of the room backwards like a humiliated hummingbird.

I close the door behind me.

Holding a shaking hand over my eyes, I take a deep breath.

Then I look up and try not to notice the dozens of beautiful, glossy, neatly dressed girls lining up quietly along the corridor with shiny portfolios tucked under their arms.

Brushing their hair and checking they look presentable.

Waiting to be called into the casting.

Being professional. Poised. *Prepared*.

i.e. all the things I failed to be.

Because apparently my surname is ironic.

"How did *she* get in so early?" someone mutters as I grab my phone and scuttle back down the corridor as invisibly as possible. "I travelled two hours to be here. I will *kill* my agent if the job's already gone."

I think I can say with some certainty it's not.

Cheeks burning, I retrieve my phone from a tangle of scarf.

Then with a twist of my stomach I click on the email that's been sitting in my inbox for nearly an hour.

Re: URGENT CASTING

Harriet,

As promised, here are maps, train timetables and suitable connections. Casting starts at 6:30pm sharp, and you're meeting Peter Trout – Creative Director of DBB. A well-known American brand is launching a new fizzy drink and this will be very competitive so I suggest the close-up snowflake shot goes in the front of your portfolio, followed by the lake shot. We can rearrange properly next time I see you.

**FYI my new agency is called PEAK MODELS.
You've got this, my girl!**

Wilbur

I blink at the screen.

All the words in the message are acknowledged by the Oxford English Dictionary, so I'll assume this was written by his new secretary.

Then I click on a flurry of texts from Nat that could not have arrived at a worse possible moment.

Are you nearly back yet? We're almost hungry enough to eat your sandwiches. xx

LOL only joking. The world will end and your sandwiches will remain uneaten. x

TOBY JUST ATE ONE WHAT IS WRONG WITH HIM. Where are you? X

I glance at my watch.

It's been fifty-eight minutes since I left the park. Every single calculation I've made this afternoon has been wildly wrong.

Quickly, I type:

So sorry – please wait just a little longer! Hx

Phone still in hand, I head towards the front door, past the two white sofas now filling with yet more girls.

Actually, you know what?

I don't think I'd really want to promote fizzy drinks anyway. We consume six million litres of them every year in Britain: they don't really need any more attention.

Plus, they're bad for us.

In fact, fizzy drinks indirectly kill 184,000 people a year, and have been shown to cause hyperactivity, memory loss and –

And –

And…

I'm tugging on the mirrored front door when my phone starts ringing and ANNABEL appears in a flash across the screen.

With a swooping stomach, I tug on the door again. I know I wrote a text to Dad but did I actually *send* it?

Still staring at my phone, I tug a bit harder.

Then again.

Finally, I look up at the door with a jolt of surprise.

My reflection has started tugging back.

24

At least, I assume it's me.

All I see is bright red hair and pale white skin, a pointy chin and button nose. Lots of freckles, pink cheeks and large far-apart green eyes.

It's only when I scowl and my reflection doesn't scowl back that I realise the door's actually transparent.

Also that my side says PUSH.

Only ten species on the planet are able to self-identify: I'm officially less intelligent than a dolphin.

My double and I stare at each other. No longer distracted by my phone, I can see we're not actually identical: we're just similar enough to be disorientating.

Her skin is translucent and spot-free: her eyelashes are long and dark. Her hair is perfectly curled and shiny; her eyebrows tidier, her lips slightly fuller.

She's smartly dressed in a black dress, black coat and black leather boots, and nothing she's wearing has been personalised with marker pen.

102

She's not sweating or flushed, which indicates she walked here calmly, knowing where she was going.

Basically, she's me but better.

Harriet Manners 2.0: upgraded with all my bugs fixed and crashes wiped, my best qualities enhanced and my instabilities improved.

And I already know her.

This is the model who replaced me in the Levaire watch advert last year. The girl who wandered the Sahara dunes, looking ethereal, content and super-coordinated.

And who at no stage got attached by the ear to a Moroccan market stall or threw herself into the sand and attempted to dance like a crumpet.

My phone starts ringing once more and I finally snap to my senses and stop battling with the door. My doppelganger pulls it open with a polite smile: one that indicates she sees nothing of herself in me whatsoever.

She flashes two sweet dimples I don't have.

Then the superior, upgraded version of Harriet Manners glides smoothly into the mess I've just left behind me.

Again.

25

OK, I officially give up.

The Whistler Sliding Centre in British Columbia is the steepest and fastest bobsleigh track in the world. It starts off at 938 metres high then hits a 152-metre vertical drop, allowing amateurs to hurtle downhill at 125 kilometres per hour.

Headfirst, without any brakes or control or idea how to stop it.

Pretty much exactly like today.

Breathing out, I blink at the London streets.

In less than fifteen minutes, it's gone from being dusky to night-time and I have a feeling I'm about to be in a lot of trouble. Annabel didn't even bother leaving voicemail: that's how little interest she had in shouting at me indirectly.

I hesitate for a few seconds – maybe she'll get bored and give up redialling – then I realise the sun will explode

before that happens and click the green button.

"Umm, hello?"

"Where are you? It's dark, Harriet. I know you're sixteen but you can't just disappear for hours without telling anyone where you're going."

"I'm in the… park," I edit optimistically. "Just enjoying the wonder of nature, flowers and… whatnot."

I *am* walking past a patch of semi-dead grass right now. The fact that it's in our capital city is neither here nor there.

There's a tree, a pot plant and a pigeon.

It's a park.

"Right," Annabel sighs. "Well, we've lined up a documentary about stars and we thought you might like to watch it with us."

"Ooh *yay*," I hear Dad say loudly in the background. "Tell my eldest it just wouldn't be the same without an elaborate running commentary *all* the way through."

I sense sarcasm.

In my defence, I *do* know nearly as much as the official narration.

"We have popcorn," Annabel adds cunningly. "And chocolate buttons. Also some kind of chilli-mango worm."

"*Salsagheti*," Bunty says cheerfully into the phone.

"I bought them in Mexico and there's a picture of a duck wearing sunglasses on the box so they should be immense fun."

"When can we expect you?"

"I'm really sorry, Annabel," I say, glancing at my watch. "I've already got plans."

I turn down the road towards the tube station. London is glowing and lit from within. Every building I walk past has something exciting happening inside it. Friends huddled in restaurants and coffee shops: eating, laughing, talking.

Having fun in their happy little groups.

All I want is to get back to mine.

"This is important too." There's the *click* of a door being closed quietly. "Harriet, you're coming home right now. I'm not asking you. I'm telling you."

Oh, *what*?

Quickly, Harriet. You have an IQ of 143: make up an impressive reason not to. Weighty, unquestionable. Profound in its deep reflection of the human race.

"But I don't *want* to," I hear myself whine. "I *want* to hang out with my friends."

"Well," Annabel says sharply, "sometimes growing up means doing things you don't want to do, Harriet. I'm sorry that spending a single hour with your family is one of them."

"That's not what I—"

"You have fifteen minutes and then I expect to see you walking through the front door. Do I make myself clear?"

And the phone goes dead.

26

Apparently the human brain doesn't stop growing until your early twenties.

I am clearly very advanced.

Given my complete inability to:

  a) lie convincingly and

  b) think on my feet, mine has clearly decided to grind to a halt at sixteen.

My phone beeps.

Scowling, I click on the message.

It's dark and cold. Went home half an hour ago. India

This day has officially thundered down the slope, crashed through a fence and shot into a snowbank.

Grumbling, I switch my phone off and start scuffing my trainers along the pavement.

108

Stupid parents. Stupid ruined sandwiches that nobody fully appreciates. Stupid castings and fizzy drinks and men named after fish and unstable door locks and unstable knees and doppelgangers and exams and friends leaving and—

Something in my peripheral brain goes *ping*.

Huh. That's weird.

I take a few steps backwards and peer in through the brightly lit window of a small Italian restaurant. There are red-and-white checked tablecloths, almost burnt-out candles and lots of couples ordering spaghetti and pretending to be in *Lady and the Tramp*.

Making a slight *blugh* face, I peer a bit closer.

There's a man sitting in the corner, surrounded by piles of paper. He's wearing a faded grey suit and a grey tie. He's peering blearily into a laptop, slumped as if he's been popped with a pin.

He looks exhausted and like he just wants to go home.

So far, so usual for rush hour in London.

What's a lot less commonplace is *who* is doing all of this. Because as the man shakes his head wearily at a waiter, my mouth pops open in shock.

I nearly walked straight past: that's how unfamiliar this man looks.

But he's not a stranger – I know him very well.

The sad grey man is Wilbur.

27

A couple of months ago, on one of his long art rants, Jasper told me that most people can see one million colours.

Those with colour-blindness can see far fewer.

But once or twice in a generation, someone is born with *tetrachromacy:* an ability to differentiate between a *hundred million* different shades.

Jasper said that for those people, snow isn't white: it's lilac and pink and red. Rain is purple and turquoise, grass is blue and orange, skin is violet and green.

The only difference between them and everyone else is just one extra kind of cone cell in the eye, and the whole world erupts into colours the rest of us can't see. Colours that we don't even know exist.

For them, everything is a rainbow.

As I tiptoe through the restaurant door, I realise that's what Wilbur is like. You think the world is full of colours,

110

and then he turns up with ninety-nine million of his own.

There must be a logical explanation for this sudden monochrome.

Maybe it's laundry day.

Maybe Wilbur is operating as the world's least convincing James Bond, or pretending to be a lawyer. Maybe he's going to jump up and reveal a sparkly pink cape hidden inside that wrinkly suit.

I'm carefully creeping through the restaurant door – preparing to shout BOO! at the top of my voice – when another man in a suit walks out of the toilets and sits down heavily in the chair opposite Wilbur.

I quickly grab a menu and hold it in front of my face.

Ah ha. Things are starting to slot into place: *nobody* knows how to dress on a date, do they?

"So," the man says brusquely, "where were we?"

"About halfway through my fourth breadstick, honey," Wilbur says, waving one in the air. "I'm on my fifth now."

The man sighs.

"This isn't a joke, Wilbur. Did you listen to a word they said at the bank? There are insolvency consequences, balance-sheet issues, lack of liquidity, fees to apply…"

Wilbur tries to smile, but he's shrivelling up like an old grey balloon. "It can't be *that* bad."

"It is that bad. You're in a mess."

Flushing, I lift the menu higher and start trying to tiptoe backwards out of the restaurant.

This has got to be the worst date *ever.*

"But—"

"Wilbur, your bank manager just told us you spent far too much in America. You were already in debt and now you have no job and no income."

Apparently lizards can't move and breathe at the same time: neither can I.

What?

"You can't expect me not to buy sassy typographic advice pillows from Brooklyn flea markets," Wilbur says indignantly. "That's my fundamental *human right.*"

"Food is a fundamental human right. Water. Shelter. Warmth. Having access to a decent accountant like me. None of which you'll be able to afford unless you file for bankruptcy."

Huh?

But Wilbur's only just started his business. He's signed all his biggest models and designers. It's really exciting and it's been planned for ages: he told me so himself.

So what are they *talking* about?

"I've got my agency," Wilbur says quickly, waving a hand around. "I just need a week to get things off the ground. Ten days. Just give me a fortnight."

Peering closer, I look again at the papers on their table: scribbled phone numbers, Google search print-outs, maps of Soho with advertising agencies circled.

There are piles of modelling photos stacked in heaps: photocopied hastily, with the tops of heads and arms accidentally cut off. Wait: is this restaurant his new office? *This* is Peak Models? I don't want to be rude, but it doesn't even look like peak Italian food.

My brain is making ominous clicking sounds.

Is the grey outfit Wilbur's attempt to be taken seriously? Was the lifeless email from *him*? Is he so sad and trying so hard it's knocked the colour right out of him?

And suddenly I can hear our conversation again. The formality. The forced breeziness. The scripted speeches. If I hadn't been so distracted, I'd have heard the panic in his voice too.

Harriet, will you come with me?

"You're hot-desking in Pizza Pronto, Wilbur. And you don't have an agency." The accountant points at a pinboard I didn't notice before, propped up against the wall. "You only have one girl."

Blinking, I stare at the photo pinned to it.

Red hair. Green eyes. Freckles. Pointy nose. Snow

caught in the eyelashes. For the first time this hour, I'm definitely staring at myself.

"She's not *only* one girl," Wilbur says fiercely, lifting his chin. "She's *Harriet Manners.*"

But his shoulders are hunched, his skin is grey and it's as if his hundred million colours are spilling out on to the floor.

The accountant stands up and puts a form in his suitcase. "Well, let's hope you're right," he says firmly. "Because now Harriet Manners is all you've got."

28

Somehow, I escape unnoticed.

Against all odds I manage to scuttle out of the restaurant without falling over, knocking anything to the ground or taking a tablecloth covered in china plates with me.

Then I round the corner, slump to the kerb and cover my face with my hands. The Pygmy Marmoset is the smallest monkey in the world, but I feel so tiny right now I could climb on to its back and it wouldn't even notice.

Wilbur doesn't know about the casting.

He doesn't know that his only model went into that big, important audition he so carefully arranged and screwed it up. That I did so badly I actually made him look unprofessional for even sending me.

Swallowing, I feel myself shrink further: to approximately the size of an Etruscan Shrew, the tiniest mammal on earth.

Wilbur's not just my agent.

Nearly a year and a half ago he swooped in and pulled

me out of a pile of broken hats, and – in one way or another – he's been swooping in ever since.

Saving me from meltdowns, sabotage and anxiety attacks; defending me against boys and protecting me from designers. Complimenting my Winnie-the-Pooh jumper when nobody else ever does.

Without Wilbur, I wouldn't be a model.

Wouldn't have found the confidence to stand up to my bully or make new friends; wouldn't have flown around the world.

I'd still be a scared little girl breathing hard into a salt and vinegar crisp packet and reciting the periodic table backwards.

My life wouldn't have changed at all.

And he asks for my help – just once – and what happens?

I don't even *listen to him.*

I mean, who are we kidding?

I put ten times more preparation into the bunting I made for the Team JINTH picnic.

And – with a hot wave of shame – I shrink further and further: to the size of a bee hummingbird (two centimetres).

A sea urchin (one centimetre).

A *mycoplasma gallicepticum:* the smallest living

organism on the planet, and (quite fittingly) the tiny bacterium that lives in poop.

Because… Peter Trout was *right*.

I fell into modelling by accident and I've been attempting to wing it ever since. Letting other people save me, over and over again.

Pretending to try, without actually *trying*.

I sit for a few more minutes, thinking hard.

Then I take my hands from my eyes, uncurl from the pavement and stand up straight.

I might only be one girl, but I can do this.

I know if I just redirect some of my attention and focus, I can get modelling jobs, make money and save Wilbur's agency.

Because now it's my turn to be the fairy godmother.

I'm going to flip this fairytale over.

And change Wilbur's life instead.

29

I just need to survive long enough to do it.

By the time I get home it's sixty-two minutes later than my allocated fifteen and the house is dark, locked and ominously quiet.

I creep round to the back door: that's firmly secured as well. I glance up at my bedroom, but unfortunately I took Toby's Stalker Route down six months ago for his health and safety (and also mine) so that's no longer an option.

Then I slide around the squashed hydrangea and carefully evaluate the bathroom window. If I can somehow squeeze through it, I can pretend I've been on the toilet the whole time and nobody will ever push for details.

Genius.

I've just stripped down to my vest top to make myself as aerodynamic as possible when there's a voice behind me.

"It's not going to work, you know."

I spin round: Dad's standing behind me with an overexcited Hugo on a lead.

"It *might* work," I say defensively as Hugo jumps up and affectionately paws my stomach. "I've calculated my shoulder width to window ratio and if I go in at an angle it should just about fit."

"Ah, but you didn't calculate for what's on the other side," Dad says in a wise voice. "The sink's too close. You'll slip and end up with your left foot jammed down the toilet bowl until Annabel breaks through the bathroom door and then gets the neighbours to help pull you out again."

He looks into the sky. "Or something like that, I'd imagine."

How have I never heard that story before?

"So what do you suggest?"

"If you want to sneak in without disturbing your stepmother, the window in the laundry room is the best option. But Annabel and Bunty are meditating in there while they wait for you so it's also a no-go."

I glance at the kitchen window.

"Locked," Dad says, shaking his head.

Catflap?

"Too small. I've tried."

"Any chance you could pick me up by the feet and

hurl me down the chimney? I don't have time to be in trouble right now. There's something really important I have to do."

Dad laughs. "Get behind me." Then he opens the front door.

"Annabel?" he calls into the empty hallway. "It turns out Harriet did text me. We've just been for a walk and she slipped in the mud. She'll need to sort herself out before movie night."

I beam at him: that should buy me long enough.

Also, it's a *very* believable excuse.

I've got the Best Dad Ever.

"Thanks," I whisper, running up the stairs. "I'll be as quick as I can."

"Good. Those stars aren't going to narrate themselves." Dad grins widely. "Oh. Wait. Yes, they will."

Now, I know many things.

I know that there are more life forms living on your skin than there are people on this planet. I know that hamsters can store half their own weight in food in their cheeks, and that astronauts' hearts become rounder in space.

I even know that the scientific name for a llama is *lama glama* and have written a very funny rhyming poem about it in the back of my diary.

But of all the things I know, how to Make A Plan is right at the top of the list.

And I'm going to put that particular skill to good use.

By the time I've been given a ten-minute warning, there are just three things left to do.

Swallowing, I make the first call.

There's an immediate *click*.

"Greetings, bumble-boo! This is Wilbur with a *bur* and not an *iam*. Say something interesting and I'll decide if you're worth ringing back. Toodle-poo!"

Beep.

"Hi Wilbur! It's Harriet. So, I was just thinking... I'm at school all week but I've just realised how much money I need for uni next year. Could you fit in as many castings for me on Saturday as possible? You'd be doing me a *huge* favour."

Wilbur has to think I've become incredibly money-hungry overnight or it's not going to work.

"And..." I hesitate. How do I say *I hope you're OK and I'm here for you please don't worry about anything it's going to be OK* without giving it all away? "...Gravy."

I put the phone down and tick the next point off my list.

Then I send a group message.

Team, I know you're busy but it's kind of important. Could you spare just half an hour tomorrow morning? Hxx

Finally, I open my laptop.

Wilbur needs all the help he can get.

On the way home, I *may* have worked out a way of doubling his new agency's chances; of giving him the best shot at happiness I possibly can.

I've just got to hope this works.

With a deep breath, I click a button and watch the webcam light turn green. I watch the dark screen slowly flicker to life. And I make a call that's going to travel to the other side of the world.

A call that could change everything.

30

How To Be A Perfect Model

1. BE PROFESSIONAL. Modelling is a business and you are the product. Conduct yourself accordingly.

2. SHOW CONFIDENCE AND STYLE. Make the most of yourself and highlight your best features.

3. KEEP IN GOOD HEALTH. Your body is your job, so eat well, exercise, sleep and make sure it is kept in tip-top condition.

4. DO YOUR RESEARCH. Make sure you prepare properly before any opportunity.

5. SEDUCE THE CAMERA. Prettiness is not enough: learn how to work it.

This is exactly why I love my friends.

Last weekend, we had to cancel our plans.

But now I *really* need them, they're here.

Yawning and wearing the top half of their purple pyjamas in India's case because it's 9am on a Saturday, but here just the same.

Rallied around in my bedroom like friendship superheroes.

I'm the luckiest girl in the world.

"What do you think?" I say once I've finished explaining Wilbur's dilemma. "Do you think I can do it?"

They pass around my latest list in silence.

With thought and care, they give it the respect and attention it deserves.

Then – one by one – they start snorting with laughter.

Honestly, I don't understand why.

This is the least funny thing I've ever written.

"Sorry," Nat says eventually, wiping her eyes. "It's just… Harriet, this is going to be… *hard* for you."

Charming.

"It's not going to be *that* difficult," I say, lifting my chin. "What exactly are you insinuating?"

They stare pointedly at the chocolate croissant in my hand. It may or may not be the third I've had this morning, and I may or may not have spread it with strawberry jam, butter and Nutella.

I slam it back on the plate defensively.

"Do you think Kate Moss asks her friends if they'd like a Mars Bar whizzed up into a milkshake for breakfast?" Jasper asks faux-innocently.

"It tastes really nice," I snap. "And if I'm going to be stylish and adopt a healthy living regime, I'll need all the extra energy I can get."

"You've hidden in the stationery cupboard during every netball match for eleven years," Nat observes, still grinning. "You once wrote THIS IS THE ONLY KIND OF EXERCISE I LIKE on the front of your maths book."

"That was a keenly observed pun!"

"*Hahaha.*" Toby's *still* laughing. "*Seduce the camera! Harriet Manners! Seduce! Hahaha!*"

Apparently only one in twelve friendships last. If they don't stop undermining me right now, they're going straight in my eleven.

"Actually, I can be *very* alluring," I say, folding my arms crossly, cheeks going pink. "*Many* boys have been completely overwhelmed by my attractive and seductive strategies and charm."

"*Haha!*" Toby laughs, rolling over on my bed. "Harriet, do you remember that time *we* kissed? No offence, but you were terrible. Diabolical. Really quite horrifically, atrociously, unspeakably—"

"*We've got it*. Offence taken."

"Wait," Jasper says, pausing from examining the notes on my revision pegboard. "Hang on, you kissed *Toby*? When did *that* happen?"

"243 days ago." Toby opens his diary at a starred bookmark. "In Japan. Sadly while I adore Harriet mentally, physically we are not chemically aligned. I believe she's been rebounding in pain ever since."

"So…" Jasper frowns, "I don't think I understand the timeline. Was this before or after N—"

"*Anyway*," Nat says smoothly, lobbing a balled-up yellow Post-it at him, "*all* I'm saying, Harriet, is of course we'll help. We like Wilbur and we love you. Whatever you need."

The sudden relief is intense.

If I'm being honest, I didn't see this list being particularly easy to tick off either. Of all the instructions I've given myself to follow, not surviving off a form of sugar like a bumblebee is probably the hardest.

Also, I'm kind of hoping if I distribute tasks cleverly and sensitively it'll help cheer them all up too.

This could fix six birds with one well-organised and perfectly aimed stone and they won't even know it.

"*Brilliant*," I say, pulling out four individually bound

files in different colours. "Because I've delegated each of you a specific skill set to lead on."

Jubilantly, I hand out the folders and wait for the collective Team JINTH delight.

"FASHION AND STYLING," Nat reads from the front of a large blue folder.

"RESEARCH AND PREPARATION," Toby says, flicking avidly through a huge red one. "Ooh! This is *just* like the Sorting Hat, Harriet! Except with a lot more paperwork."

"*Coffee*?" Jasper says, flicking his single piece of yellow paper. "My specific skill set is *hot beverages*?"

"And cold," I remind him. "It's important to stay flexible."

Then we turn to look at India, sitting quietly in the corner. Her face is expressionless and she's carefully examining the purple timetable stuck in the back of her folder.

"*Confidence*," she says without looking up. "You've given me a new revision schedule, Harriet. With time slots."

"You're welcome," I beam modestly. "That should make everything *much* more streamlined for you and help boost those girls."

Then I sit down at my desk and prepare for the hardest homework of my life.

For the first time, I'm not modelling to transform or undergo some kind of metamorphosis. I'm not running away or chasing towards anything, and I'm not seeking popularity or power.

No: I'm just going to step up and be a professional. Starting right now.

31

As predicted, Nat doesn't need telling twice.

Judging by the speed with which my Best Friend bounces off my bed, shouts "Me first! *Sit down, Toby, I SAID ME FIRST,*" and jumps into my wardrobe, she's clearly been waiting to give me a makeover for quite some time.

Eleven years, quite possibly.

I'm trying to pretend she didn't roll her sleeves up first: I assumed this was more of a tweak rather than a demolition job.

"No," she says brusquely as the Winnie-the-Pooh and Eeyore jumper I wore to Russia comes sailing out of the wardrobe.

"Nah." The Halloween black-spider-onesie lands on top, eight legs flailing. "Nope nope nope," she says as my red bobble hat, lobster shoes and gold star top hit the floor.

"Not this either." The red halter-neck dress decorated

129

with hearts lands at my feet with a *plop*.

My own heart gives a little painful twist.

So many seminal outfits: so many precious, irreplaceable memories. I can literally see the last fifteen months of my life piling up in front of my eyes.

Also – "Nat, *you* bought me that."

"I know," she says, head momentarily reappearing from the depths of my wardrobe. "It's gorgeous and that's the problem. When you walk into a go-see, do you want the thing they notice to be the clothes?"

I suppose I hadn't thought of it like that.

"Have you still got your Cream of Tomato Soup costume?" Toby asks curiously. "It shows Harriet is versatile enough to model both clothes *and* food."

"Plus," Jasper adds, "nothing says *hot* like a bowl of steaming liquid."

They all laugh and I scowl.

Up to the age of sixteen, girls have an average of one point higher in IQ than boys, and I think this proves it. Although frankly Jasper's seventeen: there's no excuse.

India says something about needing the bathroom and slips out of the door.

"Now." Nat rummages for a few more minutes, then holds up a pair of plain black leggings I didn't even know I owned, a slim black V-neck T-shirt and black pumps.

"Harriet, take those clothes off."

Jasper abruptly stops laughing.

"Uh." He takes a few steps sideways, like a crab. "I've – uh – just remembered I've got to… Uh. Tables. Work. Coffee. Bye."

And he quickly strides out of the room.

Even though it's a Saturday morning and the cafe doesn't open for another hour and a half. And I'm pretty sure he doesn't have a shift today.

Brilliant. Boys now physically *run* away from me at the first sign of a bra strap.

Nat stares pointedly at Tobes, then sighs, pushes him out of the room and slams the door behind him. "Hey, Jas!" we hear him call out. "Wow, you got down the stairs fast."

"Here," Nat says more gently, handing me the pile of plain black Lycra. "Put this on."

"But," I object as my BFF carefully ties my hair into a tight bun and pins up my fringe, "I don't look fashionable at *all*."

Honestly, I look like I'm about to attend a yoga teacher's funeral.

"Exactly," Nat says, patting my face with a little tinted moisturiser, then applying one layer of mascara and a swipe of pink lip balm. "Fashion's *their* job, Harriet. Yours is to be the blank canvas. Let them see it properly."

She carefully tweaks my outfit a few times, then pulls me in front of a mirror.

For the first time in my personal history, there are no cartoon hamsters or ponies, no attached multicoloured feathers, no mini-pigs, no fringe in my eyes or straps breaking. No mismatched shoes, no sweat, no gold on my face or chocolate on my top lip.

I look like me, except neat and tidy.

Nat's a style prodigy.

Although I can't believe that after fifteen full months of trying, my spider onesie was actually the closest I ever got to getting it right.

I sneak a look at the reflection of Nat behind me. Her cheeks are pink, her eyes are shining and there's a bounce back in her step. She really does love fashion: just not the essay-writing part of it.

I'd say that's the Happiness Goal for 'N' achieved.

So I'd better leave her alone to get on with her studies: the best gift I can possibly give her.

And the most difficult to offer.

"Harriet?" a voice calls through the door as Nat glances at her watch, mutters *shoot* and grabs her bag again. "You just got an email from Wilbur. Also one about fifteen per cent off pencils at the Natural History Museum.

It's a very good deal, I strongly advise going for it."

I pull open my bedroom door sharply. "*Toby*. How do you know my password?"

"I'm Head of Research and Preparation," he says in surprise. "It's my job."

I should have thought this through more carefully.

Fine. I'll just change it when he's gone home. "What does it say?"

"These pencils are made of the finest quality wood with engraved lettering and…"

"The email from *Wilbur*, Toby."

"He can sort something for next Saturday but he doesn't want to exhaust you. There's also a very strange photo of a kitten with a moustache."

Even at his lowest, Wilbur's still trying to make me smile. "Please email back and tell him to cram as many appointments in as possible. I'm not fussy."

"Done," Toby says after a slight pause. "I've also purchased you four pencils because it really is an excellent deal."

I make a mental note to change my bank details too.

Then I stick my head into the hallway. "India? It's your turn! I've got books I can pile on my h…"

The bathroom door is open.

"India?" I hop downstairs. "India?" I try the living

room. "*India?*" I hop into the garden, as if she might be wandering desperately around our flowerbeds, looking for somewhere alternative to urinate.

Bunty pokes her head out of the kitchen.

"Are you looking for your friend with the lovely hair, darling? She left ten minutes ago."

I stare at my grandmother blankly.

"She can't have," I say in confusion. "She didn't say goodbye."

But when I run to the front door the purple suede boots have disappeared, the purple car is nowhere to be seen and there's a big purple folder, lying on the doormat.

India has gone.

32

The next six days are spent in training.

With the help of a few carefully analysed and highlighted women's magazines, I do my best to blend my academic school duties with my target of temporary physical and mental perfection, in time for the weekend.

This includes:

* Lifting two Bunsen burners repeatedly in biology in an attempt to improve my arm muscles.
* Getting a detention from Mr Harper for being a 'fire hazard'.
* Trying to get a little extra 'beauty sleep' in the common room.
* Waking to find notes with the word GEEK written on them in my mouth.
* Eating a lot of ketchup because it's the only thing in the school canteen with vitamins left in it.
* Wondering why those vitamins aren't working.

By Friday, I finally understand why so many models abandon education at a young age: school is not compatible with a healthy-guru lifestyle. My stomach is no more toned *at all.*

Luckily, I've made up for it with research.

Thanks to intense lessons every evening with Toby in the cafe, I know *everything there is to know* about fashion.

OK, that sounds kind of arrogant. Correction: I know a *lot more than before.*

Which was zero, so that's not difficult.

And now – after disappearing into a week of solid college classes and lectures – Nat's turned up at the cafe to give me my final Model exams with a clipboard, a white shirt and a fake pair of diamante glasses.

She's possibly taking this a little *too* seriously.

"Ready," I say, putting my mug down. "Go."

"Where was Guccio Gucci born?" Nat fires at me, pointing her fountain pen. "And when?"

"Florence," I answer promptly. "1881. He was the son of an Italian merchant."

"One point," Nat nods sternly, drawing a little tick. "What is the current value of the fashion industry to the UK?"

"Twenty-six billion pounds. There has been an increase

of twenty-two per cent in nominal terms since Oxford Economics measured it in 2009."

"Yes." She draws another little tick. "Who inspired Louboutin's red shoe sole?"

"His assistant. She was painting her nails at the time."

"*And*," Toby says, leaning back and making his fingers into weird little triangles in a frighteningly sinister echo of Peter Trout, "how do you walk like a cat?"

"Yes," Nat snaps, business-like and sharp. "How do you walk like a… wait, what?"

"Cats are digitigrades," he explains. "I've told Harriet that she needs to walk on her toes and put her front leg and her back leg forward at the same time."

Nat rolls her eyes.

"So close," she sighs, smacking him gently on the nose with her pen. "Yet so far."

"Speaking of *far*," Jasper says, putting more cake on the table, "has anyone seen India this week?"

We look at each other.

Apart from a brief flash of purple on Monday morning, there have been no sightings at all. In spite of the handwritten letter I slipped in her locker, the note I pinned to the physics door and the email I sent her with an attached document detailing all of the Team JINTH whereabouts this week.

I'd think she'd fallen off the surface of the planet entirely if I hadn't set up a Read Receipt.

My stomach's starting to go rigid.

"Oh, umm," Nat says, clearing her throat, "I *totally* forgot. I got a text from Indy yesterday. Her parents grounded her while she was at yours, Harriet, and she had to peg it home. She said she's really sorry but not to take it personally."

And I swear it's like magic.

With one swoop, my entire body relaxes. There was a tiny part of me that thought we'd done something to upset her.

In relief, I look at my list. "OK, can anyone take Confidence for her? I don't mind who fills in."

"Sorry, H," Nat says, standing up and taking her fake glasses back off, "I've got more revision to do. Honestly though, there's nothing left for you to learn. You're going to be amazing."

"Apart from at *seduction*." Toby's chortling. "HAHAHAHA."

I must be the only person in the world with an ex-stalker who thinks she's physically abhorrent.

Thank goodness Jasper's gone back to the counter so he can't add a little dig there too.

They have *not* let up about it.

Still chuckling, Toby hands me a stapled document with *Harriet Manners' VIP Saturday Castings – the Research* at the top of the page in marker pen.

"Nice one, Tobes," Nat grins, high-fiving him.

Toby looks genuinely chuffed.

"It was nothing," he blushes. "Just a few library sessions here, a few night classes at Central St Martins there."

And just like that, I realise Team JINTH Happiness Goal number two is already achieved. All Toby ever really wants – has ever really wanted – is to be included.

TICK.

"You're going to walk this," Nat says brightly, kissing my cheek. "I can feel it in my bones."

A lump rises into my throat.

In an animal-rescue centre in Orlando a fully grown tiger, lion and a bear share a pen: rescued as cubs together and now totally inseparable.

That's what the three of us are.

The best of friends, even though nature, geography and common interests usually mean we'd never normally meet, and in other circumstances might literally kill each other.

"Gotta run. Text us later?" Nat calls over her shoulder, grabbing her bag and hurrying towards the exit.

"Love you."

"We've talked about this," Toby exclaims with an elaborate sigh, standing up and following her. "I just don't feel the same way, Natalie."

"Oh shut up, Toby," Nat says affectionately.

And the door swings shut behind them.

33

With a happy grin, I settle into my armchair.

Now everything's ready for tomorrow, I can finally start to relax and take stock of my progress.

Snuggling into a cushion, I take a sip of my healthy, model-approved mint tea and try to pretend it's delicious and doesn't taste like the toothpaste melted in hot water I forced my family to drink when I was five years old.

I try to ignore the fact that my right arm is still aching from all the Bunsen-burner lifting (they're surprisingly heavy).

And I watch Jasper over the top of my cup.

He's saving for art college next year, so he's been working every single night this week: striding around in his big black boots, wiping tables, taking orders, counting change, steaming milk. The muscle in his jaw only jumps very slightly when somebody spends a full seven minutes ordering an extra-hot soya macchiato with one-pump-of-syrup-not-two-oh-no-wait-is-it-one-pump-or-two?

I can't imagine how much of an effort it is for him: not being sarcastic at all when he's serving customers.

It's like the weirdest form of torture.

With a cloth in hand, he stomps over to another corner of the busy cafe, picks up a tray and stomps back again, and there's an abrupt squeal.

A tiny gang of first years are huddled tightly in the corner, and every time Jasper gets within six metres of their table they erupt into a flurry of giggles.

Apparently whales make themselves voluntarily deaf when around irritating sounds, and it looks like Jasper does too.

He doesn't even blink.

"OMG," the brunette girl whispers as he goes behind the counter and starts wiping a plate, "he's *so gorgeous.*"

"Have you seen his *eyes*? They're, like, the most beautiful thing I've ever seen."

"I *wish* I was just *five* years older."

"Don't you think he looks a bit like a wolf?" the littlest redhead says. "Native Americans believe that dogs with different coloured eyes can see heaven and earth at the same time. Shall we ask him if he can too?"

She starts waving her hand enthusiastically.

"*Lydia.*"

"Oh my God."

"Why are you always so embarrassing?"

"What? What did I do?" Then she glances around. "Oooh! Harriet Manners is here, guys! *Told* you this place was uber-cool! Fact!"

Clapping her hands, my mini-me jumps up and runs over, followed by Fee, Soph and Kiera.

I smile at my little gang from last year.

Every now and then I still see them around lower school and stop to chat, and they were so impressed with Team JINTH accessories I lent them my badge-making machine.

Although I have to be honest: 'Team FSLK' doesn't have quite the same ring to it.

"*Hey*, Harriet."

"Wow, Harriet, I *love* your Tintin jumper."

"Your hair is *so* pretty today."

"Told you a cup of chino is officially over. Harriet drinks *tea*."

"It's called a *cappuccino*," Lydia sighs, rolling her eyes. "And it comes from the word *Capuchin* because it's the same colour. Isn't that right, Harriet?"

"Umm." I literally have no idea. "Sure. Same as the Capuchin monkey."

"Not the *monkey*." Lydia looks bewildered by my unexpected stupidity. "The habit of the Italian *friar.*"

Seriously: when I get home I'm searching the house for adoption papers.

"So who are you here with, Harriet?" Fee spins round in excitement. "Is Natalie Grey here, or India Perez, or..."

She ends the sentence with a squeak.

"Your Majesty," Jasper says, appearing from behind me, "you appear to have dropped your cloak. Please, continue to hold court while I pick it up for you."

Swiftly, he grabs my red duffel coat off the floor and throws it over the back of my chair with a gallant hand flourish and I'm instantly reminded of our epic fight at school last year.

The one where I ended up on the ground, covered in mud.

Twice.

Fee gives another little squeak.

"Or perhaps this is extra padding?" he says with a small smile. "For when your seduction strategy works and all the boys fall at your feet?"

I feel myself flush tomato red.

I'm *never* going to hear the end of this. I'll be eighty years old and Toby and Jasper will be wheeling around in their electric space-chairs, sniggering at how bewitching I'm not.

"Yes," I snap, folding my arms crossly. "Well, I

wouldn't want them to smash their heads and end up as quick-witted as you."

Jasper flashes a rare grin.

"Says the alluring can of vegetable soup," he says, lifting an eyebrow and putting Nat and Toby's empty cups on a tray.

Then he disappears into the kitchen.

"*Tomato's a fruit, actually*," I finally manage at the empty swinging door. "It has *seeds*."

Yeah. That should do it. Nothing says *in your face* like botanical classification.

When I look back there are eight bright eyes staring at me. "Oh."

"Em."

"Gee."

"*Harriet*."

"What?" I quickly rub my lip on my sleeve. "What did I do this time?"

"Are you going out with *him*?" Lydia squeaks, hopping up and down. "Is gorgeous Coffee Boy your boyfriend?"

"He *is*."

"Oh my gosh, you're so *lucky*."

"I *wish* I was you."

I blink at Team FSLK, then at Jasper: visible through

the kitchen door, scowling at the lipstick smeared on a cup.

Then I burst into laughter.

I'm so loud a few customers spin round, trying to locate the source of my abrupt hilarity.

"Are you not?" Fee says in confusion when I've slowed to a snigger. "He called you Your Majesty."

"He said you were an alluring can of vegetable soup."

"He said *boys fall at your feet.*"

"Lots of falling goes on in my life," I chuckle. "But usually because I've knocked things over. Jasper's being *sarcastic*, guys. From the Greek word *sarkos* which means to *tear the flesh*. He's just winding me up."

"Aww." Team FSLK visibly wilts in disappointment. "I guess the can of soup thing *was* weird."

"That's so sad, Harriet."

"Why are you alone?"

"Maybe you could *make* him like you?"

They look so hopeful and starry-eyed, for a brief second I consider not crushing their innocent romantic dreams.

Then I change my mind.

As their experienced elder it's my responsibility to destroy these ideas as swiftly as possible.

Before life does it for them.

"You'd literally have to fly a spaceship from one side of the galaxy to the other 15,000 times before you bumped into anything else," I say firmly, "and there's still more chance of two things colliding in space than me and Jasper King getting together."

Fee gives another squeak.

"Thanks very much," Jasper says from behind me, taking his apron off and looking at his watch. "Have you ever considered writing Valentine's cards for a living, Harriet? I can really see that written across a pink teddy bear. Maybe spelt out in roses."

Then he reaches over, grabs my Modelling folder and heads towards the cafe door with it under his arm.

I jump up and bolt after him.

"Wait! Jasper! Where are you going with that? I need it for tomorrow!"

"I know," he says over his shoulder, "and it's not finished. So you're coming with me."

34

There are 6,909 known languages in the world, and the word *huh* is understood in all of them.

Which is lucky because now that's what I've got.

"You asked each of us to help you," Jasper says, pounding the pavement ahead of me, "and I'm still the J in JINTH, last time I checked. Unless you replaced me with the Jam from those God-awful sandwiches."

Wow, I had no idea he took his coffee-making so seriously; although why we're leaving the cafe I don't know.

The first ever webcam was invented in 1991 by Cambridge University scientists who wanted to stream footage of their coffee pot so they'd know when it was ready: I suppose caffeine *can* inspire great innovation.

Although the only reason I gave that brief to Jasper was so that we could keep him company while he worked.

It was supposed to make him happier.

"Those sandwiches were *delicious*," I lie, racing to

catch up. "And where are we going anyway? It's 4:28pm on Friday afternoon. How do you know I'm not extremely busy with some very important social event?"

There's a short pause while we both consider this likelihood, given that the only available person in my social group is now walking next to me.

"I decided to risk it," Jasper says. "I'm a bit of a gambler like that."

Then he takes a sharp left turn into the station, where a train to London is just starting to approach. I'm not properly prepared, and something painful unexpectedly twinges at the base of my stomach.

I swear for a second I can almost smell snow.

Firmly, I push it away.

"You know," I say, speeding up, "coffee is the second most traded commodity on earth and has been shown to reduce chances of Alzheimer's Disease by sixty-five per cent. I know *lots* about it. You don't need to worry."

Jasper stops and turns to me.

His jaw is set in its usual line and the splash of brown in his left eye looks darker than normal, but the corners of his mouth are surprisingly soft.

"Contrary to popular belief, my entire knowledge base isn't limited to liquids. I'd like to contribute too, if you'll let me."

I square myself for the inevitable mockery.

Maybe *here's the fiver I usually contribute to charity*, to which I'll snap back with *oh really, well with your coffee-making skills best keep it for yourself, you're going to need it*.

Or something sharper: I haven't decided yet.

But Jasper just carries on looking at me earnestly, and I'm not entirely sure what to do with that.

"Uh," I say, flushing slightly, "sure. What do you, uh, have in mind?"

With a screech, the train pulls up.

"Funnily enough," Jasper says, handing my folder back to me, "a different kind of paperwork."

Trafalgar Square is famous around the world.

Stretching from Charing Cross to the Haymarket and built on what used to be the Whitehall Palace mews in 1843, it's busy all year: packed with tourists, couples and fake statues dressed like Yoda.

In the middle of the enormous rectangle are two large fountains, surrounded by water, and at the centre is Admiral Nelson: standing proudly on a 170-foot column, guarded by four enormous bronze lions with big hair, curved lips and slanted eyes.

Quickly, I look away from them.

"Umm, did you know that the Harris hawk isn't *actually* a hawk, it's part of the buzzard family?" I run a bit to catch up again. "And it's native to Mexico?"

There's a short pause while Jasper strides through the bustling crowd.

Then he says: "Where did that come from?"

"Wikipedia, I think." We turn the corner. "Possibly an animal encyclopaedia. Or a documentary about hawks. Honestly, it's hard to remember all my sources."

"Nope. I meant *why did that come from.*"

Oh. Sometimes I forget that the connections I make aren't always as obvious to other people as they are to me.

Or that Jasper always calls me out on it.

Truthfully, I don't want to think about where that connection came from: I think it might be buried a little too deep.

"The Mayor of London bought a big hawk called Harry to scare off all the pigeons," I improvise. "He's still around here somewhere. If we're going to take pictures outside, I'll need to keep an eye out."

From experience, as soon as I step in front of a camera an animal tries to attack me. All I need now is a large carnivorous bird to complete the set.

"Take pictures?" Jasper stops in the middle of the

pavement. "*Now* what are you talking about?"

"Trafalgar Square," I say in confusion. "You need paperwork to shoot there, so I assumed..."

We've walked round the corner and stopped outside a big grey building with carvings over an enormous curved doorway and pillars: Trafalgar Square is no longer actually visible.

"Well," Jasper says, lifting his eyebrows, "you know what they say about *assuming*, Harriet-uccino."

"It makes an ass out of the Ming dynasty?"

I'm rewarded with a sharp laugh.

"Nope." Jasper points upwards. "It means you've jumped to the wrong conclusion, yet again. We're going in here."

35

Now, I know a fair amount about art.

I know that red paint was more valuable to Aztecs than gold and that Sir Isaac Newton invented the colour wheel.

I know that when the Mona Lisa was stolen from the Louvre the empty space attracted more visitors than the painting and when lit a coloured crayon will burn for thirty minutes straight.

I even know that in 1964 a Swedish journalist exhibited pictures drawn by a chimpanzee to see if professional art critics could tell the difference.

(For the record – they couldn't.)

But it doesn't matter how many facts I know about art, I don't totally *get it.* And I can say that with some confidence, because that's exactly what my art teacher, Mr Randulph, wrote on my Year Nine Report Card.

All of which means I may have visited every other museum and exhibition in London more times than I can

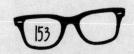

possibly count.

But I have never, ever been here.

The same cannot be said for Jasper.

From the moment we walk through the big glass doors of the National Portrait Gallery, he looks different.

Poised, determined, comfortable.

I stare at him in surprise.

Has he transformed, or is he always like this and he's just finally in the right environment? The way a wolf in a grey, dull city would just look like a big dog until you finally saw it in a forest: being who it's meant to be.

Without a word, Jasper carries on walking.

Straight through the high-ceilinged, wood-panelled rooms, past pictures of people I recognise – Shakespeare, David Bowie, Jane Austen – and people I definitely don't: rosy-cheeked children, men with austere pointy beards, and women with elaborately jewelled dresses and tiny dogs.

Finally he stops in front of a black and white photograph of Winston Churchill.

"There," he says with a nod. "Your inspiration."

I look around the room, because I'm obviously missing something.

"Umm." I glance at Jasper's profile, but he's still

staring at the picture. How do I put this politely? "I'm not entirely sure you understand the world of fashion modelling, Jasper."

In all my time as a teenage model, nobody has ever asked me to be like the man who led Britain to victory in the Second World War.

"This was taken in 1941," Jasper says, ignoring me completely. "Churchill was tired and didn't want his portrait taken. Yousuf Karsh, the photographer, refused to give him a drink, ripped the cigar out of his mouth and took the photo before he could respond."

I look at the photo more closely. Churchill looks genuinely furious: belligerent, bullish, as if he's seconds away from ripping the room apart.

"This photo helped to win the war," Jasper adds, almost as an afterthought. "It showed how terrifying and inflexible he could be."

Then Jasper turns and continues walking.

He stops in front of a portrait of a pretty lady in a blue dress.

"This was the wife of the artist's best friend," Jasper says. "He was in love with her, and she never actually knew it. This was his way of communicating how he felt."

Then, without waiting for a response, he turns and keeps walking, pausing in front of a painting of a woman sleeping peacefully with a hand curled under her face.

"This is Lady Venetia. She died an hour before this painting was made. Her husband was so heartbroken he commissioned a painter immediately and kept this next to his bed for the rest of his life. He believed her spirit had gone into the painting."

A lump rises into my throat. That's so incredibly sad, and so incredibly beautiful.

And also a bit like a creepy Oscar Wilde novel.

"Jasper…" I say, clearing my throat. "I'm sorry, but I don't understand."

"Every picture tells a story, Harriet. Sometimes we know what the story is. We know it's rage, or sadness, or love, or grief. And sometimes we don't. But they all have one."

He gestures around the room.

Blinking, I lean towards a large painting of a young girl. She's standing next to a brown and white dog, a triumphant smile at the corner of her lips.

And the meaning of what Jasper's saying is slowly starting to hit me.

It's not enough for me to just *be* there.

These portraits capture fleeting moments. They're emotions immortalised, a transient life made permanent: however personal or public, private or shared.

In a world where everything changes, these are points of time that stand still. A way to hold on to something that can't last forever.

And the same goes for each of my photos.

The fear and confusion in my face when I was trapped in a glass box full of dolls; the bewilderment as I was covered in octopus ink. The glowing snowflakes photo, taken moments after my hand was held for the first ever time. The second I fell in love, immortalised in a shining lake.

Even those first few clumsy polaroids: the anxiety of a bullied girl, thrown into a world she didn't think she could or should be part of.

All the stories I've already told, without even knowing it.

"Harriet," Jasper says, turning and looking straight at me, "as a model, you are a blank canvas. It's up to you to paint a picture."

I blink at him as the box in my head rattles a few times. That's just what Nat said too, isn't it?

I've never seen my job as anything more than meaningless expensive photos of clothes before – with me as a giant living breathing doll – but maybe it's more than that.

Maybe it's art too.

Huh. I should go get my Year Nine Report Card and ask for a reassessment: I think I finally *get it*.

I stare at Jasper.

You know, it's weird. I've always thought his face was round, but it isn't: it's kind of a heart shape. And though I initially evaluated his hair (a little unkindly) as *mousey*, up close it's actually bronzes and browns and golds and blonds.

Lots of bright colours, mixed up together.

"Thank you," I say after a short pause. "You're a good friend."

"Yeah." Jasper smiles slightly. "Probably too good. I'm expecting my medal any day now." He hands me my folder. "Come on, Harriet-uccino. You've got a big day tomorrow. Let's get back home."

36

Obviously, it's important to stay realistic.

So as much as I'd love everything to go perfectly on Saturday morning, I'm not *really* expecting to stick precisely to my Plan A itinerary.

In fact, given the Universe's refusal to ever – in sixteen whole years – follow my plans properly (or, frankly, at all), I've actively lowered my expectations.

This means I've also written a Plan B:

- *Manage to leave the house without smashing anything, breaking anything or being accidentally dressed like a duck.*

A brief Plan C:

- *Or oversleeping, panicking and ending up walking the streets in duck pyjamas and teddy-bear slippers.*

And a very cursory Plan D:

— Or getting hit by a runaway bicycle and crying noisily under my jumper on the pavement.

Mainly because these are all things that have already happened to me at some point so I need to stay on guard in case they decide to happen again.

It turns out I don't need any alternative plans.

For the first time ever, the Universe decides it's on board with my preferred itinerary.

Inexplicably, I fall asleep at 10pm and wake up a full nine hours later, feeling refreshed and full of energy. A quick experimental prod confirms that the pulsating spot on my cheek has magically disappeared overnight.

Then I roll over and read these three texts:

°°°\(*⁶‿⁶)/°°° I

。˚ +:((৲(。・ω・)৴)).˚ +。 **ARRIVING**

☆*:.。. o(≧▽≦)o .。.:*☆ **SUNDAY!!**

With a tiny squeak of excitement, I check my emails, jump out of bed and do a little Dance of Triumph around my bedroom: I'm one step further on my Get Wilbur Happy Again plan.

Then, following my clearly outlined Team JINTH instructions, I somehow manage to get ready without spilling foundation on my black Lycra or brutally stabbing myself in the eye with a mascara wand. I don't burn breakfast or resort to half a bar of chocolate instead, and I actually remember to tuck a pile of comp cards in the front of the orange PEAK portfolio Wilbur sent me.

(Yes, I Googled what *comp card* means.)

Finally – after a quick check that I'm not sporting a moustache or gold face paint or odd shoes – I start bouncing optimistically towards the door.

Plan A has been completed in its entirety.

I can't believe it: karma actually *works*.

After years of the cosmos ignoring every plan I've ever had, now I'm dedicated to helping others the Universe has *finally* started appreciating just how efficient and well thought through my arrangements actually—

"Harriet? Sweetheart, where are you going?"

Annabel appears at the bottom of the stairs, dressed in a smart white shirt and ironed black trousers, with Tabby curled sleepily in her arms.

It's 8am on a Saturday morning: at this point, my family's normally running round in a panic, trying to coordinate my sister's various body functions.

"Good morning!" Smiling, I kiss Tabby's cheek. "I'm off to London for the day. Remember?"

Annabel blinks a few times with puffy eyes.

"N-ooo. I don't... *think* so."

"Sure you do." Swiftly, I grab the smart black coat Nat's lent me so I don't 'ruin all her hard work'. "I told you over breakfast on Monday that a *musophobist* is a person who distrusts poetry and *turophobia* is a fear of cheese and a *Hellenologophobia* is a dislike of Greek terms, and then I told you I'm doing some castings in London today for Wilbur."

I'm not going to lie: I *may* have slipped it on the end of that very long list intentionally.

My facts have cunning multiple purposes.

"But don't worry," I add cheerfully, swinging open the front door, "I'll definitely be home before it gets dark."

According to the itinerary I definitely won't, but even Frodo only needed to confront one difficult mission at a time.

Waving, I start down the garden path.

"Umm." Annabel clears her throat behind me. "Oh God, Harriet. I'm so, so sorry, but I didn't hear you and I thought I'd told you but I obviously didn't and... things are a bit up in the air and I must have dropped that particular ball… and…"

I stop walking and turn round slowly: doom starting to impend.

"Told me what?"

Annabel has a very un-Annabel look on her face. "Your dad's got a second interview in Manchester today. He left an hour ago."

I blink. "Really? But that's great!"

"And your grandmother and I have an important day booked that we really can't get out of. A spa-type thing."

"How lovely!" Doom's still impending, but I can't work out which direction it's coming from. Unless they expect me to sit with them in a sauna, because that's never going to happen: I spend half my life bright red as it is.

There's a long silence while my stepmother apologises energetically with her eyebrows.

"And…" I prompt, waving my hand in a circle.

"And…" Annabel says, then – incredibly slowly, with the speed of a feather falling – she looks straight at me, and then pointedly down at Tabitha.

And there it is: *DOOM*.

The cutest, fluffiest, most adorable fat-cheeked doom known to mankind.

"But…" No. No no. This can't be happening. My

plans. My *perfect plans*. "I can't stay home to babysit, Annabel. I promised Wilbur. I've spent a whole week preparing for this."

I used up *seven plastic folders*.

"I'm so sorry, Harriet," Annabel says, her complexion changing from white to slightly grey. "We have to leave right now and it's just too late to find anyone else. Maybe you could rearrange it?"

"Sure," I snap. "I'll just ask all the top photographers and designers and editors in London to reschedule their job interviews to a time more convenient for me, shall I?"

Annabel looks up from trying to gently disentangle Tabby's clingy little hands from around her neck, like one of those gooey little rubber men stuck to a window.

"Hmm?" she says, kissing the top of Tabby's head. "That sounds like a great idea, sweetheart. Do that."

Oh my God.

Do I have to explain sarcasm to her too?

"But..." *Say something, Harriet.* "Annabel, I don't... This is... Can't you... I won't..."

According to my fact books, the Spanish national anthem has no words. In an incredibly unfair turn of events, apparently now I don't either.

"Thank you so much, darling," Annabel says quickly, plopping a sleepy Tabitha in my arms. "We're both very grateful." Then she leans into the hallway. "Mum! We're late! Are you ready?"

There's a tinkle of bells.

Then – in a floating mass of scarves, feathers and long skirts – Bunty wafts out of the living room, pink hair piled into a top-knot, large tasselled bag flung over her shoulder. Smelling of something smoky and sweet, like barbecued cherry blossoms.

"For my next adventure, darling?" she beams brightly, kissing me on the cheek. "*Always.*"

Then they both climb into the pink VW Beetle and drive off at top speed.

Leaving me holding the baby.

37

Here are a few interesting facts:

It takes ten litres of water to make a single A4 sheet of paper, and wasted pages account for 25 per cent of landfill. Globally, we destroy between three and six billion trees every single year.

I should probably stop printing my plans out: they are literally not worth the paper I've written them on.

Also, I am never speaking to the Universe again.

Blinking in dismay, I stand on the doorstep with Tabitha and stare at the road, praying they'll come straight back again.

Panic is starting to surge through me.

It's like sitting in front of a line of dominoes with a strong breeze blowing and my finger stretched out.

If today falls, everything else falls too.

Without today, I can't get modelling jobs. Without modelling jobs, there's no money for Wilbur, without money Wilbur's agency fails, he goes bankrupt and so on, tumbling in a series of disastrous clicks.

Until all my plans are lying in a pile at my feet: just another big old mess.

And I *cannot* let that happen.

Brain whirring, I glance down at Tabitha. Her thumb is in her mouth, her eyes are flickering shut and her tiny pink hand is firmly gripping Dunky the fluffy donkey.

She looks so sweet. Serene. Completely at peace.

Easily managed.

Let's be honest: I could probably do with a little moral support today anyway. And at no stage whatsoever did Annabel say I had to stay *here* to look after Tabitha. It was heavily inferred, but never actually *clarified verbally.*

So, legally, it's open to interpretation.

In a flash of inspiration, I run into the kitchen, grab a handful of milk bottles from the fridge and lob them into a large quilted bag with five spare nappies.

Hope rising, I cram a plastic musical puzzle in as well, in case she gets bored. Then I pop a floppy, sleepy Tabby in the buggy, fling my satchel over my shoulder and start off towards London as fast as I can.

These dominoes are staying up.

I'm going to conquer the modelling world today, everything's going to go as planned and now I'm simply taking my baby sister with me.

After all, how difficult can that be?

38

I get my answer within fifteen seconds.

The first five are fine: I manage to wrangle the buggy out of the front door, close it behind me and somehow get us both on the path.

Six, seven and eight are also doable.

We reach the front gate and I manage to get it open while also waving at our neighbours and praying they don't have Annabel's mobile number.

It's at second nine that it starts to go wrong.

The back wheel of the buggy gets wedged against the gate pole and I jiggle it slightly to release it.

Muttering, I jiggle again.

Then again.

But it's on the fourth jiggle that Tabby abruptly wakes up and I watch in slow motion as she flings her arm out and Dunky goes flying: over the edge of the buggy, and on to the grass next to us.

And before I can even start to bend down to retrieve

it, Victor has raced out from under a bush and grabbed Dunky in his mouth.

My stomach lurches in horror.

No. No. *No no no no.*

"No!" I yell at him as he bounds a few steps away. "Bring that back! Bad kitty!"

Victor pauses, orange tail waving.

He gives me a dark, evil look that makes it clear why Pope Innocent VIII had all cats declared as demons in the 15th century.

With a small growl, he disappears with Dunky into the overgrowth.

And that's when the screaming starts.

Statistically, a baby will cry for an average of two hours a day. Tabby has decided to ignore these basic guidelines.

With grief and rage, my sister shrieks as I clamber into the bush after Victor, to no avail. She howls as I offer up every other toy in the house and bawls as I give up and start jogging us towards the station, singing *Twinkle Twinkle, Little Star* as loudly as I can.

She squalls as I ram the buggy on to the train and weeps on the underground: ululates down Carnaby Street and vociferates into Broadwick Street.

She laments loudly in five different toyshops while I

try desperately to find a replacement Dunky.

By the time I find some kind of inferior blue stuffed horse and start running towards my first appointment of the day – already forty-five minutes late – I've run out of words to describe my sibling's fury.

She looks like a human balloon: as if she's slowly blowing herself up and preparing to pop.

"*Please*, Tabs," I plead as I awkwardly shove the buggy into a shiny elevator. "I don't know what to do. Please tell me what I can do."

Babies don't generally begin combining sounds into words until they're at least ten months old: we could be in this lift for some time.

"Did you know," I say, attempting a jolly, manic tone as she continues to screech, "that you have sixty more bones than me right now? That's interesting, don't you think?"

Apparently not: the yells kick up a notch.

"And you still don't have any kneecaps at all. You're not going to develop them for a couple more years. What do you think of that?"

Not much: the uvula at the back of her throat looks like it's about to fall off, it's vibrating so hard.

A whole week.

I spent a whole week preparing for today, and I'd

have been better off investing that time in overfeeding and/or trying to lose Victor.

Desperately, I grab my phone.

Stupid cat took D. T devastated. Any ideas? H

I don't need to elaborate any further.

Jasper bought Tabby Dunky the donkey as a Christmas gift last year, and her inability to sleep without it is well documented: if anyone knows how to find a similar one, it's going to be him.

A few seconds later, there's a beep.

Leave it with me. You've got this in the bag. J

I breathe out a few times.

Then I try to make the blue horse dance frantically with one hand while with the other I flick through Toby's folder. According to page four, my first go-see is with the biggest fashion magazine in the world, which has forty-three international editions in over sixty countries, means 'she' in French and launched in 1945.

How they feel about noises that are louder than ambulance sirens is about to be determined.

The lift goes *ping* and the doors slide open.

I brace myself for imminent humiliation – possibly an immediate arrest for noise pollution – and push the buggy out into reception.

And there's an abrupt silence.

For a fraction of a second, I assume my eardrums have perforated or maybe I've just turned into an ant. (They don't have ears.)

Then I look down in surprise.

Tabby's eyes have gone very round, the flush in her cheeks is already fading and the horse's tail has gone in her mouth. With a frown, I cautiously roll the buggy back into the lift again and she starts making an *uh uh uh* sound.

I push her out and it stops.

Oh my God. You have to be kidding. Tabitha's a fashionista *already*? She's only eight months old: she can't even stand up yet.

"*This* makes you feel better? You want to visit *Elle* magazine?"

Tabby waves the blue horse at me: trauma momentarily forgotten.

And I make my decision.

"Right," I say firmly, pulling the buggy hood back so she can see the room properly. "If it's going to make you happy, I'll show you everything. Just try and forget Dunky for a few hours. Deal?"

Tabitha beams.

I hope Annabel knows what she's in for: she's going to need another relaxing spa trip when she discovers her youngest daughter is a belligerent style icon already.

Affectionately, I straighten my sister's little green dinosaur top, wipe the tears off her little cherub cheeks and smarten up her fluffy red curls.

I do the same for myself.

And then the Manners sisters do what we've never, ever done before.

We take on the fashion world together.

39

It starts better than I could possibly have hoped it would.

Despite being nearly an hour late, Tabby and I sail straight through *Elle* reception, into the glamorous open-plan magazine office and towards a very chic-looking fashion editor in camel-coloured trousers and a light blue shirt.

Quickly, I run through my mental list.

Am I being professional? TICK. Confident? TICK. Stylish? TICK. Is my health top-notch? AS GOOD AS CAN BE EXPECTED IN ONE WEEK.

Have I done my research? OH YOU BETCHA.

The word *jeans* comes from the cotton trousers worn by sailors from Genoa; the world's first fashion magazine was published in 1586 and it takes more than 30,000 silkworms to produce twelve pounds of raw silk. I've even remembered extracts from the fifty copies of *Elle* Nat gave me, collected over the last half-decade.

Admittedly, my self-belief wobbles slightly as the

ridiculously beautiful blonde model in front of me puts a portfolio full of *Prada* campaigns back in her bag and looks in alarm at the slightly soggy toy tucked under my arm.

But I quickly recalibrate.

I've done *Baylee*. I've done *Yuka Ito*. I kind of half did *Levaire*. I have just as much chance as any of these girls.

This is *in the bag*.

"Hello," I say to the editor, before she can comment on Tabby. "I'm Harriet Manners and there was a babysitting conundrum. I promise it's not a sign of opprobrium towards fashion and I respect you very much."

"Don't worry at all," she smiles warmly, holding out a hand. "Childcare is a nightmare, I have one myself. So let's see what we have here."

I give her my orange portfolio and somehow manage to swallow an intense impulse to tell her that the fruit *orange* actually came before the colour *orange* and was a reduction of *nāraṅga,* the Sanskrit word for "orange tree".

Be professional, Harriet.

"Lovely," the editor says, opening my book and flicking the first page over. "Beautiful." She flicks again. "Gorgeous." Flick. "Very pretty." Flick flick. "Wonderful. What a lovely face you have."

Flick flick flick flick.

Then she takes one of my comp cards out, puts it on a table full of other comp cards and hands the book back to me. "Thank you, Harriet. We'll be in touch."

I blink in amazement.

Oh my God, is that *it*? Did I just get my very first job of the day? All it takes to achieve meteoric success is a well-organised binder and a bit of belief in myself.

I should have done this *ages* ago.

"When exactly, do you think?" I don't want to be pushy, but time is of the essence. "I'm free Monday lunchtime. Can you call between 1:30pm and 2pm?"

"We'll be in touch. Thank you, Harriet."

"It's just that I have a double maths lesson at three so if I can't pick up you can leave details on voicemail."

"Thank you for coming in, Harriet," she says more firmly. "See you another time."

"Or email. I can give you that too. I can check my phone under my desk."

"Thank you, Harriet. I'll bear that in mind."

Then the editor turns pointedly to the stunning, ebony-skinned girl lining up behind me, who is getting a shiny silver portfolio out of her bag.

Hang on a minute.

Is... Is this like what Nat was saying about dating? When they *say* they'll be in touch but what they actually mean is they won't be in touch at all?

Have I just been fashion-dumped?

"Umm, sorry to interrupt." I lean abruptly in front of the other model's photos. "Does this mean you won't be in touch or you will be in touch? I need to check."

The girl starts laughing.

"Ah." The editor smiles briefly. "I see. In that case, we won't be in touch. I'm afraid you don't have the right look for us at present, Harriet. Maybe come back in a few years."

"A few *years*?" I say in dismay. "But you don't understand. I don't *have* a few years."

At least that makes the other model stop laughing: she now thinks I'm dying.

"I'm sorry, Harriet," the editor says smoothly. "Better luck elsewhere."

"But—"

"Goodbye, Harriet. Have a very nice day." Politely but deliberately, the editor spins fractionally in her chair away from me.

And it looks like my first casting is over.

40

Which is absolutely fine.

I mean, I knew I wasn't going to get them *all*. I only need to secure two, maybe three, modelling jobs to make a real difference, and according to Toby's schedule I've still got seven castings to go.

That's a forty per cent success rate target at maximum, or an E grade if modelling was a GCSE.

Which I'm very happy it's not.

I tend to cry all night if I get anything less than an A-minus.

Anyway, as I push Tabitha rapidly along the streets to my next appointment, I focus on staying positive and confident. I've got a great plan and this is in the bag: all I need to do is stick to it without getting creative or veering off course.

The same cannot be said for the buggy.

First it goes into a drain, then a pothole and a shop-window. I can't get it up the kerb, then – while texting

Team JINTH to let them know how it's going – I drive it into a lamp-post.

By the time Tabby and I arrive in Savile Row, we've lost all the time we made up at the last casting. Not to mention the fact that I can barely read the notes for this go-see because there are so many hearts drawn all over them. Nat's pencilled *Kiss the doorstep!* in Toby's margins, and I don't have time to check if she means literally.

I cautiously give the doorframe a quick peck, just in case.

The door swings open with a sharp bang.

"Model!" a very short man in a black polo-neck snaps. "Why are you sniffing our shop? What's wrong with you? Come in quickly, you're letting the warmth out."

Then he scuttles away, busy and ant-like: muttering about how he "doesn't appreciate waiting around all day for tardy teenagers".

Obediently, I push the buggy past grey, tailored and very formal suits and dresses: into the kind of darkly lit back room I'm not sure I should be following a strange man into.

Then I clear my throat anxiously. "This is very—"

"Walk," the man says, straightening his glasses.

"I'm sorry?"

"Walk." He makes little stepping movements with his

fingers. "You put one foot in front of the other and move forward?"

"Of course," I say, quickly grabbing a pair of black heels out of the buggy, popping them on and thanking my lucky stars that Nat forced me to spend three hours practising walking in them this week.

Then I start ambling across the room.

"Faster," the man says, clapping his hands, so I obediently scoot forward a bit faster. "Not that fast." I slow down. "Shoulders back." I obey. "Too far." I pull them forward again. "More hip." I roll my middle section. "Less hip." I go rigid again. "Good lord, girl, who taught you to walk?"

"My dad. When I was fourteen months old."

"Bad," he snaps. "Bad bad bad. You should get a new one. You're no use to me at all." Then he starts ushering both Tabby and I out of the shop with flappy hands.

My heart lurches in dismay. That's *it*?

Scientists have worked out that the perfect slice of toast should be cooked for exactly 216 seconds. You can't make a decent breakfast in the time it's taken for my shot at this position to be over.

He hasn't even looked at my portfolio.

I haven't told him that the first pair of Levis was sold for $6 of gold dust, and I feel like that definitely might have helped.

"Umm." *Do something, Harriet.* "Would you like my composite card for future reference?" I desperately thrust nine or ten at him from the doorstep. "I've hole-punched them for easy storage."

He hands my cards unceremoniously back.

"Keep them, honey. Judging by that performance you're going to need as many as you can get."

And the door gets slammed in my face.

41

Right.

My chances are plummeting faster than Galileo's famous objects dropping from the top of the Tower of Pisa, but statistics are still totally on my side.

I obviously just need to try harder.

Lightly jogging, I wheel Tabby towards Covent Garden. She starts mewling, so I pause in a cafe to give her a bottle of milk and change her nappy. Five minutes further down the street, she starts grizzling again so I find another cafe and change her nappy again. Then again because I stuck it on the wrong way round.

And again because I sat her in orange juice.

By the time we reach a creative agency in Shoreditch, we're an hour and a half late and the receptionist rolls her eyes, yells, "We've got a straggler, do you want to bother or not?" and goes back to painting her nails.

A few minutes later, a silver-haired girl barely older than me wanders in with the expression of someone who

has just woken up and isn't particularly happy about it.

"So where's the model, then?" she asks the receptionist, yawning.

Ouch. Excluding an infant and her own work colleague, I'm literally the only person in here.

Confidence, Harriet. It's in the bag.

"Hello." I hop up and hold out my hand. "It's very nice to meet you. I'm Harriet Manners from Peak Models. Wilbur Evans sent me."

"Yeah." She yawns again. "So, like, everyone's at lunch so I've been sent to deal with you? Whoa," she adds, blinking at the portfolio I've thrust hopefully at her. "Bright."

Then I quickly narrate while she flips lazily through: yawning widely the entire time. I've never seen all four of a stranger's wisdom teeth before but I guess there's a first time for everything.

"So, you're, like, *smaller* in person than you look here?" she says finally, glancing up. "You're, like, taller in photos? Upwards?"

I'm not entirely sure what the question is.

Also, my precise height is on my comp card in both metric and imperial.

"We shrink one per cent throughout the day due to our spines compressing," I offer helpfully. "If you'd like me to be taller maybe we could schedule a morning shoot?"

"LOL," she says flatly. "Oh, you're, like, serious? Yeah, no. Maybe we'll just get someone who's, like, the right height all day? But thanks for coming in."

She stands up and stretches like a bored cat.

"Cute baby, by the way," she adds. "Your tummy is snapping back *well* fast. You can barely tell you've had one."

I open my mouth in shock.

Then she wanders out, taking another one of my precious chances with her.

Casting Number Four I miss completely.

By the time we arrive the shoe company won't even open the blinds, let alone the door. "Job's gone," they say through the slatted bits of metal.

I make my eyes as wide and beseeching as is physically possible. "Please…"

"Gone." And the slats slam shut.

Casting Number Five tell me I'm *pretty for a ginger* and then ask if I'd consider dying my hair jet black for a handbag campaign.

"Not permanently," they add when my eyes widen.

"Just until it grows back out, so two or three years. And monthly eyebrow maintenance, obviously, or that would just look *weird*."

"We could shave them off completely," somebody else offers. "That look is so hot right now."

"Oooh, *that* might work."

"Or it might look weird."

"Yeah, that too. I suppose we could give it a go?"

"I mean, what do we have to lose?"

They start inching towards me and I take a deep breath. *For Wilbur for Wilbur for Wilbur...* "Sure," I say as bravely as I can. "You can dye my hair black and shave my eyebrows off. You can shave my head completely if you like."

They start laughing. "You're funny."

"Funny can't sell a handbag, though."

"Nope. Sorry, Carrot Top. Maybe next time."

Number Six tell me I have a "fat back" and – when they think I can't hear – "nobody wants to see *that* in a bikini".

Which may have traumatised me forever.

Number Seven (a toothpaste commercial) disorientate me by being sweet, friendly and interested in the fact that snails have twenty-five teeth located on their tongue.

"We'll call you!" they say just as I'm leaving.

So that's a no too.

Honestly, this is starting to feel like I'm on a series of the horrific speed dates I read about in those women's magazines, and I'm just as bad at them as I would have expected myself to be.

And having even less fun.

By my last casting of the day, my chances have dropped to almost nothing and I'm trying not to look at Wilbur's hopeful texts.

Twinkle me when you're done! F-G. xx

I have been so incredibly naïve.

All day, beautiful models have been scattered around me with portfolios as impressive or better than mine, without an add-on baby or the need for an additional instruction manual tucked in their satchel.

I thought *planning and trying* would be enough.

I assumed if I could break modelling into bite-size pieces – if I could analyse, strategise, bullet-point and demystify it – I'd somehow be able to conquer it.

Because that's how my world always works.

But for once in my life, studying has got me nowhere.

"No," the last receptionist sighs. "You can't take a

baby in with you. This is a casting, not Mummy and Me group."

I look in exhaustion at Tabitha.

She's been perfect all day: apart from the juice incident, and nobody likes an orange bottom.

Then I glance at the seven other models I've been quietly waiting with for an hour. Every single one has red hair. Every single one has pale skin and freckles. Every single one has green eyes and the look of somebody who avoids sunshine.

And at the end of the row is my doppelganger.

We've been studiously ignoring each other for the last hour: nothing says *I am not a special snowflake* quite like eight girls who look identical to you.

I glance back in the buggy.

Tabby's fallen asleep with a thumb in her mouth: clearly worn out by a whole day of rejection.

I'm utterly exhausted too. I just need to get this over with as fast as possible.

"Please," I say, pushing the buggy behind the reception desk. "Will you look after my sister for me? I'll be two minutes."

Then I look at the other models.

My confidence feels like a spinning top that's slowing down: as if it's wobbling, more and more unsteadily. This is not *in the bag* at all.

Or if it is, I misplaced that bag some time ago.

Also, there's baby spit-up on Nat's no-longer-smart coat.

"Make that one minute," I amend tiredly, rubbing as much as I can off with my sleeve. Then I wipe my sweaty hands on my leggings, tidy my hair and remove mascara smudge from under my eyes.

And prepare to tackle *Vogue* head on.

42

The thickest skull of all time is believed to have belonged to the pachycephalosaurus: a dinosaur with a domed head-bone ten inches thick, which was used to smash its targets into submission.

I kind of wish mine was that solid right now.

This is going to hurt.

"Hello," I say with the door swinging shut behind me. "My name is Harriet Manners, and I'm from Peak Models. Here are a few reasons why I am the right person for your magazine."

Sure enough, the mewling outside has already started: just as I suspected it might.

Audition like the wind, Harriet.

"*Vogue* was first published in 1892 but didn't become a fashion magazine until 1909 when Toto Koopman was the first ever cover girl and she later became a spy during the war."

There's another, slightly louder, mewl.

Faster, Harriet.

And maybe cut some of the fascinating historical background.

"Ibelievelamversatileandflexible, capableofadapting to anykindofscenariowitheaseandskill…"

The mewl gets even louder. "ihaveexperienceworking forsomeofthebiggestnamesinfashiontodayandhavealready featuredinanadvertinyourmagazinelessthanayearago…"

But it's no good: the mewl is now a shriek.

At a volume of over 105 decibels and the right pitch, a human voice can literally shatter glass. Being left in *Vogue* reception was not part of the deal with my sister, and as punishment Tabitha is going to destroy the whole building and everybody in it.

I can feel my cheeks getting hot.

This was by far the most important casting of the day, and it's slipping between my sweaty fingers.

"I'm sorry," I tell the three silent people sitting in front of me. They haven't moved a muscle since I started. "Please. I just need a few seconds."

Then I dart back into reception.

Sure enough: Tabitha is purple with rage, her tonsils are visible from ten feet away and she's waving her fists around like a tiny, furious boxer.

"For God's sake, take her." The receptionist thrusts my exploding sister at me. "I'm not insured for this. She's going to burst something."

Tabitha looks at me with pure sadness, and my stomach spins over with shame. I made a promise to my little sister, and I broke it. It's a good thing memories don't start until children are three years old or I think I'd have a lot of relationship fixing to do.

"I'm so sorry," I whisper, bobbing her up and down gently. "I'm here. I'm not going anywhere without you again, I promise."

Slowly, she quietens down.

Then, giving her another little kiss as she nuzzles soggily into my neck, I hold my sister on my hip and step back into the casting room. "Anyway, as I was saying…"

The woman with the sharp blonde bob abruptly holds her hand up. "Stop."

I flinch.

And here it comes.

They're going to tell me they had a lovely time and they'll call me and I'll never hear from *Vogue* again.

"Are you thinking what I'm thinking?"

"Definitely," the man says, nodding and looking at the other woman. "You?"

"I certainly am. Is there time?"

"We can find it. I'm feeling quite inspired, actually. This is going to be fabulous."

All three turn back to me.

I hope they don't ask what I'm thinking because frankly they lost me at *stop*.

"Harriet, how do you feel about shooting an eight-page fashion spread for us next Thursday?"

I'm so shocked I nearly drop Tabitha. I *got* it? I finally got a job? I'm going to shoot for *Vogue*?

Toby was right: the information about Toto Koopman was data gold.

"Oh, *yes, please*," I blurt out gratefully. "Thank you. I promise I won't let you down, I'll be on time, I'll work super hard and—"

The hand goes up.

"We have just one condition. The baby models with you."

43

So, here are some statistically unlikely events:

- *Achieving an Olympic gold medal: 1 in 662,000*
- *Becoming a canonised Saint: 1 in 20,000,000*
- *Winning an Oscar: 1 in 11,500*
- *Being hit by an asteroid: 1 in 700,000*
- *Being voted President of the United States: 1 in 10,000,000*

How do I put this?

They're *all* more likely than Annabel allowing her eight-month-old daughter to start working as a fashion model.

It's been fifteen months and even *I'm* not technically allowed to take a job without a chaperone (even though I have, obviously).

Also, next Thursday is a school day: I have double chemistry, biology and maths.

Although – let's be brutally honest – skipping

education to model is not exactly unheard of for me: *not* skipping it would probably be more so. For a geek, I miss a surprising amount of lessons.

But I *need* this job.

"I…" My brain is turning frantically in circles like Hugo when he's chasing his own tail. "Could you perhaps use a similar baby that is not this particular baby?"

"I'm afraid not," the woman says. "You look identical. That's kind of the point."

Bat poop.

There's no *way* this is going to happen. Tabitha is too young to say yes for herself, and Annabel will say no and then ground me for even asking.

Unless…

Statistically there are seven people in the world who look exactly like each of us. I'm just about to suggest we look for one of Tabitha's when I realise that the solution is also the problem.

My seven are currently sitting outside.

Ready to take the job the moment I turn it down, with great enthusiasm and gratitude.

Especially the doppelganger.

And I have a nasty feeling that if she replaces me just one more time, my modelling career is over for good.

Brain still spinning, I glance down.

Tabitha looks so happy: babbling and pointing at colourful *Vogue* covers on the wall. It's not stretching the imagination *very* far to assume that this is what she wants.

I just can't believe that after a solid week of trying to become the Perfect Model, my Unique Selling Point isn't actually me.

I should have made a folder for Irony.

"Yes," I decide before I can change my mind. "OK, deal. We'll both take the job."

"Fabulous," the man grins, holding out a piece of paper. "Talk it over with your boyfriend and we'll email your agent with the rest of the details."

"My b-boyfriend?"

"Sorry, husband? Partner? Significant other?"

I stare at the three of them blankly, my heart starting to squeeze. I can hear a slight rattling in my head. "I-I don't have a boyfriend. We b-broke up a long time ago. Do I need one?"

Maybe it's some weird fashion criteria: must not be single or people will be able to tell in the photos.

"Oh God," the blonde woman says quickly. "That was incredibly insensitive, I'm so sorry. He meant the father of the little one, but just your signature will be perfectly fine."

I blink at them.

After Einstein died, his brain was pickled, sliced into 240 cubes and left in a box labelled "Costa Cider" for twenty years. I'm guessing he was still sharper than me right now.

Do they think Tabitha is my *daughter*?

I don't want to be rude about Annabel, but exactly how old and tired do I *look*?

"Oh my goodness, no," I laugh quickly, shaking my head. "This isn't…"

But then what? I clarify that Tabitha's actually my sister and they'll need a signature from our parents instead – which incidentally they'll never, ever get – and I'm back to square one.

"This isn't..?" the lady prompts in alarm. "Oh my gosh. You're so young, but we just assumed that…"

Backtrack, Harriet.

"What I mean…" I say slowly and carefully, "is that the father of this child is… in… Manchester."

That's not a lie.

It's a strategically positioned truth and I can't get in trouble for it.

"Well," the man says, holding out a piece of paper, "in that case just your signature on this release form, please."

OK: this I *can* get in trouble for.

I stare at the legally binding paper, brain flopping one way and then the other.

Sign it or don't sign it.

Save Wilbur or don't save Wilbur.

Be a good friend or a rubbish one.

"Great," I say, grabbing it and urgently scrawling my name in the box at the bottom. "We're very excited about this, uh, family opportunity."

Then I wave goodbye with Tabitha's hand and scoot out of the room before I can do or say or sign anything else.

The Kola Superdeep Borehole in Russia is the deepest artificial point in the world, drilled 12,262 metres towards the earth's core.

I think I just dug myself a new record.

All I have to do is pretend Tabitha is my fake daughter, skip school, kidnap my sister, illegally shove her into the workforce for profit, wait for a forged document to surface and lie to my parents for the millionth time.

So I'm going to have to get a move on.

Because Annabel's going to find out.

Now it's just a question of when.

44

On the upside, at least I get to do *this*:

"Wilbur, I got it!"

Then there's a silence long enough to hear somebody order pizza and a side salad in the background. Smiling, I tuck Tabby into her buggy, snuggle the little blue imposter horse next to her and watch her fall fast asleep.

It's been quite a momentous day for both of us.

"Hello?" I say after forty or fifty seconds and two slices of background cheesecake ordering. "Wilbur? Are you there?"

"Got what?" he finally says. "Alien Hand Syndrome? Because I was just reading about that, baby-can-of-tomato-paste, and I'm terrified. Your hand just *does* things without you knowing about it. What if I accidentally put on last season's shoes? Utterly horrificating."

What on earth is he talking about?

Then I realise: this is Wilbur's version of 'breezy and casual'.

Oh bless him.

"I got the job with *Vogue*," I grin as somebody near him orders a bowl of olives. "And guess what? They want Tabitha too, so she'll have to sign up with you as well! That's double the money!"

Then I cough. *Gah.*

I really need to start working on my subtlety: I have the tact and delicacy of a red-bottomed baboon.

"Money for *me*," I clarify quickly. "*The Encyclopaedia of Life Sciences* features more than 4,300 commissioned articles and is very expensive and rare and I want it badly."

There's another silence.

Then – just as I'm convinced I've given myself away – Wilbur explodes into a firework display of words I've never heard before and will be extremely surprised to ever hear again.

"*Whoopdicracking figure-skating wombats!*" he yells. "*Bingolacious dolphins! Sugarific cherry coconut brownies!*" He inhales loudly. "Bless my disco bats, I *knew* you could do it, baby baby tiger. There was no doubt in my mind."

Studies have found that a single smile generates the same amount of happiness as 2,000 bars of chocolate.

I'd love to find out how much Wilbur produces.

"I know there wasn't," I beam fondly.

Which is – I realise as I say goodbye and put the phone down – exactly why I don't feel bad, even though I'm doing something wrong.

And why there's now no doubt in mine either.

There's just a few people left to tell:

We got VOGUE! GO TEAM JINTH! :) Hxx

Within seconds, the messages start flooding in:

No. Freaking. WAY. I told you! So proud of you. Nat xxx

This is excellent news. Did you remember to tell them that 42% of VOGUE ONLINE readers are male? Toby Pilgrim

And that the first celebrity ever on the cover was Madonna? Toby Pilgrim

And 50% of the whole thing is advertising? Toby Pilgrim

IN. THE. BAG. ;) J

I beam again, then wait for the rest as I push the buggy back to the station.

I catch the train home.

I wait a bit more.

I tidy Tabitha's blankets up and make sure she's warm and that all her empty milk bottles are straight at the bottom of the buggy. I check the train timetable even though I'm already on the train.

Then I wait a little bit longer.

Finally – forty-five minutes later, when I'm pretty much all the way home – my phone beeps.

Awesome. India

And maybe I'm wrong.

But something's telling me we might need to start looking for a new vowel in JINTH after all.

45

I spend the rest of Saturday evening and Sunday morning preparing for my visitor and trying to coach my sister on the pitfalls of modelling. Tabby's been animated and glowing ever since we returned from London, and her total lack of poker-face has not gone unnoticed.

"I don't know what you two did together yesterday, darling," Bunty says warmly as I walk into the kitchen, "but Squirrel has been beaming like the moon all morning."

My sister squeaks and waves at me conspiratorially from her highchair. If we're going to start lying to our family regularly together, she's really going to have to work on her facial expressions.

She has *no* idea how to play it cool.

"Oh really?" I say vaguely, giving Tabby a firm *chill out* look. "Science has shown that children with siblings four or more years older tend to be much smarter and have fewer allergies compared to those without. I think maybe

she's just happy to spend more time around me."

"I don't doubt it, darling," Bunty smiles.

Then I start rooting energetically through the cupboards. "Do you know if we happen to have any Steak and Ale Pie lying around? Or maybe some Haggis?"

"*Haggis*?" Annabel enters the kitchen with Dad two inches behind her. "Harriet, why on earth do you want minced sheep's organs at 9am on a Sunday morning?"

OK: eww. I thought it was some kind of Scottish dessert. "Fish and Chips? Toad in the Hole? Bubble and Squeak?"

"I have a sausage roll," Dad offers, pulling a greasy paper bag out of his pocket. "And some Haribo eggs." Four emerge, stuck together. "And a liquorice lace. Maybe a few cheese crisps."

We all stare at him.

"*What*?" he says defensively. "It was a long train journey from Manchester and I got hungry."

Apparently the nematode worm has a brain shaped like a doughnut.

Sometimes I wonder if my dad does too.

"Still doesn't explain why they're in your dressing-gown pocket, Richard." Then Annabel bends down and gives Bunty a gentle kiss. "Good morning, Mum."

Annabel's eyes are puffy and her face is kind of splotchy. Honestly, she looks more exhausted than she did yesterday.

They should ask that spa for their money back.

"Good morning, my angel." Bunty smiles again and points at the wall. "Look, Bells. A rainbow. Do you know what that means?"

Annabel turns to the kitchen sink.

"Refraction," I answer for her, pulling out a tin of mushy peas. "It means white light is passing through that crystal and separating it into different wavelengths that we perceive as colours."

Then I pile a tin of mushy peas, some Cadbury chocolate, a packet of Jaffa Cakes and three packs of Walkers Crisps into a basket and glance at my watch.

Yup: I've timed it perfectly.

"Harriet?" Annabel says, turning round as I grab the basket, my satchel and three full carrier bags and start hefting them towards the door. "Where are you going *now*?"

I pause in disbelief.

"I literally *told* you," I say in frustration, plonking my bags back down. "Four times. Not including *that.*"

I point at a laminated sheet, stuck to the wall:

> *Don't forget: Harriet's visitor arrives Heathrow*
> *Sunday 11am – staying ten days! Thanks! :) X*

Underneath this message is a colour-coordinated chart for the whole family. I've highlighted it in bright yellow pen and stuck a note next to it that says

Please read me -> ->

with hot pink arrows.

I'm not sure what else I could have done.

"*I remembered,*" Dad says smoothly, putting his arm around my stepmother as she blinks at the message. "And I've bought a spare air bed. You just get back to turning the hot tap off, sweetheart, before you drown us."

Water's beginning to spray all over the kitchen.

On second thoughts, maybe I don't need to worry. It feels like I could turn Tabitha into a purple Chihuahua at the moment and Annabel wouldn't notice.

"Thanks, Dad," I say gratefully, kissing his cheek. Then I add in a whisper: "You might want to look into changing Annabel's antihistamine meds."

Dad smiles. "It's on the list."

And – for the second time this week – I pick my bags up and start heading back into London.

46

Psychologists recently made a discovery.

After a lot of research, they found that the visual perception of a geographical slant is influenced by both physiological resources, like age and fitness, as well as psychological assets, like social support and camaraderie.

In fact, their studies showed that even the *thought* of not being alone decreases a potential gradient and makes it feel like less of a physical challenge.

You know what that means?

Scientifically, a hill feels a lot less steep when climbed with a friend.

I could have told them that for free.

As I race towards Heathrow, it feels like every step I take is easier and less overwhelming: as if the hill I've been struggling up doesn't seem quite as steep any more.

Not now there's somebody to climb it with me.

Feeling lighter already, I elbow my way to the front of the

arrival gates and watch travel-weary people emerge: smiling, kissing and laughing. Looking eagerly around for the people they love most.

And then I see one of mine.

Pale yellow puffy dress covered in pictures of tiny purple lollipops; purple high-heeled shoes with ribbons on them; a short black bob curled into ringlets with a purple bow on top.

A beautiful face: radiant and rosy.

And as a rush of brightness pulses through me, there's an enormous squeak, three unicorn-stickered suitcases are dropped on the floor and I'm covered in a storm of cheek-kisses, twinkle and under-netting.

It's like being rugby-tackled by a particularly affectionate fairy.

And I've missed it *so* much.

"Harry-chan!" Kiss. "Oh my goshing! It is actually you!" Kiss kiss. "And I am here myself! In this happy place of United Kingdoms!" Kiss. "We will be having *all* of the fun." Kiss. "Just you wait and saw!"

Kiss kiss kiss kiss.

And there – in tiny yellow-frilled ankle socks, like a Japanese superhero – is the one person I knew could really make a difference to Wilbur's agency.

My second-best girlfriend in the entire world.

Rin.

47

I know: great idea, right?

As Wilbur's accountant pointed out in the restaurant, one girl isn't a modelling agency: it's just one girl. And you can say what you like about his lack of etiquette, but the maths was unquestionable.

Well, now Wilbur has *three.*

And Rin's an incredibly successful model. She's been promising to visit me ever since I left Tokyo last summer so all it took was a little extra nudge in the form of a persuasive Skype call and the offer of a spare bed at my house.

Then I sent Wilbur a cunningly subtle message asking him to find Rin some holiday work while she visits me, and BAM.

I've statistically *doubled* his chances.

And with Tabitha as well, I've *tripled* them.

Between the three of us, we've got the entire fashion world cornered. Rin can provide extraordinary natural

beauty, sweetness and many years of experienced modelling for top designers around the world.

And Tabby and I can cover accidental modelling, criminal activities, infant workforce and badly thought-through lies.

As a team, we're basically invincible.

"*And*," I say happily once Rin and I have wedged ourselves and all of Rin's unicorn luggage with some difficulty back on to the train, "did you know the bra was first patented in 1914 by Mary Phelps?"

I can barely see her any more.

With great excitement, Rin and I exchanged all our traditional Japanese *omiyage* gifts within the first thirty seconds of meeting each other, and now we're both laden down with so many presents we're practically immobile.

First, she gave me tuna sushi socks ("your feet will be like double fishes, Harry-chan!") so I gave her my British Food Basket.

Then I got a dancing *Totoro* lamp and a forehead-wrinkle-iron and she got the complete works of Shakespeare and a Cambridge University mug. A fake bubble-wrap key ring is exchanged for a light bulb (invented in England in 1880); a tiny model steam train for musical chopsticks (technically of Chinese origin, but it's the thought that counts).

By the time Rin finished emptying one entire suitcase and started on the second, I had nothing left to give her but the gift of *knowledge*. Which is the ultimate present, because you can keep it with you forever and it can't cause a pile-up on an underground escalator like a giant fluffy yellow duck just did ten minutes ago.

"*And,*" I say from somewhere underneath my bounty, "the bikini was originally declared a sin by the Vatican! Can you believe it?"

I figured I could use the opportunity to train her up on as much in-depth fashion knowledge as possible on the way home. You never know when someone important will challenge you about the history of undergarments and swimwear.

"Gosh," Rin says in a tiny voice, "that is top of the morning news, Harry-chan."

Then she stares around us with enormous eyes.

Huge fake eyelashes have been stuck to the outer edges of them, silver glitter has been carefully applied on the inner corners and there's a little black heart drawn on her left cheekbone. As always, off-duty Rin looks less like a small human and more like an enormous china doll.

But for the first time since I've known her, she's kind of behaving like one too.

Over the last fifteen minutes, her usual bubbliness has slowly flattened, and with every second that passes she gets quieter and stiffer, and her eyes get a little larger. And I didn't even know that was physically possible.

She already has the face of a baby owl.

"There are many people in London, Harry-chan," Rin whispers, shrinking towards me. "There is much of the shouting."

I blink at our carriage. It's just a regular weekend train: people are chatting, yelling into their phones, crunching on crisps with unnecessary enthusiasm.

It's noisy, but nothing out of the ordinary.

"Tokyo is one of the most populated cities in the world," I reassure her comfortingly. "This is practically empty in comparison."

Rin's huge eyes wander the carriage as she smooths out her dress self-consciously. "Am I wrong, Harry-chan? Do they not liking my tyre? Am I not England enough?"

In truth everyone *is* staring at her, but obviously because they think she's adorable. "They're just not used to so much cuteness," I tell her affectionately. "You are super *kawaii*."

She looks around again.

There's a young couple giggling and kissing incessantly a few seats across from us: hands entwined, eyes locked.

Every time the girl says anything, the boy impulsively cups her face and kisses her as if he can't control himself.

Huh. Nobody is *that* irresistible.

"I have once too, Harry-chan," Rin sighs wistfully. "In Tokyo. I am with boy for three, four minutes?"

I nod. "Do you mean four months?"

"*Iie*, Harry-chan. We have one kiss and I am dump straight off. Now I am little bit…" She gets a translation dictionary out and pauses while she looks for the right word. "…Contusion."

"Confusion," I correct automatically, sympathetically patting her shoulder. "I think you mean you're *confused.*"

She nods. "And Harry-chan," she continues, "do you have new one now? Or are you still missing N—"

"*Noodles?*" I say quickly. "No no, I'm fine. Not missing noodles at all."

Rin blinks.

"And don't you worry," I carry on, "I've got so much planned you'll forget all about that." I open my notepad at *Rin's Epic Modelling Holiday TM!* "After any potential photoshoots or castings, I thought on Monday evening we could maybe head to Greenwich to see the Meridian Line, then have a look at HMS…"

I stop.

Rin's not listening: she's gazing at a piece of wet

chewing gum stuck to the skirt of her pretty dress. "Why?" she whispers in bewilderment. "Why someone leave that there, Harry-chan? Why not in mouth?"

Then somebody yells "*Give us a twirl*!" across the train and she almost jumps into my lap.

Her whole body is trembling.

"It's OK, Rin," I say gently, starting to feel a bit sick. "Don't be nervous. London's just like a lot of other cities you've visited, except there's probably more pigeons here."

For some reason an abrupt image of the day Annabel first brought Victor as a kitten to our house has suddenly popped into my head. He was so disorientated, he spent his first twenty-four hours trying to get under the fridge.

"London not like Tokyo," Rin says in a tiny voice, shaking her head. "Or Nagoya. Or Osaka. Or Kyoto. Not like home."

"No," I admit. "But what about Paris? Milan? Barcelona? New York? It must be quite similar?"

Rin's eyes get even rounder. "I have not been visiting there, Harry-chan. All only Japan."

What?

This must be a language-barrier thing. Like when I said *iruka-des-ka* instead of *ikura-des-ka* and accidentally asked a shopkeeper if I could buy a dolphin.

"I mean as a model," I smile. "You're a successful top model, Rin. You were the face of *Baylee* before me. You must have travelled a *little* bit."

"Only top model in Japan. This first time now to leave." Then Rin lifts her chin and gives me the bravest smile I've ever seen. "I come for you, Harry-chan."

And my stomach suddenly feels like I've just clambered off a merry-go-round that wasn't very merry in the first place.

No.

No no no no no – Rin's never been out of Japan before?

She's never been *anywhere*?

Oh my God.

I was so carried away with my brilliant idea of getting her to help save Wilbur's agency, it didn't occur to me how big a favour I was asking. I didn't consider the fact that maybe not everyone finds travelling as exciting as I do, or that Rin loves me so much she'd say yes to anything just because I asked.

Or that she might absolutely *hate* it here.

And now one of the sweetest, most gentle people on the planet is 5,936 miles from home, scared and on the verge of being completely miserable.

And it's all my fault.

"Now I am an adventuriser and exploringer too," Rin says, forcing a smile and grabbing my hand a little too hard. "Just like you, Harry-chan."

I can't believe what I've just done.

48

I had so many great plans for our journey home.

Stops we were going to make through London, museums we could pop into, interesting architectural details I intended to point out (the geometrical staircase in St Paul's Cathedral being just one).

I immediately abandon all of them.

By the time we get to the next station, Rin is culture-shocking so badly it's clear I need to get her to the safety of my home as fast as possible, before she shrinks so small I have to keep her in my pocket for the rest of the holiday.

As it is, we don't escape the van driver.

"Oy oy!" he yells out of the window as we trundle Rin's many suitcases down the street towards my house.

Rin jumps so far she ends up in a bush.

"I'm not knowing *oy oy*," she says to me when I've pulled her gently out again. "Is this new English greeting?"

"Sometimes," I growl, making a face at the van

receding into the distance.

By the time we get through the front door, Rin's such a jittery, discombobulated mess she only just about manages to bow shyly to Dad and Annabel, nervously pat Hugo and greet my grandmother again with tiny, shaking hands.

It's only when she sees Victor that her little inner Rin-light begins to glow.

"Oh Harry-chan!" she breathes happily, grabbing him off my bed and holding him tightly to her face. "He is just like my *neko*-baby, Kylie Minogue. *Ne*?"

Victor looks furious but hangs there limply while Rin covers him in thousands of tiny kisses.

Then she plops abruptly to the floor in a puff of lace, rummages through her third suitcase and drags out four teeny socks, a miniature pink dress and a tiny strap-on tiara.

"Don't worry," she tells Victor as he scrabbles urgently towards the door and gets dragged back into her lap, still scrabbling. "You will be *kawaii* in no times!"

With renewed vigour, she energetically forces a tiny white sock on to each paw.

Then – with Victor tucked tightly under a surprisingly strong arm – she reaches into her suitcase and begins distributing Japanese things around the room: a ruffled duvet cover and comforter on the air bed, heart pillows, a dangling mobile with tiny photos of Kylie the cat and Rin's family hanging from it.

"I think maybe I will like England," she says with forced chirpiness, not quite meeting my eyes. "Maybe I will be very happy here in Harry-chan's England bedroom."

"Rin…"

"Don't be worry!" she says earnestly, looking up just in time to see my distraught expression. "If Wilbur has job for me I will be coming out. I promise I will be help."

That's not what I'm worried about.

My bedroom is basically Rin's version of the fridge, and she's just disappeared right under it.

"Sure," I say desperately, giving Princess Victor a sharp look that says, *You owe me and this is your karmic punishment.* "Whatever will make you happy, Rin."

49

But nothing seems to work.

No matter how hard I try over the next few days, Rin just gets smaller and smaller. On Sunday night I spent two hours begging her to come to school with me because no matter how sad I am, education can *always* cheer me up.

"I will learn here," she insisted, holding up *How To Speak Like a British Person!* and *So You're In England – Now What?* books. "My English slurps so bad, Harry-chan. I practise, *then* I come to school."

Then she grabbed Victor – who was furiously wearing dungarees and a bandana – and disappeared behind *A Thousand Fascinating Things To See And Do in London!*

On Monday I tried food: another source of great personal pleasure. The average girl eats an average of 651,525 calories a year and I look forward to every single one of mine.

"Mmm," Rin says, gagging slightly after one bite of a Marmite sandwich. "Burny mouth. Delicious, Harry-chan."

And when she thinks I'm not watching she spits it into a pink hankie and gets a seaweed snack out of her suitcase.

On Tuesday while I'm at sixth form, I leave her with piles of guidebooks to read and interesting facts about England to look up. And in the evening we watch Korean soap operas on the internet and play *Janken* (Japanese Rock Paper Scissors). I even try to make sushi to make her feel more at home (it all falls apart within seconds).

By the time I get in on Wednesday afternoon, Rin hasn't left my room – apart from brief trips to the bathroom and the one time Victor escaped and she had to run down the stairs and drag him back again – and I'm starting to panic.

If I don't do something fast, Rin's going to shrink so much I'll be able to post her back to Tokyo stuck to the back of a postcard.

"Harriet," Annabel says anxiously on Wednesday after school, "sweetheart, as responsible adults we can't just leave your friend locked away upstairs. What will her parents think of us?"

"That we treat our prisoners excellently," Dad says cheerfully, wiping down the kitchen table, "and that the Manners family run the best teenage jails in the country."

Annabel's eyes widen in alarm. "*Richard.*"

"I'm joking, darling. Harriet's barely ever in the house. We clearly suck at it." Then he looks at me. "But it's a valid point. Any suggestions?"

"I've tried *everything*," I say, admitting defeat. "Monopoly, graph-drawing, map studying, dictionary perusing…"

Dad lifts his eyebrows. "I didn't realise Rin was an eighty-year-old physics professor."

I stick my tongue out at him.

But a little light bulb has just gone on in the back of my head.

Maybe I need a new perspective.

Grabbing my phone, I text:

JINTH emergency at my house. Please bring all resources. Hxx

Fifteen minutes later, I knock on my bedroom door. "Rin? I've got a few people here who want to say hello."

There's a short silence.

Then the door opens a crack and a tiny white face appears: completely stripped of all make-up and twinkle and somehow even prettier than it was before.

Rin is alarmingly beautiful.

Even in old grey tracksuit bottoms, big white socks, a huge Winnie-the-Pooh T-shirt and some kind of ratty green blanket I think Bunty must have snuck in while I was at school.

"Hello," Nat says cheerfully. "I'm Natalie, and I've been sent by the fashion police to destroy those sweatpants. Kind of like Bruce Willis in *Armageddon* except instead of a meteor it's a style abomination."

"*Nat*," I say indignantly. "They're *mine*."

"I know. No *wonder* Rin's not having much fun. That outfit has literally sucked the life out of her."

"Hello," Jasper says, stepping forward. "I'm Jasper. And I'm here to protect you from Natalie."

Rin giggles softly.

"Did you know," Toby says from the back, staring at the ceiling, "that there's a worm called the *Eoperipatus totoro* because it was discovered by Studio Ghibli fans and looks just like the Catbus?"

Rin takes a step forward.

"You know Catbus?" Then she frowns. "I know you. Were you being in Tokyo with Harry-chan? You wear piano shoes and your name is Ted."

"Toby Pilgrim, actually. Sadly those laces were not musical although the packet gave the *distinct* impression they were."

Nat face-palms herself.

"So," Jasper says, clearing his throat, "Rin, we were just heading to the local coffee shop. Would you like to come with us? We have excellent hot chocolate and I can make the cream into a bear shape, if you like?"

Oooh. That's an *excellent* idea.

Rin's face has gone rosy pink, and I give Jasper a grateful smile.

He subtly winks back.

"Y-ees," Rin says slowly. "I think I will like very much to see this. Just wait one tickity."

The door closes abruptly and there's the sound of a lot of zipping and clacking and meowing and banging.

Then it opens again.

Rin has transformed. She is now wearing a blue silk dress covered in tiny blue flowers, white ankle socks and little blue shoes. She hasn't had time to do any make-up, so her face is still naturally pearly and slightly flushed: her hair a tidy black bob.

Victor is also in a blue dress, and I can't help feeling again that this is his cosmic comeuppance for stealing Dunky.

"I am ready for the cream-bear now," she says with great dignity. "Please lead me the way."

And for the first time in four days, Rin braces her

shoulders like a warrior, lifts her chin and takes a courageous step forward.

Back into the world again.

50

Things are starting to look up.

As the five of us start walking towards the coffee shop, I trail behind and watch Rin visibly relaxing: expanding like one of those magic little flannels that absorb water.

She obviously feels more at home in a group.

Or – more specifically – in *my* group: AKA the *best gang in the world.*

"I've never been to Japan before," Jasper says as they walk a few steps ahead of us. "What's it like?"

"It is smashing," Rin replies sweetly. "Fishes and games and flash-lights and Kitty-chan. In Japan we have many horses for our courses."

"Horses for your… Oh. Got it. And… uh. Where specifically are you from?"

"Nichinan. It is a village near palm tree with festive every year. We have dances and *takoyaki* which is made of the octopus." Then Rin giggles. "I think you shall ask Harry-chan about the octopus and the spray and

the blue Smurf."

"Huh?" Jasper spins to look at me. "Harriet, I think I need to hear this potentially humiliating story right this minute so I can never, ever stop reminding you of it."

Sugar cookies.

I managed to keep Octo-gate a secret from Jasper for *five whole months*. When he finds out I got attacked by an irritated cephalopod and covered in bright blue ink I am never going to hear the end of it.

"Oh look," I say, abruptly looking at the sky. "Altocumulus clouds. How interesting."

"Isn't there a castle in Obi?" Toby says abruptly from just in front of them. His new satchel has a plastic shark fin poking out of the back. "It was built in 1588 by the Tsuchimochi clan. I read about it in a Japanese history book."

"*Hai*," Rin says wistfully, then her voice wobbles slightly. "My home is very beauty. Very, very beauty."

Uh-oh.

Quick, Harriet. Change the subj—

"So what kind of bear would you like, Rin?" Jasper says evenly. "I can make one out of cream, or chocolate, or cinnamon, or milk froth…"

"Does she have two ears?" Rin asks, immediately perking up. "And a nose?"

"I think I can even manage a bow."

And – still chatting about the intricacies of a bear's hair accessories – they draw further ahead until all we can hear is Toby randomly shouting *"squirrel!"*

Nat and I watch them for a few seconds.

Then she links her arm through mine. "I'm glad you dragged Jasper into our group, Harriet. Under that gruff exterior, he's actually really sweet."

"I didn't *drag* him," I say indignantly. "He joined entirely of his own accord."

"Sure he wasn't kicking and screaming?"

"Screaming, no. Maybe a tiny bit of kicking, but I was wearing metaphorical shin pads and couldn't feel a thing." We both laugh. "Speaking of Team JINTH..." I clear my throat. "India still hasn't replied to today's group text message."

I've been trying not to think about it, but that's actually the seventh team message this week she hasn't responded to now. And without sounding neurotic... I'm starting to think she hates me.

OK, maybe that sounds neurotic.

"It's not just you," Nat says, reading my mind. "I ran into her last night and she's *crazy* busy with some kind of Head Girl disaster. Intense hallway monitor fights or something."

A wave of relief crashes over me.

"It's a lot of responsibility, poor thing," I say, shaking my head. "Those school corridors aren't going to manage themselves."

"Exactly." Nat squeezes my arm. "And can we please just take a moment to fully register what you've achieved this week, H? I mean, *VOGUE*. How do I put this in Harriet-terms? What's the tallest tree in the world?"

"A redwood in California. It's 115.7 metres tall and its name is Hyperion."

"How do they know what its name is?" Nat laughs. "Anyway, that's what *Vogue* is. You're at the top of the fashion tree. You literally can't *get* any higher."

It's true that in the panic of trying to get work – any work – I didn't really stop to absorb the fact that I, Harriet Manners, part-time model and full-time geek, just secured an eight-page spread in the world's most prestigious fashion magazine.

The girl who hides under tables.

The girl with tiny Boston Terriers currently pictured all over her leggings and a dried porridge oat stuck to her jumper.

How did that get there?

"But what if I took a ladder up with me, Nat?" I grin, starting to feel just a little bit proud of myself. "Wouldn't

I be higher then?"

"Nope, because there'd be nothing to lean it against. You'd still be the highest point. Plus, that would be *insanely* dangerous."

"What if I was in a *hot-air balloon*?"

"Well, then you'd be cheating. Face it, Manners. You're at the top. You're a big, important, glamorous supermodel and there's *nothing you can do about it*. So *there*."

Nat beams proudly.

I beam back at her.

In the Arctic there lives a Woolly Bear caterpillar, one of the most remarkable creatures on the planet. Every winter, it burrows underground and freezes solid, and every spring it thaws and its heart starts again and it carries on living, just as it always did.

That's what my best-friendship with Nat is.

No matter how much time apart we're forced to spend, no matter how busy we are with college or school or anything else in life that will keep trying to get between us, all we ever really do is press the pause button.

Our relationship is timeless.

(Apart from when it eventually turns into a Woolly Bear moth and then it'll be even more *awesome*.)

"And," Nat says, squeezing my arm gently, "I know

you pushed that box full of He Who Must Not Be Named under your bed, and I think that shows real guts. You're a warrior, H. I'm proud of you."

My stomach spins slightly and I flush and put my head on her shoulder. "Thanks."

Then I look back up the road and my proud, warm glow starts to seep slowly out again. Rin has sat down on a bench, and is waving her phone at Jasper and Toby, probably showing them photo after photo of Kylie Minogue – both cat and pop star – and it looks like we're teetering on the precipice of sadness again.

"Oh good lord," Nat says. "Why is Toby trying to show her the owls on his socks?"

"He shows everyone the owl on his socks," I say in frustration. "Nat, I don't know what else we can do. As soon as we get home, Rin's going to lock herself back away in my bedroom like a princess in… a…"

Wait a minute.

"Castle?" Nat says as my eyes suddenly widen. "Disneyland? Prison?"

"*Tower,*" I finish, grabbing her arm and pulling her into a bush.

I've just had the idea for a genius new plan.

51

Have I mentioned before that every day, we each have 70,000 thoughts? Well, we do.

That's 3,000 thoughts per hour, fifty a minute, or just under one contemplation per second.

But some of them are of greater quality than others.

I think this is my best one yet.

"*Nat,*" I breathe as the one hundred trillion synapses in my brain start firing simultaneously, "*look.*"

It's like spending days and days trying to finish a difficult jigsaw puzzle, then finding that the one piece you need has been stuck to the bottom of your foot the whole time.

Or – you know.

Another analogy that doesn't make it sound like I don't shower.

One day I am hoping I will be in romantic twosome too, Harry-chan.

231

I have that once. And now I am a bit… contusion.

Rin wasn't trying to say *confusion* at all: she was trying to say *bruised*.

She's not just homesick, she's crushed.

My friend has wanted to be part of a big love story as long as I've known her, but her very first tentative attempt ended in immediate rejection. And OK, last year she specifically said she wanted an Australian boyfriend, but… (*shut up, box*) I don't know any of those any more.

But Team JINTH need to drag this particular princess out of her tower for good.

Maybe a British prince will do instead.

"I'm *looking*," Nat sighs impatiently, picking a leaf out of her hair. "Why are we in a bush? And by the way, was your cat wearing fake *pigtails*?"

"Sssshhh," I whisper, mentally turning the final piece of the puzzle round and round until it fits. "I'm still thinking."

Jasper's usually so sarcastic about everything, and yet here he is: patiently looking through photos of a black cat wearing a white catsuit without a single sardonic comment.

Not one snip; not a derisive or scornful snort. Not a contemptuous observation or a caustic reflection: not even a scathing expression.

Just sweet, genuine *interest*.

In Year Five, we did a basic experiment with magnets and we learned that the south pole of one magnet is attracted to the north pole of the other. (And then Nat and I used this knowledge to clip our magnets to the end of our noses.)

i.e. We learnt that opposites *attract*.

And the law of electromagnetic nature seems to be at work here too.

I narrow my eyes analytically. I tell everybody constantly that science can be practically used in everyday situations, and this is the perfect example.

Rin's sweetness balances out Jasper's sharpness; her sugariness is the perfect counterpart to his bluntness. They even *look* good together: he's broad and tall and wearing dark grey, and she's tiny and dainty and pastel-coloured like a butterfly.

Despite their differences, they're a *perfect* match.

Actually, no: *because* of them.

"Seriously, Harriet," Nat says, "these are brand-new Seven jeans and now I've got mud on the... *Oh my God.*"

I beam at her. I knew she'd catch up eventually: I just had to wait for our magical best-friend telepathy to do its thing.

"Right?" I say triumphantly. "Can you see it too?"

We look back at the bench.

Jasper's genuinely not scowling for the first time in ages: he seems lighter. *Happier.*

"Huh." Nat looks at me, visibly impressed. "You know, I can't believe this, Harriet, but you're right. Those two are *made* for each other. How did I not spot this before you?"

"Experience," I say, nodding sagely. "I am wise and learned, Nat. Like Yoda, but with a better grasp of sentence construction."

"Like guru, you are."

We laugh and look back at the sweet little scene playing out in front of us. The rebellious box in my head is starting to rattle uncomfortably, but I don't really have a choice. I'd locked everything away tightly for *myself*... but maybe I need to open the lid a tiny bit, just to make sure my new plan works.

Just a couple of centimetres.

Enough to get a smidgen of what I know about romance out, make two of my best friends so much happier than they were and then put it away again. Like a handyman delicately picking the best tools out without touching the chainsaw.

Yes: I think that's perfectly safe.

As long as I'm super careful.

"I'm going to do it," I say decisively. "I'm going to get them together."

"Wait." Nat looks at me in alarm. "Hang on, Harriet. Why can't you just let it happen naturally?"

"Because we don't have time," I explain. "The chemistry's there: I just need to speed it up a bit. I'm the catalyst, like iron when used in the synthesis of ammonia from nitrogen and hydrogen. I'm not *changing* the future, just making it get here faster."

"But Harriet…"

"Don't worry," I say reassuringly, standing up and pulling a twig out of my fringe. "I know exactly what I'm doing. Everything is under control."

52

Now, I know that the L-word is not an *exact* science.

But I also know that – with the right knowledge and a little practice – science can get pretty darn close.

Studies have shown that it takes between ninety seconds and four minutes to decide if you're interested romantically in another person, and those physical symptoms can be monitored carefully.

Dilated pupils. Flushed cheeks.

Hair twiddling and wrist-exposing; mirroring the same body gestures. Too much eye contact or too little eye contact; laughing too much, listening hard and leaning towards the other person.

Unfortunately, it's a language so complicated – so nuanced and subtle – that scientists have found that there's only a 28% chance of accurately detecting flirtation, even if you're the person being flirted with.

So it's lucky I know what I'm looking for and have a naturally data-collecting kind of mind.

"*Also*," Rin continues once we're seated comfortably in the cafe. She's nervously holding out a big bunch of large, bright key rings and going through them, one by one. "*This* is Rilakkuma. Kuma mean *bear* in Japanese, so he is Relaxy Bear. He likes eating odango."

"Ah," Jasper nods. "And this one?"

"This is Anpanman. 'Pan' is bread, 'An' is bean. He is Bread-Bean man, and he is always saving the world with eating of his head."

Jasper blinks a few times. "Come again?"

"The world is eating his head." Rin frowns with concentration. "Am I saying it wrong?"

"People eat this man's head?"

"*Hai.*"

"He's alive and made of bread and gives people chunks of his own head to eat?"

"*Hai*. And he fly with cape."

I carefully watch Jasper deal with this information, waiting for the inevitable "Who the *hell* came up with this nonsense?"

"Ah," he says eventually, nodding with patient understanding. "Gotcha."

Oh my God. I *knew* it.

It's like watching a destabilised Superman: I think Rin might be Jasper's kryptonite.

In the meantime, Rin's body language could not be easier to read. She's still shy and anxious, but her blue skirts have been spread across the velvet armchair like something from *Gone With the Wind*, her cheeks are getting pinker by the second and her eyes are starting to darken and sparkle.

We are *definitely* on the right track.

Although maybe I should distract her from the presentation of tiny toys. We all get super nervous around people we like, but I'm not sure that this is the most efficient way to attract boys.

"Rin," I say, clearing my throat, "why don't you… uh… tell everyone about your experiences as a beautiful top model in Tokyo?"

That's a little bit more universal, isn't it?

"I'd imagine they can't possibly be as – how should we put it? – *colourful* as yours, Harriet," Jasper says, standing up and running a hand through his hair.

Bat poop. She told him.

Rin starts laughing. "Blue! So blue all over! Harry-chan is so funny."

"Funny's one word for it." Jasper ties the stripy apron around his middle and raises his dark eyebrows. "I can think of a few others."

I scowl. "If there's a problem with your vocabulary,

King, I can lend you my thesaurus."

"Please do. I'm sure it will just *blue* me away." He picks up a plate from the other table. "Now if you'll excuse me, there's something I've promised to do."

He smiles at Rin.

Then he strides off behind the counter, grabs a damp cloth and turns on the noisy cappuccino machine.

"*Blue...*" Rin says experimentally. "*Blue* me..." Then her eyes widen. "I understand that English joke, Harry-chan! Blue and blow are similarity words!"

Her shoulders have relaxed, her smile is lighter and the sweet sparkliness I love so much about Rin seems to be slowly coming back.

I think this is actually *working*. I am a genius at making my friends happy, if I do say so myself.

"Rin?" Toby says, leaning forward and pointing at a little green key ring. "Is this *Mameshiba*? Body of edamame bean, face of shiba dog?"

"You know him?" Rin glows a bit harder. "He is *most kawaii* of all and know many interesting fact."

"Oh I've seen the adverts," Toby nods. "Chilli Bean Mameshiba tells us that cows produce a hundred litres of saliva a day."

"*Hai*. And Jelly Bean Mameshiba say a koala's appendix is two metre long."

"Chickpea Mameshiba informs us that catfish have tastebuds all over their bodies." Toby thinks about this for a few seconds. "That would be awful. Imagine if you stood in dog poo. You'd basically be tasting dog poo with your feet."

"*Itadakimasu,*" Rin says with a little bow.

They both start inexplicably chortling.

"It means *bon appetit* in Japanese," Toby explains to the room in general. "Hilarious."

Nat looks up from her magazine and makes her eyes into circles at me. I widen mine back: our silent communication as seamless as always.

She's right: this is going *so well*. Rin's almost back to her normal self and I haven't even *started* on my big plan for tomorrow yet.

"Here you go," Jasper says, returning to the table with a tray full of drinks and plopping them down in front of us. "My one discernible skill, as promised."

On top of each drink is a delicate picture sprinkled with cocoa in the foam: a robot, a high-heeled shoe, and a three-dimensional bear, made from foam rising out of the cup in a dome shape, with little ears sticking from the top.

They're incredibly beautiful, and I have never seen anything like it before. How long has Jasper been able to do this? Why has he never done it before?

Oh.

"*Su-goi!*" Rin cries happily, clapping and picking up her teddy hot chocolate. "Oh I *love* him, Jasper! You are so kind! Thank you!"

"Woah," Toby says, grabbing his robot. "Epic."

"So cool." Nat picks up her shoe.

I stare at the single remaining cup.

You have *got* to be kidding me.

Sketched in the Harriet-uccino foam in dark cocoa is a blob with eight arms, two eyes and a domed head.

There's no doubt about it: it's an octopus.

"Haha," I say flatly. "Hilarious."

"Sounds like it really was." Jasper sits next to me. "Maybe you wanted to practise your seduction strategy with Charlie first, or were you just going in for a cuddle?"

I flush bright pink.

Yup: this is *exactly* why I didn't tell him about Octo-gate. Or any of my other modelling experiences.

He finds my embarrassment *way* too amusing.

"Anyway –" *change the subject before he asks about Paris* – "guys, I have a favour to ask. My *Vogue* shoot is tomorrow, and I think I'm going to need a back-up model in case anything goes wrong. Rin, would you be able to come with me?"

Nat frowns. "I don't think you get to pick your own…"
I kick her under the table and glance pointedly at Rin then
Jasper. "*Oh.* Got it. Err… bench-subbing yourself is totally
standard procedure in the British fashion world."

"Of course," Rin says brightly. "I am happy to do it."
Tick.

"I'll come along t—" Nat begins before I give her
another swift boot to the shins and a *no, you will not*
expression, "—or I would, but… *Vogue* is so over right
now." Nat shrugs whilst going a little pink around the
ears. "I mean, *yawn.* Boring. Whatevs."

I literally have the best friend in the world.

"I've got quadruple physics," Toby says, rubbing a
dusting of cocoa off the end of his nose. "It's actually my
double physics lesson and then another one I go to that
isn't mine."

"But…" Nat says, frowning, "aren't you…"

"Such a shame," I interrupt smoothly, then turn to
Jasper. "Please can you come too? Tabitha's going to
need an extra pair of hands and she likes you."

His eyebrows lift. "Really?"

"Well, she's too young to know any better."

"*Touché.*" Jasper throws a napkin at me. "I've got a
class first thing but I can try and make it afterwards. Can't
miss seeing you in action, can I?"

Tick.

Delighted, I grin and resist the urge to rub my hands together and burst into loud Mad Genius laughter.

Everything's lining up, just as I hoped.

A few more strategic but subtle nudges here and there and I think my job is done.

"Gah," Nat says, glancing at her watch, grabbing her handbag and standing up. "I'm late for a night class again. Have fun tomorrow, OK guys?"

Then she gives me eloquent Best Friend eyes.

Harriet, they say, *what exactly are you planning on doing?*

I grin at her triumphantly.

Oh, nothing, I wink back. *Just a little bit of chemistry.*

53

With one plan completely under control, it's time to focus on a few of the others.

Like stealing my sister.

By first thing the next morning, I've packed a bag full of baby stuff, sent Toby off with a forged sick note for school and worked up a series of elaborate ruses for Tabitha: ranging from pretending Rin's taken her on an incredibly long walk (simple), to rigging up an electronically motored balloon underneath a pile of clothes with a doll's head on top and putting it in her cot (much more difficult and potentially the beginning of a really bad film).

After much deliberation, I opt for National Bring Your Pre-School Sibling to School Day.

It's a brand-new holiday – according to the newsletter I've just made on my computer – designed to foster *a love of education and knowledge* among relatives.

Especially babies.

It says that very clearly on the form.

Unfortunately, it's taken me so long to make this fake government-approved initiative that by the time it's ready I'm getting texts from Wilbur telling me that the taxi to the *Vogue* shoot is already on its way.

Rin is still making herself look *kawaii* yet professional.

And I haven't even started on my verbal excuses yet. At this rate, I'll have to shove Tabby under my coat, run as fast as I can and hope for the best.

"Go ask all the Starbucks lovers," Rin's warbling sweetly from the bathroom, "they'll tell you I'm in Spain…"

"Rin!" I shout, rapping on the door. "You've got five minutes and then we have to leave whether you're ready or not!"

She's been in there an hour and I'm concerned she's going to set fire to the shower curtain with her Hello Kitty hair-irons.

As of last night, it wouldn't be the first time.

"OK, Harry-chan!" she calls chirpily. "I am just varnishing my toes! I be out in a tickity!"

Then I run back to Annabel and Dad's room and take a deep breath.

OK: my best lie is locked and loaded.

Ready, aim…

"Annabel?" I call, knocking on the door. *Fire.* "So

245

there's this thing at school I *totally* forgot about. You won't *believe* what the government has decided to—"

The door swings open.

"Good morning, Batman," Dad says, Tabitha dangling from one of his arms.

I blink and look down at my outfit. Black leggings, black T-shirt, black shoes, black cardigan, black coat, black woolly hat.

Fudge nuggets: he's right.

All I need is a black mask and *Vogue* are going to think they accidentally shone the bat signal.

"Where's Annabel?" I say, peering round him. "Because there's this important thing that I have to…" I stop. "Dad, are you doing *laundry*?"

"No," he says, putting a red jumper in a conspicuously white pile. "I'm doing *pre*-laundry. It's even worse."

He's obviously in big trouble for something.

"And I'm afraid your stepmother has gone out for the day," he adds, putting something else that clearly isn't white on top of the pile. "She went shopping with Bunty. There was apparently a last-minute urge for a fragranced candle."

"Oh." I look flatly at the complicated form in my hand: now completely unnecessary. That's another bit of wasted forestry. "Dad, can I take Tabitha to school with me today?"

"Go for it." He immediately bundles her into my arms, and she gurgles happily.

"Great. Thanks."

Then I turn to go. OK: kidnapping my sister was *significantly* easier than I thought it would be.

A little *too* easy, in fact.

I pause in the hallway. "And you honestly don't mind that I'm taking a baby to a building filled with sharp pencils, stairs and hormonal teenagers?"

"In fairness, we've got all of them here too," Dad points out reasonably.

"It doesn't bother you that she's probably going to get passed around a class like some kind of netball and possibly dropped at some stage?"

"She's surprisingly bouncy."

"And you think this is a reasonable request? You don't even need to see a form or a typed-out newsletter confirming this idea or anything?"

"Not particularly."

I stare at him. "Dad, I say this with a lot of love and affection, but what the hell is *wrong* with you?"

"Well, in my humble opinion," he says calmly, grabbing another armful of laundry out of the basket, "I'm a misunderstood genius and it's the greatest sadness of our time."

My stomach twists in sympathy. "You didn't get the Manchester job, did you?"

That's the fourth interview this month alone.

"I did not," he confirms. "And, dearest elder daughter, I know you're taking Tabitha to your shoot this morning."

I freeze. *What*?

Then I look down at Tabitha. *How? How did she tell him?* Though I wouldn't be surprised if her first word turned out to be *Vogue*.

"I…" I swallow. "I don't know what you're—"

"Harriet, did you really think Wilbur wouldn't check with me or Annabel before signing *both* our children to a modelling agency?"

"Yes," I say without hesitation. "Obviously."

Wilbur once accidentally sent me to his dental appointment instead of a photo shoot.

"So…" I'm still trying to work out what the *sugar cookies* is going on. "If you know, does this mean it's OK? We're allowed to go?"

"Are you kidding?" Dad grins. "This means I have *two* supermodel daughters instead of one. I'm the common denominator which means I am officially genetically perfect. Me-five."

He holds a hand up and high-fives himself.

"But Annabel…"

"Annabel doesn't know," he says in a weirdly firm voice. "And she doesn't need to right now. We've got two guests and the house is chaotic enough already. It can wait."

I blink at him in amazement.

"You want me to lie to Annabel?" I check. "To her face?" I mean, that's what I was going to do anyway, but I didn't think I'd get parental approval for it.

"Nope," Dad says, picking up another sock. "Just be selective about what exactly you tell her. It's surprisingly easy to miss the things right under your nose."

He grins, pinches my nose and then Tabby's. "Now, go get 'em, my baby tigers."

"I think we're a panther and a leopard, actually," I grin, pointing at Tabby's spotty onesie.

And as I give the bathroom a final loud knock and carry my sister downstairs, I realise that it just goes to show.

I was so focused on Annabel not finding out, it never occurred to me that this time the savvy parent would be my father.

Or that he'd be on my side.

54

Now, I love knowing things.

I love knowing that a mantis shrimp can swing a claw so fast it boils the water around it, and that we swap our main breathing nostril every fifteen minutes. I'm transfixed by the knowledge that there are more possible iterations of a single game of chess than there are atoms in the Universe, and that all the clocks in the film *Pulp Fiction* read 4:20.

And I haven't even seen that movie yet.

But of all the things I love knowing, *exactly where I'm going* is right at the top of that list.

Which means that, as Rin and I climb into the back of the taxi three minutes later with a bundled-up Tabby safely tucked into her car seat and start the unbelievably short drive towards today's shoot, I can feel myself starting to fizz with excitement.

The body produces 25 million new cells every second, and I swear I can feel mine: snapping and crackling all over me.

I know every *inch* of this journey.

"Take a left here, please," I tell the taxi driver, wiggling my fingers in front of Tabby's face. "Then a right."

"Third exit and then a sharp right again," I say a few minutes later as we head towards a roundabout. "Don't miss the turning."

"You might want to indicate," I remind him after thirty seconds. "It's a busy road."

"Do you want to drive, miss?"

"I'd love to," I say sadly, "but unfortunately I'm still five months too young. Thanks for asking, though."

Then I point out the window so Tabby looks as we slowly make our way up a huge gravel driveway and the fizz inside me gets cracklier and sparklier.

And there it is.

A magnificent red-brick building with intricate lead windows. A grand, circular lawn and enormous fountain; ivy-covered walls and white pointed turrets. One of the most historically important buildings in England, and the destination of so many of my rainy Saturdays I've actually lost count.

Although Nat hasn't: we're currently at eighteen.

I just can't believe that of all the possible locations to do this shoot, *Vogue* chose one less than ten minutes from where I live.

That's serendipity for you. Or just really good planning.

"Oh *Harry-chan*," Rin breathes as the car stops, her entire face lighting up like a glowstick, "it is *castle*. We are in real England castle, like fairytale."

"Nope," I beam as the doors swing open. "Better than a fairytale, Rin. This is real, living *history.*"

This is Hatfield House.

Some places just feel steeped in time. Like tea leaves that have been left in hot water for centuries, so there's no part of the water that hasn't changed colour as a consequence.

That's what this place is like.

And as Rin, Tabby and I crunch up the gravel path towards the enormous wooden studded doors, for just a second I can see it all. Over four hundred years swirling around us: of soldiers and kings and queens, princesses and warriors and clergymen, horses and bright gowns and banquets.

It's like being dipped in the past: submerged in the stories of the people who came here before us.

I just can't see the *Vogue* team anywhere.

Which – given that we're technically not here for an extra-curricular tour of Tudor England – is a little bit disconcerting.

I spin back towards our taxi, but it's already driving away. *Bat poop.* It's only a ten-minute car journey, but quite a long walk along either fields or a dual carriage motorway.

Especially wheeling a buggy.

"Umm," I say anxiously, as Tabby grabs my thumb. *Wilbur's done it again.* "There's quite a good chance we've been sent to the wrong place and the shoot's happening in another place entirely. Possibly another country."

At which point the huge wooden, studded door at the front of the building suddenly swings open with a creak.

A boy steps out.

Broad shoulders, bronze hair, six freckles on his nose and bright, disorientating eyes. Tabby immediately squeaks and holds her arms up.

"Jasper!" Rin cries happily, skipping steps towards him. "You are here already! I am so glad of it!"

"My class was cancelled last minute," he smiles, taking Tabby off me. "So I decided to walk."

I look down: there's yellow and purple paint and mud all over his black trousers and a little dark splash on one cheek, a little green one on the other.

"Through a rainbow swamp?"

He lifts his eyebrows. "Not so many of those in

Hertfordshire, Harriet-uccino. Or on Earth. But let me know if you find any."

"Harriet?" The blonde lady from *Vogue* pokes her head out from the door. "Oh, you're both here! Wonderful! We're ready if you are! I'm Charlotte, by the way. It was such chaos the other day, I don't think I properly introduced myself."

A wave of relief rushes over me.

And guilt. Wilbur wouldn't get this one wrong: it is far too important.

"Please," Jasper says, bending gently with Tabitha and lifting one eyebrow, "you go first, *Your Majesty.*"

I glare at him, flushing.

It's one thing mocking me in the private sanctuary of our friendship group, but not in front of *Vogue.* I'm a *professional.* This is my *job.*

"If you're going to be like that," I hiss, "then you can just swim straight back through the rainbow swamps to where you…"

The door finally swings open completely.

"…came from," I finish limply.

Because standing at the bottom of the spiral staircase is something that immediately makes my argument void.

A real, live queen.

55

Everybody needs a hero.

Someone to look up to: to remind us of the kind of person we would be if we were the very best version of ourselves.

Of what real people can actually achieve.

For Annabel, it's Marie Curie: the only woman to ever win two Nobel Prizes in two different fields. For Dad, it's Einstein (a "maverick with great hair, just like me") and for Toby it's Galileo: the father of observational astronomy.

Bunty loves American pioneer Amelia Earhart, Nat worships Alexander McQueen, India adores feminist icon Frida Kahlo and Jasper is a big fan of French artist Henri Matisse.

For Tabitha it's currently me, but we'll see what happens when she knows more than three people.

I've had the same hero since I was six.

She was my chosen class project in Year Two, my voluntary class project in Year Three, my debate club

subject in Year Four and by Year Six I was asked to pick someone else because I was getting "a little obsessive".

So I picked her older sister instead.

Now – as I stand in the doorway of Hatfield House and stare at the fascinating face of its most famous resident – I can feel something in my throat start to tighten.

This woman is still everything I want to be.

Elegant and dignified, with pure white skin, green eyes and bright red hair, piled high on her head.

A long, structured black dress: tied at the waist and puffed out four metres, covered elaborately in white buttons and a big, spiky lace collar.

The wise, calm face of somebody fearless and independent, courageous and strong.

I love her.

And not just because she's the most famous ginger person in the history of the world, although – I'm not going to lie – it's nice to have somebody representing us other than Prince Harry.

"Hello," the queen says warmly, holding out her hand. "I'm Sophia, and I'm guessing you must be the baby versions of me."

I look back at Tabitha and Jasper.

And with a BANG, it suddenly makes sense: why everyone at the casting had red hair, why *Vogue* wanted my sister to come too, why we're in one of the most famous Tudor houses in the whole world.

Why Jasper looks so pleased with himself and is trying quite hard not to laugh.

Finally, after a decade, my most obsessive dreams have come true.

I *am* Queen Elizabeth the First.

56

In 1990, Steve Woodmore broke the world record for fastest speaker of all time: reciting *Hamlet* at 637 words per minute.

I hope somebody's recording me, because I'm so excited I think he has some fierce competition on his hands.

Finally, what I already know is *relevant*.

"Did you know," I tell the stylist as Charlotte takes Tabby to get her ready, "that paleness was so popular in Elizabethan times that the women used to physically *bleed* themselves to look whiter?"

"Gosh," Rebecca says, leading me into the pantry: the house is shut to the public until the end of March, so it's now a makeshift dressing room. "Well, we won't be doing that today, I assure you."

"And," I say as she wipes my face clean with a damp cloth, "pink lips and cheeks were created from rouge made from ground-up cochineal beetles combined with

red ochre?"

"Crikey." She applies a thick layer of moisturiser. "No ground-up beetles today."

"Also, Queen Elizabeth made her skin whiter with a combination of white lead and vinegar, which was poisonous and left craters in her skin. Which meant the more she used, the more she had to use."

We both look at the white foundation.

"No lead," Rebecca smiles. "Or acid. I promise. And I won't be shaving your hairline to give you a higher forehead either."

I smile at her gratefully.

I was totally ready and willing to throw myself into this experience at any cost, but I have to be honest: I'm a little relieved that she's using contemporary tools of the trade instead.

With an immense effort, I stop chatting just long enough for Rebecca to make my skin look flawless, paint a little black dot under each of my eyes, flush my cheeks with gel blusher and daub a faint red spot in the middle of my mouth with lipstick.

"We're doing Elizabethan but *modern*," she explains, styling my hair and then attaching very long red hairpieces that match it exactly and fall down all the way to my bottom. "Something a little fresher and younger."

Then she holds out a long dress.

It's bright yellow silk, huge, floor length and covered in tiny embroidered black skulls, with elegant black ridges spiking out of the shoulders.

I'm kind of hoping this is an update too, or my Year Two project may need revisiting.

"There is just *one* concession to tradition, I'm afraid," Rebecca says with a small grimace. "And I'd like to apologise in advance."

Oh my God: I knew it.

After all that, they're taking both my eyebrows.

You can do this, Harriet. You are a brave, resilient queen, capable of rising above such slight and unimportant topics as facial hair.

Nobody knows what they're really for anyway.

"OK," I say, closing my eyes firmly. "But please teach me how to draw them on afterwards or my best friend is going to kill you."

"Breathe in, sweetheart," Rebecca laughs. "This is going to hurt."

She's not wrong.

Ten minutes later, my eyes are prickling with uncomfortable tears.

Normally the surface of our lungs would stretch to the

size of half a tennis court, but the corset I'm now wearing is so tight and so rigid, mine have been reduced to the size of a postage stamp and an assistant has to put my shoes on for me.

On the upside, at least I can still communicate thanks to my still fully unedited eyebrows.

"Gorgeous," Rebecca says in satisfaction, tying a jet-black ribbon round my now ridiculously small waist. "You're a sixteenth century vision, my darling. Let's get you in there."

This proves harder than you'd think.

Somewhat embarrassingly, I need four assistants: two to fold my dress inwards so I can fit through the pantry doors like a telescope, one to hold my hand so I don't fall over in my elaborately jewelled heels and another to carry my enormous hair extensions so they don't get caught up in the shoulder spikes.

I'm starting to realise that with great majesty comes great responsibility.

And also great balancing skills.

Breathing much more shallowly than I'm used to, I shuffle stiffly through the narrow corridors: into the Long Gallery, running the entire length of the South Front of the building. It's nearly two hundred feet, there's an enormous fireplace, the walls are elaborately carved wood and the ceiling is coated in gold leaf, glowing in the sunlight.

Then I stand in the grand entrance, blinking.

In one corner is Sophia, now changed into a six-foot-wide red dress covered in tiny, pink embroidered bees: carefully having her eye make-up retouched.

In another is Charlotte, chatting to Rin.

Across the middle, in front of an elaborate throne, is the standard photo shoot set: large cameras, huge metallic lights and assistants milling around, looking busy and anxious.

But I don't care about any of that.

Because as I scan the room a little faster, I can feel icy panic starting to run through me: across my shoulders, up my neck and down my back, into my chest and ears. And as I scan it for the third time, my stomach flips over with a bolt of terror.

No. No no. No no no no no no no no no no...

"Tabby?" I say, spinning around. "Tabitha? Tabs? TABITHA?"

But nobody responds.

No gurgle, no squeak, no little red curls bouncing up and down. No rosy cheeks and bright eyes, watching me with unquestioning adoration.

The human heart beats more than three billion times in the average lifetime, but you can take at least three of those off my total.

My whole chest has frozen solid.

Where the hell is my baby sister?

57

There are apparently pivotal moments where your whole life flashes before your eyes.

This is one of them.

Except instead of my life it's Tabitha's, and instead of flashing it's just one big, blinding glare of white-hot terror.

Oh God Oh God Oh God Oh God Oh God Oh God...

How could I have just *left* her?

How could I have been so distracted by my Elizabethan ambitions that I let a bunch of strangers walk off with the person in the entire world I love most?

I am the worst big sister *ever*.

And this is the exact place where Mary Tudor tried to get Elizabeth imprisoned for treason in the Tower of London.

"Tabby?" I shake my assistants off and wobble dangerously into the middle of the room. "*Tabs*?" Fear is starting to close my throat. "TABITHA MANNERS?" I grab a passing photographic assistant by the jumper.

"WHERE IS SHE?"

All week, this felt like a totally reasonable plan.

In the glossy, safe *Vogue* offices and in the sanctity of my bedroom, what I was doing didn't seem *that* reprehensible.

Irresponsible, yes. Selfish and poorly thought-through, quite possibly.

But not *bad*.

Except it's finally hitting me: I've just ripped a defenceless eight-month-old baby away from her mother without permission and left her in the hands of a bunch of fashionistas I don't know, to do with as they will.

What the fudge nuggets is *wrong* with me?

"The baby?" the assistant blinks nervously: I'm shaking him more than a little roughly. "Are we talking about the baby?"

A human bite is approximately 120 pounds per square inch, while a crocodile has the strongest jaw of any animal on the planet at 3,700.

I know it's not this poor boy's fault.

But I swear if he doesn't answer me this very second, I'm going to turn into a reptile and chew his head right off.

"YES OF COURSE THE BABY WHERE IS THE BABY GIVE ME TABBY OR I SWEAR I WILL RIP THIS WHOLE

PLACE TO—"

"Blimey," a voice says behind me. "Are we in character already?"

I spin so fast I nearly poke the assistant's eye out with my shoulder spikes.

"*Tabby?*"

She's curled up in Jasper's arms, beaming, in a pretty cream lace dress with a train so long it's thrown over one of his shoulders.

The relief is so intense it's a good thing I'm wearing the corset because it's basically the only thing holding me up.

"*Babababababa*," she tells me happily as I launch myself across and start covering her in kisses that leave little red lipstick spots all over her face. "*Babababababa*."

"They have a farm," Jasper explains. "We went to look at the goats. Goats don't say *Baa*, Tabitha. They say *Meh*. I told you, they're the most unimpressed creatures in the animal kingdom."

I blink at them both.

My heart is still hammering, and I'm struggling to breathe: adrenaline, fear and an already reduced lung capacity are a heady combination.

"I didn't know where she…" I gulp. "I wouldn't know what I'd do if…"

Jasper hands her to me without a word.

"*Bababa*?" she says, smacking me in the face with something damp, small, grey and fluffy. "*Bababa*?"

Wait. "Is that…?"

Gripped tightly in my deliriously happy sister's hand is the original Dunky.

"He was in a tree at the end of your street," Jasper shrugs. "That cat of yours is an impressive climber. I had to fight a squirrel who thought it was its baby."

A grateful lump rises into my throat.

After my panicked hunt under the bush and a long and fruitless conversation with Victor, I had just presumed that Dunky was gone for good.

"*Babababababa*," Tabitha beams, whacking me with her beloved toy again. "*Babababababa*."

"Thank you, Jasper," I say awkwardly. "For… looking after her for me."

He lifts his eyebrows. "That's what I'm here for, isn't it?"

I blink. "Uh. Absolutely."

"Harriet?" Charlotte calls, hurrying across the room. "Are you ready to… Oh." Her eyes widen at Tabby, covered in little red dots, and me: now lipstick-less. "Let's get you both tidied up and then we can start."

58

Over the last year and a half, I have been transformed a dozen times.

I've worn dresses covered in tentacles; long pink wigs and net tutus; found myself liberally doused in gold paint and mud and ink and sequins; been lit up by a switch and covered in a sack.

I've been a doll in a box, a nomad in a desert.

A glowing Ophelia in a lake.

I've jumped in snow and danced in sand; sat down on catwalks and wandered around a sumo stage. I've whizzed round in circles and upside down at hundreds of miles an hour; attended parties and crashed into castings.

I've turned into so many different people.

But as I walk close behind Tabby, past an enormous mirror to my right, I realise with a jolt that this is a version of me I haven't seen before.

The yellow dress is flared and glowing in the sunshine; the spiky collar is so high it touches the sides of my head.

My face is steady and pale, and my red hair is waved in glossy tumbling curls. The crown on my head is gold and delicate.

I look regal. Powerful. Majestic.

Holding my chin up, I stare at my reflection without flinching or blushing or looking away.

It feels like something has changed.

I don't feel out of my depth or anxious or out of control any more. I feel as if I know exactly what I'm doing and what I want and how I'm going to get it.

And for just a moment it's as if I can see both of us, standing side by side: the Harriet Manners of nearly sixteen months ago in a borrowed leopardskin coat and red high heels – terrified and wobbly and uncertain – and this one.

A girl who needs nobody.

A girl with nothing to answer to or bow down in front of: totally in command, strong and free with an untethered heart.

A girl in control of her own story.

Just like Elizabeth.

"I can't believe we were only going to use two models," Charlotte says as Tabby and I are led in front of the bright lights. "I'm so glad you brought your little one to the casting, Harriet. Three is *so* much more interesting."

"Mmm," I say quickly. "She's… uh. *My* little one all right. AKA belonging to me."

Then I look round.

We've been positioned in a triangle: me, standing up, with Sophia seated to my left in a throne – enormous red gown spread regally out and hair piled high – and Tabby gurgling happily on her lap.

I glance up just in time to see Jasper lean down and say something quietly in Rin's ear.

She laughs and claps her hands together.

"*Well*," someone says as I lean forward to hear a little better, "Harriet Manners. I didn't think I'd be seeing *you* again."

I freeze, mid-earwig.

Where do I know that voice fr—

Oh my God: no. You have *got* to be kidding me. The radius of the earth is 6,371 km: it's a *really* big place. Of all the photographers on the planet to choose from, there's no way that *Vogue* would have picked…

"Aiden," I say, spinning around.

"Little Miss Stickers," he says over the top of a huge camera. "A pleasure, as always. How do you plan on ruining my photo shoot this time?"

59

The Universe clearly thinks it's *hilarious*.

Just for *once* I finally feel in control of my life, and it sends someone to loudly and repeatedly remind me of a time when I wasn't.

And to regale everyone else with stories about me while he's at it.

"So she's making these crazy poses," Aiden says as I try my best to stay focused on the job at hand, "then I look closer and she's covered in tiny *stickers*."

Concentrate, Harriet. You are a professional.

I shift a little, keep my neck as long and regal as possible and move my body very subtly towards the camera.

You are a Queen. A leader, a pioneer, a powerful force of gravitas and majesty.

"*Stickers*?" Jasper says from behind one of the lights. "What *kind* of stickers?"

"Maths equations," Aiden laughs, clicking a button. "Home-made, handwritten. Unbelievable."

271

"*They were physics* and I *typed* them," I mutter through gritted teeth.

"It turns out she was trying to revise for an exam while simultaneously shooting a huge perfume commercial for Yuka Ito."

I stick my nose in the air. "An exam which I *aced*, by the way. Top in the year, thanks for asking."

"*Then* she got tangled up in the changing-room curtains and couldn't get back out again."

OK: I'm not quite as proud of that. It definitely wasn't one of my most regal moments.

I turn to glare daggers at Aiden.

"*Yes!*" he shouts, clicking the button a few times. "Perfect! Let's see that anger! I'm thinking controlling! I'm thinking imperious and dictatorial and overbearing!"

"I'm thinking that'll be a challenge," Jasper says in a low voice.

So I turn my icy death-glare on him instead.

"Oh I *love* this," Charlotte declares happily from the side where she's watching carefully. "Harriet, you're *fierce* right now. Sophia, you're a noble, wise goddess, as always. And Tabitha… You are the star of this show, sweetheart."

I look around in surprise.

I'd almost forgotten Tabs was there, she's behaving so perfectly. She isn't crying, grizzling or sucking her thumb.

She's not blowing spit bubbles or vomiting or giggling or trying to climb up Sophia's hair.

Her blue eyes are wide, her chubby little face is relaxed, her tiny pink mouth is very slightly pouted and she's staring curiously at the camera.

Not at Aiden, not at Jasper, not even at beloved Dunky: now being held carefully by Rin.

The camera.

Uh-oh. Apparently we snap as many photos in two minutes as the whole of humanity did in the 1800s, and it looks like Tabitha is preparing to be in *all* of them. She's a born poser, just like Dad.

Annabel is going to *kill* me.

I reach over and pat her cheek so she knows I'm still here: she beams and grabs my finger.

Click. "Gorgeous!" *Click.* "Adorable!" *Click click click.* "Sweet!" Aiden frowns. "But as touching as this is, I think I actually preferred the earlier icy look, Sticker Girl. So let's go back to that, shall we?"

I glance at Sophia, standing up and shifting from one foot to the other. She's a total professional: her chin is up, her eyes are hard, and she's making tiny movements every few seconds so that no photo is the same.

"I have *got* to pee," she whispers regally under her breath. "My bladder is fit to burst."

OK: maybe the movements serve a double purpose.

"Harry-chan is wonderful, *ne*?" Rin sighs as I attempt to take a deep breath without breaking my ribcage. "She is beauty and rare, like unicorn."

"Yup," Jasper says drily. "She's unbelievable."

"That's better!" Aiden shouts as I turn towards him crossly. "Let's keep that expression, Harriet! Haughty and high-handed! Love it!"

He clicks a few more times and I can't help noticing that Rin and Jasper have been standing next to each other in silence for at least fifteen minutes. And it's not a comfortable silence either: it's awkward and stiff.

This isn't what was supposed to happen.

The idea was for them to connect while I worked: to bond romantically, adhere together and let the fireworks fly. Like Jane Eyre and Rochester, or Romeo and Juliet: the two other famous R and J couplings.

Except hopefully without all the dying, blindness and fires.

"OK," Aiden says, flicking through the photos on his camera. "We've got this shot. Let's try something else."

I look back at my friends.

Maybe they just need another little nudge in the right direction.

"Yup," I say, as my brain starts whirring again. "Let's do that."

60

A lot of people don't know this, but Cupid actually had *two* types of arrow.

The famous one was made of gold and dove feathers, and when shot into the heart it caused intense feelings of love and desire. The other, less well known, type was made of lead and owl feathers, and resulted in indifference and apathy.

I'm starting to wonder if I've shot the wrong one.

After an elaborate costume change – I'm in bright green silk covered in tiny blue embroidered butterflies, with a pearl tiara with gold wires wound round it – all three Elizabeths are led carefully outside into the enormous park.

My assistants are helping me not to trip over my dress, slip or face-slam the ground in any way, and Tabby's being wheeled in her buggy ahead of us by a mildly besotted Charlotte. Which means I can focus on trying to subtly listen to Rin and Jasper, walking ten metres behind me.

275

And I have to be honest: it's not going as I'd hoped.

I mean, obviously flirting is not exactly my key speciality or talent.

But the last thing Rin just said after a five-minute silence was "I like apples," to which Jasper replied, "Really? I prefer pears," and I don't think that's *typically* how many eternal fires of the soul are started.

I deliberate for a moment.

Then, with a quick wiggle, I ram my heel into the mud and loudly exclaim: "Oh dear, I'm stuck!"

"Speaking of apples," I say airily when they've caught up, "did you know that the Ancient Greeks used to declare love by throwing apples at each other? Fascinating, don't you think?"

I'm not saying Jasper should start throwing apples at Rin, but a *little* more wooing would be nice.

Although that's how the Trojan War started, so you do have to be quite careful.

"Why would you know that?" Jasper asks bluntly. "Seriously, how much Ancient Greek history do people normally have to hand?"

"*Okashii desu, ne?*" Rin laughs. "I love how Harry-chan is always saying the things."

At least they're agreeing on something.

"Right," Aiden says as we reach the edge of a

beautiful, cultivated garden with flowers in neat shapes and a tiny fountain in the middle. "I've had an idea." He points at me. "Can everybody please keep an eye on *this* one in case she decides to cover herself in Shakespearean quotes while I'm gone?"

Then he hurries off towards an outbuilding.

In the meantime, Sophia's put her huge gold crown down on a small bench and is now massaging her neck, while Tabitha attempts to cement her reputation with *Vogue* by forcing Dunky into the face of its fashion editor.

Rin and Jasper have lapsed into silence once more.

Do something, Harriet.

Reach into the box and pull something romantic out.

"Umm," I say, swallowing, "why don't you play a game? Maybe with…" I swallow. *A roundabout.* "A wheelbarrow and…" *Stamps.* "Stickers and…" *A race to the postbox with a letter.* "A skipping competition?"

They both stare at me blankly.

"What?" Jasper says after a lengthy pause.

"Or…" I'm carefully picking through, trying not to touch anything too dangerous. "Maybe you could…" *Throw mints at the window early in the morning.* "Chuck chewy sweets at a… greenhouse? Or…" *Buy her sixteen purple balloons. Walk across New York hand in hand. Sit on the pavement together.* "Sit down on the grass?"

"What?" Jasper says again, still staring at me. "Harriet, have you been electrocuted in the last two minutes?"

It's no good. I can't rifle through any more.

"Or... you could just have a staring match?" I say abruptly, slamming closed the lid again. "Let's say, I don't know... A hundred and twenty seconds? *Go.*"

Scientists have discovered that staring into a stranger's eyes for two minutes increases the likelihood of falling in love on the spot.

I don't know if it works but it seems worth a shot.

"*Nani*?" Rin says, brow crumpling up.

"You're being really weird, Harriet," Jasper frowns, folding his arms. "Even more so than normal and the bar's pretty high."

Fudge nuggets.

The atmosphere between them is so awkward you could open your mouth and take a chunk of it out of the air.

Ugh. Maybe Nat was right.

I'm really not making anyone happier here, am I?

They were getting on so well yesterday, but I've taken a natural, organic connection and put too much pressure on it, too soon and in public.

I need to give them *space.*

"I'm back," Aiden announces unnecessarily, carrying

a ten-foot ladder under his arm. "I'm thinking *action*. I'm thinking *movement*. I'm thinking this is where they shot *Batman*."

It is, actually.

And *Harry Potter, Shakespeare in Love, Tomb Raider, Sleepy Hollow* and *Get Him to the Greek* (although nobody ever talks about that one).

"Ready!" Sophia says cheerfully, standing up and putting her crown back on. "Where do you want us to go?"

Aiden points to his left. "We're doing the next shot in *there*."

We all turn towards the huge maze that looms behind us.

It's made of two-hundred-year-old yew trees, it's eight feet high, and my insides have just done an immediate dolphin-like backflip of excitement.

I *love* solving puzzles.

Especially when my progress is being recorded.

Plus, I've always wanted to do this particular maze, but it's not open to the public: it's another moment of sheer wish fulfilment.

I'm going to be *so* good at this.

"We'll do single shots first and then end with a shot in the middle," Aiden adds. "So assuming the models are focusing on modelling and not the maze –" he looks at me sharply – "somebody needs to go ahead and find the centre for us. Guys?"

He gestures at the four poor assistants and my brain suddenly lurches.

Hang on…

Privacy and quietness. Nothing to distract them. Solving problems together and overcoming strife. *Potentially getting lost for the next two hours with nothing but each other for company*.

"*Wait*," I blurt suddenly, "why don't you send Rin and Jasper? They can find the centre of the maze for you."

Tabby's in safe hands with Charlotte; in fact, she seems positively delighted to have some more fashionista one-on-one time.

"Uh," Jasper says after a pause. "Sure. Why not."

"I go in big dark hedge," Rin agrees in a tiny voice, nodding nervously. "It is not *kowai* at all."

"Fabulous," Aiden says, clapping his hands. "Off you go, then. *Chop chop*. The rest of us have work to do."

They look at each other in bemusement, then disappear without complaint into the life-size puzzle.

Nat was totally right, as always.

Now we just need to let nature take its course.

61

The first model up is Tabitha.

"OK, little one," Aiden says gently as Charlotte passes her to me. "Harriet, can you take her in for us?"

He's standing on the ladder, ten foot in the air, with his camera strapped to his shoulder.

Carrying my sister in my arms, I walk into the centuries-old maze. I take a right, into a particularly green and glossy corner, and wait as the stylist puts an elaborate, pale blue silky pillow on the floor.

Then I gently plop Tabby on top.

She grabs one of her tiny feet, stares at the little green boot on it for a few seconds, then beams and starts waving her arms around.

I don't think I need to worry about any potential future damage to her mental health: I've never seen her more in her element.

"OK, up here, sweety-pie." Aiden waves Dunky in the air. "Look at me."

With a tiny gurgle, Tabs immediately looks up.

Her blue eyes open wide.

And she stares at that camera with the sweetest, most open and trusting expression I've ever seen her give anyone that isn't me, Annabel or Dad.

Or Dunky, obviously.

Although right now she's not even looking at him. Tabby's love is clearly fickle.

"Ridiculously cute," Aiden says as the camera goes *click*. "Adorable." *Click click.* "*Vogue* should be all babies, all the time." *Click click click.*

Gurgling happily, Tabby plays with the tassels on the cushion, examines an interesting leaf next to her, then reaches out for a sparkling bead on my dress.

And before we know it, she's done.

My sister has completed her first solo photo shoot with more natural charisma, grace and charm than I've managed in my entire career.

I am so incredibly proud of her.

Maybe when we get home she can give me lessons.

"OK," Aiden says, climbing off the ladder so he can shift it to another part of the maze. "Perfect. Sophia? You're up next."

Watching Sophia work is mesmerising.

I have no idea how old she is – she could be forty, fifty, sixty, a hundred – but she's completely ageless: her skin is lined but flawless, her features beautiful and delicate, her figure elegant and tall.

With a quick wink at me, she rearranges her knickers underneath her enormous dress and repositions her boobs. She takes a deep breath and blows a loud raspberry.

Then she pulls her shoulders back, lifts her head and walks enigmatically further into the maze. Curiously, I let Charlotte tend to Tabby while I stand on a bench and peek over the top of the hedge so I can see what's going on.

Sophia grins up at me from between two bushy green aisles.

"Let's DO THIS," she shouts loudly.

Then her face suddenly goes very still, her long arms become effortless and every muscle in her body relaxes. Dozens of expressions start shifting across her face, changing every few seconds, and she begins to move as if she's dancing: floating, striding, bending, turning, flicking.

She spins and pivots, waves and crumples.

And every time the camera clicks, she gives the picture something else.

A new emotion, a new pose, a new angle.

It's like watching Queen Elizabeth come alive again,

over four hundred years after she died and became a legend.

Sophia is a *master* of storytelling.

"Right," Aiden says after the final camera click. He hasn't said a single word for the entire shoot: not a single direction or comment. He just let Sophia do her thing and took as many pictures as he could. "Nailed it, as always. Sophia, you are ever the consummate professional."

"Forty years of practice," she grins, swigging from a can of Diet Coke. "You can wheel me on in forty more."

Then she unceremoniously tucks her crown under her arm like a rugby ball and swaggers back to the palace behind us to "find a cheese and pickle sandwich".

There's a pause, then Aiden turns to me.

Charlotte's taken Tabby back to the house to get changed into her onesie and the assistants are preparing the elaborate dining room for Sophia's next solo shoot.

Jasper and Rin are still gone.

"You know," Aiden says thoughtfully, cracking his knuckles, "nobody could work out why Yuka Ito allowed you to do what you did in her photo shoots without ripping you to pieces and distributing you through her breakfast cereal like tiny Harriet marshmallows."

That's a very alarming image.

And also very accurate: she remains the most terrifying person I've ever met.

"But I think Yuka knew what she was doing," he continues, flicking through his camera. "She saw something the rest of us didn't. And you're ten times the model now that you used to be, Harriet."

He holds the back of his camera out to me.

The photos are tiny and untouched, but they're beautiful. The colours, the clothes, the history of the place we're standing in.

And I look… right.

Dignified, poised and beautiful.

A rush of unexpected warmth floods through me. I've wanted to be many things in my life: an award-winning palaeontologist, a history-changing astrophysicist, an acrobatic woodlouse (I was five).

But a good *model* was never a goal.

Except… I'm genuinely touched by this compliment.

Maybe – after sixteen months of falling through it – I'm starting to take the fashion industry and the people in it seriously after all.

"Thank you," I say, blushing slightly.

"I'd have fired you if it was me," Aiden grins. "Just for the record. Now get into that maze, model. Let's see what else you've got."

62

This time, I give it everything.

As I walk purposefully into the maze with my silk gown trailing behind me and Aiden bouncing around three steps in front with a camera shoved in my face, I focus like I've never focused before.

Not just for Wilbur, or for Aiden, or for the money I'm being paid, but for me too.

I want to be the best model I possibly can be.

With immense concentration, I narrow my eyes, throw back my shoulders and try to harness the majestic ghost of Elizabeth.

Click. I am fierce.

Click. I am regal.

Click. I am a powerhouse of nobility, capable of defeating the Spanish Armada in 1588 thus securing one of the greatest military victories in English history and…

"No," Aiden says, stopping abruptly. "No, this is all wrong, Harriet. Who are you trying to be?"

I blink at him.

Then up at my tiara and down at the princess dress and the palace garden I'm standing in. "Do I really need to answer that question?"

"You're not an actress, Harriet. I want to see something genuine. Try again."

Swallowing, I keep walking.

The maze is getting darker the further we move into it: the floor is dappled and green and the leaves are getting glossier and packed closer together, the paths more twisty and narrow. Aiden runs ahead and dives into little nooks in the hedge as I do my best to find something else to give him.

Except I'm not really sure what he wants.

Honestly, I'm not actually sure I have anything else left.

We take a sharp left and I turn so I'm facing the light and give the camera my most imperious, haughty stare: the kind Elizabeth must have given the Pope when she was excommunicated in 1570.

"Nope," Aiden says patiently. "That's not it either."

So I lower my chin and try sheer rage.

"Nu-uh."

With growing desperation, I turn towards the hedge, shake my waist-length hair then spin back and attempt unbridled joy, even though a strand of it is now caught on a bit of maze bush.

"Looking a bit mad now, sweetheart."

And I can feel myself starting to panic.

I can't screw this one up too; I *can't*. Not after Levaire last year. It's too important. I owe it to everyone who has believed in me and helped me over the last fifteen months: to Wilbur, to Yuka, to Rin, to Bunty and Nat, to Ni–

Click.

"*That's* better," Aiden nods. "*Now* we're getting somewhere. Let's try even softer. You're only sixteen, Harriet. Even Elizabeth wasn't in charge at your age."

This is true. As a teenager, Hatfield House was actually the prison she was locked in.

I think about Nat, holding a cut-off ponytail and a pair of art-room scissors.

"More," Aiden says as he jumps in front of me. *Click click.* "I'm thinking vulnerable. I'm thinking real. I'm thinking something that *matters*."

So I dig a little deeper.

Alexa commanding a classroom full of hands up; banana sweets flying at my head; a pinstripe suit and a crossed-off list…

Click. "Yes! This is better! Keep going!"

Vomit on my lap and a stall full of broken hats.

Click. "More!"

A table. A table. A table.

And – without any warning – the box in my head starts to tremble.

Singapore chewing gum. Dovetail joints. A wooden chest full of treasures, pushed under my bed.

I'm trying to hold it down, but with a deep rumble it's beginning to shake uncontrollably: contents flying around and crashing against the sides with enormous bangs.

Click click. "Brilliant, Harriet!"

Now tiny memories are starting to slip out from under the lid: spilling and splashing all over the floor.

A cuddly toy lion. A hundred yen note.

A blue sock.

Three stars, a necklace of planets.

Click click click. "Beautiful! Keep going, Harriet!"

A sunset, a mountain, a lake full of lights. A bridge and a peregrine falcon and a pair of gloves; skates and a cinnamon-scented kiss by a sparkling Christmas tree.

Click. "Stunning!" *Click.*

And I'm not sure I can hold it any more.

Everything I put in the box and locked up so tightly all those months ago is still in there, and now it's trying to get back out as hard as it can. And I don't know what

I'm going to do if it does. I've used all my energy up just holding it together: just keeping everything under control.

I can feel tears starting to prickle.

The maze is getting even darker and narrower and I suddenly don't know where I'm going: I don't remember what I'm doing.

Click.

I don't know how to get out.

Click.

I don't know how to make it stop.

Click.

Make it stop make it stop make it—

"Harriet?"

Trembling, I emerge with a *pop* into the bright sunshine at the centre of the maze as the lid of the box slams shut just in time.

Jasper's sitting on a bench with Rin.

They're laughing and lit by sunshine: right at the start of making their own memories.

Happy.

Which is why it makes no sense that with a sharp sob, I fling my hands over my face, feel my chin crumple up into a little paper ball.

And burst into noisy tears.

63

Yup: this is exactly why you should always be careful what you wish for.

Vogue wanted emotion, and they got it.

Loudly and in soggy, snotty streams all over my beautifully styled hair, make-up and priceless dress.

Let's see if they want a photo to immortalise *that.*

There's a stunned silence for about thirty seconds while I bawl into the crook of my arm. A thick layer of powder and foundation is melting all over the fabric, my eyes are inflating and my eyelashes are sticking together in clumps, but I don't seem to be able to stop.

And that's when the yelling starts.

"*What the hell is going on? What did you DO?* WHAT DID YOU SAY TO HER?"

"Umm." Aiden's confusion sounds genuine, even through my sobs. "I have absolutely no idea. I was just directing her."

"TO WHERE?" Jasper shouts. "To the edge of a cliff? Into a gas oven? Off a bridge somewhere? What the HELL IS WRONG WITH YOU?"

"You are a very mean man," Rin adds with more ferocity than I knew she was capable of. "I am cheese off and not full of beans for you. Go and get yourself lost!"

"Well, I'm sorry for doing my job," Aiden retorts as I start to slow down to a hiccup. "I just asked her for an emotion that was real."

"It wasn't him," I manage, wiping my face on a no-longer-white glove. "I-It's me. I'm sorry, I'm just... tired."

I suddenly realise that's true.

It's exhausting: keeping everything and everyone under control all the time.

Also, this corset is not helping.

I haven't inhaled properly in two and a half hours.

"If it helps," Aiden says, holding up his camera, "those pictures are going to be amazing, Harriet. Probably worth the unattractive mental breakdown."

Jasper makes an aggressive growling sound at the back of his throat and I shake my head at him gratefully.

Now I'm calming down, I'm actually starting to feel acutely embarrassed.

This is all my own doing, isn't it?

I let myself get carried away, and I promised myself

months ago that I wouldn't.

"Right." I give myself a firm shake. I just need to re-find my focus, and maybe a bit more oxygen. "Guys, I'm OK, really. So what's next? I'm ready."

"No, you're not," Aiden says. "You look like you've just been steamrollered by a Boots make-up counter."

He holds up the camera so I can see my reflection in the lens. I'm red, white and black stripes and it looks as if I'm made of hot wax and all my features have slipped four inches down my face.

I'm basically *The Scream* by Edvard Munch.

"I think your shoot is over for the day now, Harriet," Aiden continues firmly. "So I may as well head back to the house to shoot Sophia…"

There's a silence.

Then, slowly, we turn to stare at the enormous maze that surrounds us.

Inexplicably, it looks even bigger.

"OK," Jasper says. "Any suggestions of *how we get out*?"

"Left?" Aiden suggests, scratching his head. "Or… no, it's definitely left. Then straight on. Then left? Or possibly right."

"Wrong," Rin offers. "I mean…" She grabs a dictionary out of her handbag. "*Right*. We go right. Or

293

left. *Then* left."

"We're going to die in here, aren't we," Jasper says, deadpan.

Seriously. No wonder I have to concentrate so hard all the time: what would they do without me?

"I've got this," I say, wiping my eyes. "Just follow me."

64

The word *maze* comes from the Old English word *maes*, which means *to bewilder or confuse.* Clearly the people who designed this in 1833 had never met *me* before.

With total ease, I lead everyone swiftly towards the exit, taking sharp turns at exactly the right points, without a single wrong step or hesitation.

And OK, I *may* still remember the fun interactive Hatfield House maze puzzle I made for one of my Elizabeth projects, but I've never actually put it into practice before.

I still think that's quite impressive.

"Wait," I hear Jasper say in a low voice to Aiden. "Did Harriet actually know the way the whole time?"

Oops.

Before they can ask any more valid questions, I grab Rin's arm and scoot out of earshot.

"So, how was it?" I whisper. "Are you having fun?"

"Oh Harry-chan," Rin says fervently, clutching her hands together. "It is *most* excellent. In this England

castle I am having time of my life."

I look at her carefully.

Her cheeks are glowing, her eyes are bright and her step is significantly lighter. The sad, shrunken Rin of two days ago has disappeared completely.

A wave of relief rushes over me.

Thank you, Jasper.

"And you're not missing Japan?" I ask cautiously. "You don't regret coming here?"

"Not even little bits, Harry-chan," Rin beams. "I am so happy to be with you and new friends. England is top of the notch and knees of the bees."

I laugh, then look down.

Hang on: is she wearing *jeans*? How did I not notice that before?

"I borrow from Charlotte," she says, blushing slightly. "She says they are very cool England cut."

"They look awesome on you," I smile. "Especially with that top."

"This is mine," Rin says proudly, pointing at her smart, V-neck black jumper. I peer a bit closer: although from a distance it looks like a professional model-like item of clothing, when you're very close to it you can see little embroidered cat faces near the hem.

"I can see that," I grin, squeezing her arm.

With one more right turn, Rin and I come to the final twist of the maze and exit into the sunlit green park: Hatfield House looming, stately and majestic in the distance.

And that's when I hear it.

Bibbidi-Bobbidi-Boo, playing at top volume from my satchel: propped against the bench.

It stops for a few seconds, then starts again.

Oh God oh God oh God.

Dropping Rin's arm, I race over and rummage through my satchel, pulling out lists and plans and physics homework until I finally find my phone.

There are twelve missed calls.

All of them from Wilbur.

He knows.

He knows I lied to *Vogue* about Tabitha being mine; or about the contract I signed. Or Annabel's just found out or school has just rung or…

I press the green button.

"Wilbur?" I mumble, hands starting to sweat. "Is everything OK?"

"No, poppet," he says quietly. "Everything is not OK at all."

65

A lobster's brain is in its throat.

Judging by the fact that I can no longer either breathe or think properly, mine may have just slipped down there too.

There must be *something* I can say.

I just need to find the right words in the right order, and everything will be OK.

"So here's what happened," I blurt after a few seconds of guilty silence. "There was this mirror except it wasn't a mirror and a girl who looked like me but *wasn't* and…"

I clear my throat. Nope. Definitely wrong words.

Try again, Harriet.

"And Mister Trout was there with a sandwich but I showed him Dostoyevsky and he got angry…"

Wrong order.

Sugar cookies.

"Wilbur," I say, playing for time while I think of an excuse that sounds a bit less bonkers, "I can definitely explain."

"I think you just did. You're a magical peanut-butter-

cup of joy and beauty and a single day with you is like being the bunny in *Alice In Wonderland*."

"I..." I blink. "Sorry, huh?"

"Everything isn't OK, monkey. It's *spectacularific*. Do you want the good news first, or the *fabulous* news, or the *fantabulous* news, or maybe all at once?"

This conversation is not going as I thought it would. "G-good news?"

"The *best*, my little marshmallow top. This is the news that good news tells other people to prepare for. Ready? *Vogue* just rang: they *love* you and Mini Manners and want to work with you again ASAP."

"Really?" I frown. "Are you sure?"

"Sure as a stick of deodorant," he giggles. "Ready for number two? They also want Rin to meet with their head honchos for a go-see! I'm sending them her portfolio as we speak!"

I stare in amazement at my friend.

She's sitting cross-legged on the floor, playing with a daisy and singing "dancing clean, feel the beat from the tangerine, ooh yeeeah".

It hadn't occurred to me that Charlotte had been cornering Rin for a job, but of *course* she was.

How could anyone in the world not love her?

"Wilbur, that's *amazing*!"

"It certainly is, chipmunk-breath!" he cries jubilantly. "And now do you want the *most* tremendalazing news?"

My hand tightens on the phone.

"You got another job, baby-baby-turnip! KABOOM! And this one's an actual *payer*, so you can put money towards those adorable little textbooks after all!"

I blink at my phone, then at Hatfield House.

Then down at the tight, incredibly painful corset I've been struggling to breathe in for the last three hours.

"Umm, what do you mean by 'a payer'? What about the job I just did?"

"*Vogue*'s pretty much unpaid," Wilbur laughs breezily. "Huge kudos, lovely photos, almost no money. It's always been that way. And yet oh how we love them so!"

You have got to be *kidding* me.

I did all of that – the shoot, the crying, the criminal fraud, the lying and stealing (then temporarily losing) of a precious infant – for *free?*

Oh my God: of the many things I have researched over the last few days, why was *How much am I being paid* the only thing not on the list?

I am *such* an idiot.

"So, ah, what's this new one?" I ask, crossing my fingers hopefully and trying to swiftly push away the swoop of disappointment. *Focus on the positive, Harriet.*

"Is it… uh. Lucrative?"

I really hate hearing myself say that.

"Baby dumpling," Wilbur laughs breezily, "by the time you've finished this job, you'll be able to blow your nose on ten-pound notes if you want to."

"Who is it for? And when?"

"You got the fizzy drink campaign, bunny. And you're shooting tomorrow."

66

I know: it makes no sense, right?

After everything – the falling over, the being-shouted-at, the disrespect and the lack of preparation – Peter Trout's agency *gave* me the fizzy drink job anyway?

I mean, doesn't that just prove his point?

Isn't it yet further evidence that I still just crash around the fashion industry, without design or intention: being *handed* top jobs on a plate?

Nope.

Because Rin wasn't the only part of my plans I didn't tell you about.

That first night, after my disastrous casting with Mr Trout when I'd seen Wilbur in the restaurant and realised how much he needed me to get this job, I pushed movie-night with my family back an hour and sat down at my desk.

I got my best folders and rulers and notepads and highlighter pens and laid them out neatly on my desk.

With great care, I set up the new binding machine I got for Christmas that Nat said I'd never use and I have used *plenty.*

And I started my new, multilayered plan.

I researched how much revenue fizzy drinks brands generate (the top two make a hundred billion dollars a year) and how Coca-Cola create so many types you could try a new one every day and it would take nine *years* to sample them all.

I discovered that soda flavours in Japan include octopus, wasabi, kimchi, cheese and eel, and that 7*UP* contained the mood-stabilising drug lithium until 1948 (hence the name); that the twenty-three ingredients of Dr Pepper are still one of the world's top secrets.

I even found out about the vending machines in the 1990s which varied price according to the temperature outside: the hotter it got, the more expensive it was to drink them.

And made notes to strongly advise against following this ethically dubious practice.

Then I typed it all out and carefully constructed an A4 booklet including relevant photos, charts and graphs.

And I took THE HARRIET MANNERS' FIZZY DRINK REPORT back into Mr Trout's agency, along with my modelling portfolio – carefully reorganised as Wilbur suggested – and a long letter, apologising profusely and in detail.

Plus personalised flapjacks, because it's not really an apology without baked goods.

It must have actually *worked*.

Ha. I *knew* all you really need to win anyone over is a decent session with a binding machine: flowers are so overrated.

"Did they say anything about the shopping psychology infograph?" I ask curiously. "Apparently eighty-five per cent of consumers are primarily drawn by colour. Royal blue could be a contender."

"What the Mary Poppins are you talking about?" Wilbur laughs. "You lost me at *psychology*."

"The Fizzy uh… never mind."

"It's the funniest thing, monkey. Do you remember the Levaire advert you shot in Morocco last year? You know, while I was in New York and Stephanie was trying to be me, which is physically and spiritually impossible?"

I bought a monkey, was nearly throttled by four snakes and watched the sun set in the Sahara Desert. So: "Yes."

"Well, the girl who replaced you – I want to say Hannah? – got this job too."

Hannah.

Oh my God: I can't believe this didn't occur to me

before. The girl with the elaborate CV; the girl with the dancing awards and gymnastics abilities and operatic singing.

The girl I pretended to be for the entire trip to North Africa.

She's my doppelganger?

"But…" I wipe my face and a trail of thick black eyeliner smudges across my glove like a sooty snail. "If she got it then…"

"She broke her leg this morning!" Wilbur shouts triumphantly. "Right in the middle! Apparently she was doing some kind of backflip and landed in the wrong place! Haha! That'll teach her to be so unnecessarily bouncy!"

Then he clears his throat. "Officially Peak Models is very sorry for her loss."

Ah.

OK, maybe it wasn't *all* the report. It looks like I'm the replacement for my replacement who it transpires I actually replaced to begin with.

Although surely the home-made diagram showing international fizzy drink consumption on a full-colour world map must have tipped the balance a *little* bit.

"Tomorrow?" I double-check, swallowing. "The shoot's *tomorrow*?"

"Hannah was actually flying tonight, poppet, but you've got another fifteen hours to get ready while they process an emergency visa."

I blink.

Apparently the first ever pacemaker was used to plug into a wall socket, and my heart is racing so fast it feels like I've been hooked up to the mains.

Flying. Emergency Visa.

I'm going abroad I'm going abroad I'm going abroad I'm going abroad I'm...

"Where?" I manage, heart thudding like a drum.

"Trumpet-cake," he says, "you're going to India."

67

Now, I may not know much about hosting guests.

Thanks to the constant cancellation of my sleepovers, parties and picnics, I haven't had much of a chance to practise.

But I *do* know one thing.

You can't compel a friend to fly thousands of miles across the world to your side and then fly off and leave her to her own devices in a totally strange country.

As social gallantry goes, it's just not on.

"Just one minute, Wilbur," I say, swallowing hard. "I'll call you back."

Then I look at Rin: sitting on the floor, humming "bald-headed woman, bald-headed woman to meeee" and brushing the fluffy tail that's hanging off her handbag.

She looks up with a bright smile. "*Hai*?"

My heart is still racing, but a whole new wave of guilt is starting to surge as well. "That was Wilbur. You got a

go-see with British *Vogue*."

She nods happily. "*Hai*. Charlotte ask me a few hours ago. Jean editorial. Good Wilbur times."

Ah. That makes a lot more sense.

It did seem strange that *Vogue* were just handing out extra pairs of trousers like a benevolent Oxfam: they were obviously already in Charlotte's kit.

My smile falters. "But I've been offered another job too, and it's really far away. Four thousand one hundred and sixty-eight miles away, to be specific. And it would mean leaving you on your own for a…"

Rin's already jumped off the floor and her arms are around me. "Harry-chan! My gob is smacked! This is corking! Double happy Wilbur times! I am so delight for you!"

A warm glow begins to radiate from my cheeks. She's genuinely more excited about my opportunities than her own: I wish I cared less about the adventure itself too.

"Are you sure?" I check anxiously. "You won't be lonely? Or sad? Or… homesick?"

You won't hide back in my bedroom again, refusing to come out?

"No, Harry-chan," she says sincerely. "You must go make money for Wilbur. I will be dory hunky."

I can still feel my brain flipping like a pendulum

between excitement and guilt. "You honestly don't mind being on your own in a strange country for a couple of days?" I study her pretty face a bit harder. "*Honestly*?"

She doesn't seem to be lying or faking it: there isn't a flicker of doubt there. "Harry-chan," she says confidently, kissing my cheek, "you are also on your own in strange country. We are sister peas in pod and we must both now seize the carp."

I laugh. "Rin, do you mean *carpe diem* which is Latin for *seize the day*?"

"Yes," she giggles. "Exactly. When you find your carp in the sea you must hold on tight!"

"Do you think I should grab this carp?"

"Grab it, Harry-chan!"

We both laugh and I hug her again in gratitude.

Yes, this still leaves skipping one day of school to worry about, but I only have two lessons on a Friday and with an extended sick note, I think I should be able to work my way round it.

As for my parents, I'll work out what to do about them later. With Annabel's current vagueness, almost any excuse will do.

Actually, you know what? This could be a *good* thing. With me away, Rin will have extra time to hang out with *other* people instead.

Other, taller, grumpier people with thicker eyebrows. In fact…

Oooh. That could work.

Scientists have recently discovered that the power of our brains could charge an iPhone in approximately seventy hours, if they could just find a way to plug it into our heads: I've just had a moment of inspiration that could blow an iPhone right up.

Seize the carp, Harriet.

With a lurch of excitement I hold my phone so Rin can't see it and quickly text:

I got another modelling job! :) Please will you keep R happy while I'm gone? Hxx

I send it to everyone on Team JINTH.

Then I open a new text message.

There's just one complication left: if I'm leaving the country tomorrow, I won't be able to carry out what needs to be done alone or keep an eye on everything. So I'll need to outsource: delegate to somebody geographically closer.

Somebody who fully appreciates how important a good itinerary is. Who understands how to follow a set programme properly and accurately.

Who – unlike the stupid Universe – won't just make it up as they go along.

And I think I know the perfect person.

Toby - be You Know Where at seven pm tonight. TOP SECRET - TELL NOBODY. Hxx

I wait a few seconds until my phone beeps.

Pbcl gung. Neeviny ba qbg. Bire naq bhg. Gbol

That's Caesar Cipher for: *Copy that. Arrival on dot. Over and out. Toby.*

I definitely picked the right person.

Then, starting to prickle all over, I make the final call.

Every can of fizzy drink contains an average of 18.9 million bubbles, and – rather fittingly – I'm suddenly so excited I feel like I might too.

"Wilbur?" I grin happily, staring at the bright blue sky. "Prepare the unicorns. I'm in."

68

We make it home *just* in time.

I need to drop by the post office with my passport so my visa can be emergency-processed overnight (it's a good thing I always keep it on me: you never know when you might have an adventure abroad).

I have to have my little visa pictures taken three times because I blink in two of them.

Apparently *Vogue* doesn't train you for photo booths.

By the time the taxi drops off Tabby, Rin and I at the end of our driveway, it's already getting dark. Thankfully I've been getting a countdown from Dad:

The heron and robin land in eight minutes. x

Seven minutes. x

Can I have one of these Jaffa Cakes I just found in the picnic hamper? Six minutes. x

312

Me versus Jaffas: 9-0. Five minutes. x

And there's only time to sprint into the house with the buggy, hand a happy and gurgling Tabby to Dad and leg it up the stairs with Rin before the pink VW Beetle pulls into the driveway, Annabel driving.

That was far too close.

I have no idea what terrible excuses my father would have come up with for Tabitha's absence if left to his own devices, but this is a fully grown adult man who just ate nine biscuits in one minute and considered it a triumph.

I don't think that's a risk anyone should take.

With a sleepy smile, Rin grabs an alarmed and now wide-awake Victor from my beanbag and collapses on the bed with him in a puff of denim and subtle kitten-print, spreading out like a baby starfish.

And I run to the bedroom window and watch as Annabel stops the car and sits in it for a few seconds, talking to Bunty. Then she rubs her face, gets out of her side and I scamper to the top of the stairs.

A moment later, the front door opens.

"We're back," Annabel calls tiredly, walking straight into Dad's arms. "Finally," she mumbles into his shoulder. "I don't think I can do that again. Worst day *ever*."

Dad glances up the stairs to where I'm standing

anxiously on one foot, waiting for Annabel to use her spooky Gandalf skills to somehow *smell* our treachery.

He winks at me over the top of her head.

"What did you expect from fragrant candle shopping?" he says, kissing her forehead. "Silly, silly people."

I start backing cautiously into the bedroom.

Unbelievably – against logic or expectation or frankly historical precedence – I think we actually got away with it.

For now, anyway.

It looks like Annabel has temporarily handed the reins to my father completely. Which is very fortuitous. Getting him to agree to my trip should be a doddle.

"Rin?" I say, still staring out into the hallway, "there's just something I've got to... do... in... the... shed... for... school."

My brain is so exhausted I can basically *hear* it buffering. All I need is to escape for an hour to get things ready. Just one hour, and then I'm good to go.

There's a silence.

Frowning, I turn round, ready to come up with a different, possibly even more obvious lie.

But there's no need.

Both Victor and Rin are sprawled out on my bed, fast asleep.

69

I move as fast as I can.

With the speed, accuracy and elegance of a sailfish – the fastest fish in the sea – I grab my heavy binding machine and wrench it off my desk.

Breathing laboriously, I somehow waddle down the stairs, past my parents and grandmother without being asked any questions and into the garden shed.

I hook it up to the electrics.

With absolute focus, I do a little Google research on my phone, write down some neat underlined notes and put together my Top Secret Plan in a beautifully bound black folder.

I add a few relevant stickers I had lying around, because presentation is always important.

And a few badly drawn sketches.

Then I glance at my watch, tuck the folder under my arm and crawl into the space inside the rhododendron bush outside my house.

Toby's already in there: wearing skin-coloured knitted earmuffs shaped like pointed Star Trek ears.

Seriously: *where* does he go shopping?

"Reporting for duty and hitting on all eight," he says, giving a sharp salute. "Took it on the heel and toe and used my noodle. This is going to be duck soup."

I blink at him for a few seconds. "What?"

"I'm clammed after the dust out, eggs in the coffee. Ready for the flimflam. Grab a little air."

He holds his hand up.

I stare at it. "Toby, don't make me regret texting you."

"It's *Detective Speak*," he says in surprise. "This is how they do it, Harriet. This way nobody but *us* knows what we're talking about."

"I don't know what you're talking about either."

"That could be a problem," he concedes. "So what's the plan?"

I straighten my shoulders and proudly present the Top Secret folder with both hands.

"*This*," I say solemnly. "It is a very important task, Toby Pilgrim."

He takes it with an expression of reverence. "Have you discovered why tomatoes have more genes than humans, a subject that still baffles scientists to this day?"

"No," I say with some certainty.

"Do you know where all the missing lithium in the Universe is, given that there's only a third as much as we would expect there to be?"

"N-no."

"Is this a folder containing information on why some nutrient-rich areas of the ocean have very little phytoplankton, otherwise known as the Antarctic Paradox, and you would like me to submit it to NATO anonymously?"

OK: he's totally ruining my moment.

Mine's not going to sound anywhere near as impressive now.

"No, Toby," I snap slightly. Then I adopt my mysterious voice again. "Toby Pilgrim: this is your mission, should you choose to accept it. It is of utmost importance, time-sensitive and needs to be carefully handled while I'm in India on a modelling shoot."

He nods in awe. "Copy that."

"Follow it exactly," I say cryptically. "It is delicate. Subtle. The complex intricacies are beyond the understanding of most mere mortals."

"Will I understand it?"

"Probably not fully," I admit enigmatically. "Just do what it tells you to and all will be well."

"Harriet Manners," Toby says in wonderment, "I

am your man." Then he starts laughing. "Not literally, obviously. *Hahahaha*. You can't seduce me."

I glare at him. "Are you going to take this seriously or not?"

"I am," he says, straightening his face. "I will carry this out exactly as laid out in the oracle. I will die to defend it. *Nobody* will know."

"Apart from Nat," I say, thinking about it quickly. "You can tell Nat if you want."

"Apart from Nat," he repeats obediently.

"And India." I think about it a bit more. "You can tell her too if you like."

"And India," he agrees.

"And if my dad asks then it's all right if you want to—"

"Harriet," Toby interrupts. "I don't feel like you understand the words 'Top Secret'."

I nod: he has a valid point. "Repeat after me: I, Toby Pilgrim, will carry this project out perfectly in preparation for Harriet's return in three days' time, at which point she will take over."

"Two days."

"Sorry?"

"You come back in two days and three hours. It's a surprisingly short trip."

It's at times like this I remember quite how good at stalking Toby is.

"Just say it, Toby," I sigh.

He makes the oath, slides the folder with great respect into his rucksack and I feel a weight lift off my shoulders. A weight I didn't really notice was so considerable until it was gone. I can leave now, knowing that everything is perfectly in place.

"Pipe that," Toby says, crawling out of the bush with a cautious and unnecessarily elaborate look each way. "All silk so far. Scram out."

I crawl out too and we high-five each other.

Then I run back to the shed and drag my binding machine out to lug up to my room again.

And by the time Rin wakes up, forty-five minutes later, it's as if I was never gone.

I am a plan-making *ninja*.

She will never suspect a thing.

70

Now, obviously, this trip to India isn't about me.

This trip is about:

a) Helping Wilbur
b) Proving to Peter Trout that I'm not the arrogant model-idiot he thinks I am, and -
c) Doing the best job I possibly can.

But.

If I *happen* to get incredibly excited about this new adventure in the process, it's not really my fault.

And if I manage to tick another fascinating destination off my Countries I Want To Visit list while I'm there, I don't think I can really be blamed.

If three or four of my best travel guidebooks accidentally slip into my suitcase while I'm packing, it's not because I'm being unprofessional.

I just like being *prepared*, that's all.

Admittedly the scrapbook, notepad and fiction novels set in India are a little less easy to explain away: *The Jungle Book* is not essential reading for a modelling job.

But it's handy as a reference anyway.

Just in case I accidentally get abandoned in an Indian village and have to be taken in by a wolf family to protect me from a tiger.

You never know.

I spend the rest of the night packing.

And showing Rin how to forge a fake school-trip letter from a template I find on the internet: I think she finds my skills quite an education.

We're just trying to force a full-size map of Delhi into the corner of my already stupidly full suitcase when there's a knock on my door.

Swiftly, I slam the lid shut, hop off the floor and try to ram the entire thing under my bed.

Sugar cookies. It's not going to fit.

I didn't think I'd ever say this, but this might be one too many books.

"Just a minute!" I shout urgently, shoving it again. "We're just…" *What*? "Practising our synchronised swimming moves…." Shove. "In front of the mirror." Shove. "Wearing our swimsuits."

What is wrong with my lying abilities?

"Goodness. That sounds like my kind of evening, darling. I've got my two-piece on right now."

I stop shoving. *Phew:* it's only Bunty.

Standing up, I quickly throw my dressing gown over the rest of my suitcase. "OK, you can come in now!"

The door opens and Bunty's pink head pokes through. "I thought I'd see if you wanted a green tea, sweeties. It's *jam-packed* full of antioxidants and bacteria-killing goodies. And it tastes like drinking summer grass, which is lovely."

"I love green tea!" Rin says, jumping up enthusiastically. "I make it! Be back in a tickety!"

She hops out of the room, still in her *Vogue* jeans.

Then I wait anxiously for Bunty to leave, trying to subtly stand in front of the suitcase so she doesn't realise it's there.

"Going somewhere exciting?" my grandmother says, lowering herself slowly on to the edge of my bed. "Tell me *all* about it, darling."

Sugar cookies.

I forgot my satchel is still propped open on the floor by the wardrobe with my spare pyjamas and Winnie-the-Pooh wedged inside it.

"I've… got a three-day biology field trip in Norfolk,"

I recite stiffly, trying to make definite eye contact and handing her the piece of paper I've prepared on my desk. "Here is the official form. It should be of high coursework value… I look forward to it immensely."

That's my lie and I'm sticking to it.

"*Lovely*," Bunty says, beaming. "And India?"

The painted turtle can withstand temperatures below zero, and even survive ice formation within their tissues. I've frozen so suddenly I'm kind of hoping I can too.

"S-sorry?"

"Your purple-haired friend, India? She does biology too, doesn't she? I could have sworn you said she did. Is she going to Norfolk as well?"

Oh thank *goodness*. She meant *that* India.

"Yes," I say quickly, nodding. "Absolutely. We are both looking forward to it immensely."

I'll text her and let her know that she is.

"It's a lovely name, *India*," Bunty says airily, gazing around the room. "And a very fascinating country too. So dynamic, so rewarding, so interesting. One of my very favourites, in fact. I've spent many years living there."

I take a quick step forward. "I read that in one of its states, police officers are given a pay rise for having a moustache. Is that true?"

"Quite possibly," Bunty laughs.

"And I also read that it has the world's lowest meat consumption per person."

"It is indeed a vegetarian's dream, darling. Lentil dhal you would chew your own arm off for. So when are you leaving?"

"Tomorr—"

I slap my hand over my mouth.

How did she – What did she –

Oh. A stray India guidebook is sitting on my pillow, and there's a bright yellow Post-it stuck to it that says:

<u>Harriet's Guide to Speaking Indian</u>
<u>On her Indian trip!</u>

Namaste = Hello
Mera nam Harriet hai = My name is Harriet
Tayalet Kaham hain = Where is the toilet?
Ruko! = FIRE!

I am so, so, so bad at this.

Toby's completely right: I've got more chance of getting a Hogwarts letter than one from MI5. Unless it's one asking me to never even think about working there.

Bunty and I stare at each other for a few seconds.

Then she coughs politely and cups her hands round her mouth.

"ANNABEL?" she calls. "Darling? Can you come here for a second? I think there's something we need to tell you."

71

No. No no.

This can't be happening.

It can't be, but somehow it is. *No no no no no no no NO NO NO...*

All the hard work, the sneaking around, the emotionally traumatic castings and photo shoots and lies and excuses and plans and crying... all of it, wasted.

The second Annabel finds out, this is over.

From top to bottom. Before I've actually managed to achieve anything that matters. Before I've actually managed to help anyone.

And I was *so close*.

"No, Bunty," I beg, hopping towards her with my hands clutched tightly together. "Please. Don't tell Annabel. I need to do this, she'll say no, I need to go, I need her not to find—"

"What's going on?" Annabel says, stepping quickly into my bedroom, face suddenly pale. "Are you all right?"

326

"I can explain," I blurt quickly.

"She certainly can," Bunty says firmly. "Bels, darling, Harriet's just shown me this holistic juice retreat in Turkey." She pulls a bright pamphlet with a photo of a sunset out of a tie-dyed pocket and holds it out. "It looks just the ticket and I want to go, please."

Annabel blinks. "You want to—"

"I want to go," Bunty repeats. "It says they have herbal shots, mountain walks and meditation sessions. That's *just* what I'm craving right now. And I want you to come with me."

"But…" I can basically see Annabel's brain scrabbling around like a hamster. "I don't understand. When?"

"I'm thinking first thing in the morning. No time like the present."

"*Tomorrow?*" Annabel's tired shoulders slump. "Mum, that's just not going to happen. I've got work to do. Tabitha. Harriet. Rin. The dog and cat. A house to clean and a husband with no common sense. Maybe in a few weeks, maybe I can get someone to cover…"

"No," Bunty says firmly. "We're going tomorrow morning. Early. Until…" She glances at me. "I've forgotten the dates, darling. When did I say?"

"Sunday," I say in bewilderment. "Afternoon."

"There you go." Bunty beams. "Come on, Bels.

Doesn't it sound fun? You, me, sunshine, wheatgrass juice and clean intestines. I promise I won't make you do any yoga, hand on my heart."

A pink flush is climbing into Annabel's cheeks. "But the flights…"

"I can sort them out," Bunty says breezily. "I have a pilot friend who owes me a favour or six. It won't take thirty seconds."

"The accommodation?"

"I know *tons* of people in Turkey. If the retreat can't fit us in, I'll just ask one of them to."

"I suppose it *does* sound…"

"And I've got the kids," Dad says, appearing from nowhere. "Both ours and the one from Japan, who – by the way – is currently in the kitchen trying to carve out Hello Kitty toast and putting something that smells very odd into our teapot. They're all in the safest of hands. You're going."

Annabel swallows. "But the—"

"You're *going*, Annabel." Dad puts his arm round her. "I know I don't win arguments often, but I save my Powers up and right now I am Hercules."

There's a pause, then my stepmother breathes out in resignation.

"*Fine*," she says in a voice tinged with a definite

tone of relief. "In that case, I need to write down the doctor's number, the vet's number, the dentist's number… Rearrange the food delivery…"

She turns and runs down the stairs with the words "Has anybody seen my yellow legal pad?" trailing behind her.

"Fantastic idea," Dad grins when she's gone, playfully knocking my chin with his fist. "You're turning into a very thoughtful girl in your old age."

Yup: I'm going straight to hell.

With how tired Annabel's been looking lately, this is something I *actually* should have thought of.

"Richard!" Annabel shouts up the stairs. "Come on, we need to sort out the family itinerary for while I'm gone!"

"Because nothing says mellow hippy relaxation time like ten typed-out pieces of A4, stapled together," Dad says with a smile. "Unless it's in Comic Sans."

Then he disappears too.

Yet again, nurture versus nature continues to astound me: Annabel and I are essentially twins.

"Bunty," I say slowly, turning to look at my grandmother in astonishment. "I don't know what to say."

"Say you'll have an amazing time," she says with a wide smile. "And don't drink the water."

72

The rest of the night is manic.

Annabel's so frantic – organising everything and making Dad promise to text her in Turkey with updates on how we're doing every four hours – she doesn't notice I'm packing too.

And as she races round the house, coordinating different folders for Dad ('Laundry', 'Food', 'Tabitha and Harriet'), I make sure I've got everything I could possibly need.

Sunscreen: *check.*

Rubber shoes and insect repellent: *check.*

A stomach full of butterflies and a head full of dreams, hopes and relevant facts: *CHECK.*

For instance, India is geographically the seventh largest country in the world and the largest democracy, with a surface area of over 1.27 million square miles. There's an enormous dichotomy of wealth: more than a million Indians are millionaires but the vast majority of its population live on less than two dollars a day.

India is home to the wettest place on earth – Mawsynram, a village in the East Khasi Hills – and it produces more cow's milk than any other nation in the world.

It has a *floating post office*.

And – most excitingly of all – both Snakes and Ladders *and* Chess were invented there, originally called *Moksha Patamu* and *Chaturanga* respectively.

It also has one of the highest rates of murder, at 40,000 per year, but I'm not going to think about that statistic.

All I'll say is, I haven't felt like this since just before I left for Moscow, for Tokyo and for Morocco.

I enjoy modelling, but I really *love* travel.

"And it's called *India*," I tell Rin as I somehow stuff the last few bits into my suitcase the next morning, "because it's a corruption of the word *Sindhu*, which was pronounced *Hindu*, the country's main religion."

"*Sooo desu?*" Rin's diligently sticking all my toiletries into a pink glittery wash bag that's appeared from nowhere. "What else?"

"They actually invented the decimal system and the

concept of zero as a number."

She shakes her head incredulously. "Stop with your jokes."

"And the Taj Mahal was built by Mughal Emperor Shah Jahan for his wife and took 22,000 people 22 years to complete."

"You can knock me down with bird feathers, Harry-chan."

"They also invented yoga too, darlings," Bunty adds, yawning from where she's propped up on my bed with her battered old suitcase snuggled next to her. "Many thousands of years ago."

Well, I suppose no country can be perfect.

Grinning, I stuff my earplugs into my satchel and – just in time – remember to grab my *How To Be A Perfect Model* list and tuck it in too.

Whoops. Almost forgot about that.

This time I *really* need to try and remember why I'm flying to a foreign country in the first place.

"Rin?" I say, pausing. "Are you *sure* you're OK with me going?"

"Yes," Rin says calmly. "Of course. I am happy here with Victor and Nat and Toby."

"And Jasper," I say with a sly smile. "Don't forget about Jasper."

She grins back shyly. "I'm not forgetting about Jasper, Harry-chan. Don't you worry."

"Somebody's meeting you at the airport, I'm assuming?" Dad says, poking his head round the door. "The answer's an immediate and truthful 'yes' or we have a problem."

Yup: my dad knows exactly where I'm going now too.

Bunty told him – she said I needed an emergency contact who was staying in England – but he's being surprisingly *zen* about it. She's obviously convinced him of just how mature and grown-up I am these days.

Either that or she's hypnotised him with a crystal.

"They're sending a car to take me to the airport and meeting me directly at the other end," I reassure him. "I *promise* I'll be looked after the whole time."

He just doesn't know by *who*.

I think I'll add the fact that it's the advertising agency that fired him last year to the long list of unpleasant consequences I'll have to deal with later.

"Good," he says, folding his arms. "Or your daddy will tell them where to go."

"Mmm," I say, zipping my suitcase up.

He actually already has.

Rin and I wave Bunty and Annabel off at the front door

just after lunchtime.

Then we wave them off again.

(Annabel came back to check Dad has Tabitha's Development Schedule in case she progresses too rapidly while she's away.)

And they disappear just in time.

Less than fifty seconds after Bunty's pink VW drives off to Gatwick airport and I've quickly got changed into my professional-model-appropriate clothes, a big black car rounds the corner for me.

A very big, very black, very shiny car. *Very* big and black. *Very* shiny.

OK, it's a limousine.

"Woah," Rin says, eyes widening. "Harry-chan, you are now the *big* time."

"Crikey," Dad says as Tabitha starts clapping her hands. "I think you might be earning more than the rest of this family combined, Harriet. Any chance I could borrow a fiver?"

I blink in amazement as a chauffeur in a neat blue uniform climbs silently out of the front and waits for me politely with his hands clasped together.

Then I take a deep breath.

You can do this, Harriet.

You are a Professional. You are Confident and Stylish.

Healthy and Prepared.

You've found the bag, and this is now IN IT.

Dad pivots my suitcase of books around and helps the chauffeur load it into the back of the limo. Then – without warning – he grabs me in a too-tight bear hug.

"Are you sure that you're ready to do this on your own? Because if you're not, just say the word and we can walk now. No questions asked."

And – in a flash – I suddenly remember the first time he said that exact thing to me. Sitting in a tiny back room in the Infinity Models agency. Just me and my dad.

Moments before my life changed forever.

I nod, an unexpected lump abruptly stuck in my throat.

"Yes," I say without a flicker of hesitation. "I'm ready."

Because I think I finally am.

73

I've been on quite a few planes in my life.

There was the flight to Moscow with Dad on my first ever modelling trip, and to Tokyo with Bunty; to Marrakech with Annabel, and New York with Tabitha (she was definitely the most prominent passenger, anyway).

I flew to Nice with Nat and her mum when I was twelve, and to Krakow on a history school trip with my whole class at thirteen, with Alexa throwing peanuts at my head all the way.

But this is the first time it's just me.

Me, 4,168 miles, nearly eight hours and an Airbus A380: the largest passenger airplane in the world, equivalent to the size of two blue whales.

And I've been put in Business Class.

With seats that lie completely flat like beds, a wireless tablet and my own private minibar full of soft drinks, just in case I wasn't excited enough by this experience already.

This is my first time flying solo, my first time as a proper adventurer and explorer, and I intend to make the most of every *second* of it.

Ding.

"Yes, madam?" the air hostess says graciously, turning my call button off. "How may I help you?"

I beam at her in delight.

Nobody's ever called me a *madam* before, unless I was in trouble, and I don't think that counts.

"Did you know that if you laid out all the wires on this plane end to end, they would stretch from London to Edinburgh?"

"I didn't know that, no, madam."

I snuggle comfortably into the big leather seat-slash-bed.

"And that its wings are actually made in England, the tail in Spain, the fuselage in Germany and it's all put together in France. Did you know that?"

"No, madam."

"And that the Airbus A380 fits three *thousand* suitcases?"

"Yes, madam. Can I get you anything to eat or drink on this journey?"

I think about it carefully. "What can I have?"

"Whatever you like, madam," she smiles. "This is Business Class. It's all included."

A wave of happiness suddenly floods over me.

Being a model *rocks.*

"Then yes, please," I yawn, snuggling in a little further. "I think I'll have it all."

Sadly, I don't get to enjoy any of it.

Next thing I know, I'm being nudged gently awake, the plane is descending and the lights are being turned on.

Fudge nuggets.

My first solo flight and I slept through the entire thing. I guess that'll teach me to stay up all night teaching my friend how to play Indian chess.

"Are we there?" I mumble, sitting up abruptly, wiping a little dribble off my face and flinging open the window shutters. "Is this India?"

Outside is a bright blue early-morning haze.

Even with the plane's air conditioner turned on full blast, the air looks so warm and thick you could hold it in your hands, and it's the exact, cerulean shade of Tabby's eyes.

Or the W of a Word document.

And, beneath that dense blue, in an arch that stretches out and disappears into the shining mist, are tiny buildings: browns and greens, oranges and reds and blues.

A whole country built on colours.

"Madam," the air hostess says, handing me a wet wipe, "welcome to Delhi."

74

Indira Gandhi International – named after India's first ever female Prime Minister – is the largest airport in India, and has doubled in size since 2007. Twenty-seven million passengers pass through on their way in, out and through the country every single year.

As I have my passport and visa checked, collect my luggage and walk out into the arrivals terminal, it looks like they may have all decided to pass through at this precise moment.

The building is *crammed.*

Stuffed with people of every description, age and possible nationality. Businessmen, backpackers, tourists, locals; children, teenagers, old people; babies, men, women.

All chatting and jostling for space or sitting on suitcases and leaning against the shiny white walls of an incredibly glossy hall.

I blink anxiously around the room.

339

How is anyone *possibly* going to find me here? There's just no way that in this total chaos and noise, they're going to be able to—

My phone starts ringing.

Oh. I suppose there's that.

"Hello?"

"Is that Harriet?" a woman says with a very faint Indian accent. "My name is Deepika. I'll be coordinating your entire trip in India so you don't have to worry about a thing."

Oh thank God.

Obviously, I really enjoy being independent and mature and at the top of the organising tree, but I also enjoy not getting lost in the middle of the second most populated country on the planet (experts believe it'll overtake China in 2023).

"Hi Deepika," I say warmly. "Thank you so much. I'm really, really happy to be here."

Too happy, possibly.

Now I'm not stranded indefinitely in a crowded foreign airport, I'm so excited, I'm struggling to stay physically still.

My Dance of Triumph is about to break out, unedited and uncontrolled: I can feel it.

With a subtle wiggle, I look up at the huge sculpture

hanging over my head. It's incredibly beautiful: enormous gold copper coins with brass three-dimensional hands emerge from the middle in a variety of graceful gestures.

I'm sure it must mean something culturally important and artistically significant.

I can't *wait* to find out what.

"Understandably," Deepika continues as I do a merry shoulder shimmy, "we'd like to get moving as fast as possible. As you may have noticed, it's *extremely* busy in India at the moment and time is of the essence."

"Absolutely," I nod, exuberantly waggling my bottom. "Where shall we meet? Is there a car outside? Shall I come and find you?"

Then – excitement getting a little too much for me – I hop from side to side a few times and jerk my head like a pigeon. Then I waggle my arms slightly and blow a raspberry, just for good measure.

Finally, I end my tiny impromptu *I Can't Believe I'm Actually In India Right Now* dance with a leap and a quick spin round.

The final *Yessss* dies on my lips.

"I don't think that'll be necessary," Deepika smiles, hanging up her phone. "I'm standing directly in front of you."

75

*N*ice one, Harriet.

Just over an hour and a half in India, and you're already waggling your bottom at the organiser.

That is *not* how a professional behaves.

Not a professional model, anyway. Maybe a few of the dogs who get taken to Crufts do.

"I'm sorry I can't give you time to orientate yourself," Deepika says, glancing at her watch. "There's no flexibility on this particular shoot and we're already running behind."

With poise, she's walking swiftly towards the exit very slightly ahead of me. There's something curiously cat-like about her: composed and kind of detached.

She even *looks* a bit like a cat, with dark skin, long, insanely glossy black hair pulled back in a ponytail, thick black flicked eyeliner and a beautiful, silver-coloured *Punjabi* suit: a long, embroidered tunic with sleeves and

342

loose green trousers.

I really have to stop doing The Dance of Triumph.

"Don't worry," I say earnestly, skipping to catch up. "I slept the whole journey. I'm not tired in the slightest."

"Excellent," she says with a small smile. "Ideally you were supposed to arrive yesterday and there would have been plenty of time, but our initial plans had to be... adjusted."

That's a very sweet way of saying *the girl we originally chose broke her leg so we had to fly you here at the last minute instead.*

Deepika pushes open the glass door and I gasp.

It's like being hit in the face with an enormous fist, except instead of flesh and bone this fist is made of hot, solid air and blinding, forty-six-degree sunshine.

Why on earth would they pick two *redheads* for this shoot?

I'm going to get roasted like a pepper.

Fumbling desperately for my SPF 50, I'm led through soupy, dense air towards a faded red car. We climb into the blessedly air-conditioned back seat and I wipe the sweat already dripping from my flushed forehead.

"I'm afraid we have some way to go," Deepika says calmly, leaning forward and nodding to the driver. "And it's essential we get there on time or the whole shoot is ruined."

I put my seat belt on and look curiously out of the window as the car pulls gently and smoothly away from the kerb. "I understand."

Honestly, I just want to get going too: I want to see India, not an airport car park.

"So we're going to have to go fast."

"No problem." I peer out at the enormous palm trees, lining the edges of the sunshine-soaked road.

"Mmm." Deepika puts on her sunglasses and smooths out her *punjabi*. "Harriet, you might want to shut your eyes."

And so the nightmare begins.

76

Last year, I went on a rollercoaster.

It was in New York, it was called *Cyclone*, it was eighty-five feet tall and it shot upside down and round and round at sixty miles per hour.

And for the whole ride, I was convinced I was probably going to die.

This time, I'm *sure* of it.

As the car heads through the dusty outskirts of Delhi – the pastel-painted and grey cement buildings getting smaller and less regularly shaped and the air getting hazier and smokier – the roads begin to fill up.

And I don't mean just with cars.

There are cars, vans, trucks, lorries: weaving in and out, beeping and braking and swerving. Food carts wheel across the road without warning, full of fruits and corns, beans and fried breads. Little green and yellow rickshaws and bicycles bolt haphazardly between spaces; nimble motorbikes lace their way in and out.

A cow ambles across next to a horse-drawn carriage. People run into the road from the streets, inches from beeping lorries. Scooters perched on by two, three, four, five people – whole families – dip between the traffic: a tiny baby without a helmet held firmly on a lap at the front.

A bus with thirteen people sitting on the roof and seven standing on the suspension shoots by, followed by a bicycle with a sofa strapped to the back. A big, white, bony cow with prominent shoulder blades draws a packed carriage; a car with fifteen cardboard boxes piled precariously on top takes a sharp left, wobbling as it goes.

And we just keep driving faster.

Faster and faster: braking, accelerating, beeping, swerving. Curving around enormous trucks and holes in the road; bolting through dirt and dust until the air and the windows are thick with orange.

There appear to be no rules at all.

No regulations. No actual lines on the road. It's like the polar opposite of Japan: as if somebody took one country and flipped it over.

From what I can tell from my cowering position on the back seat, everybody just ploughs forward as hard as they can and the biggest vehicle wins: as proven by the five-thousand-kilo lorry hurtling towards us on *our* side of the road.

I whimper and put my hands over my eyes.

There is one death and four road injuries every *minute* in India: in one year, half a million people will be involved in an accident, a hundred thousand of those fatally.

These are statistically, literally, factually the most dangerous, deadly roads in the world.

At times like this I really wish I didn't know quite so much.

"Are you OK?" Deepika asks, glancing at me from over the top of her sunglasses.

My hands are clutched in sweaty fists, my stomach feels three times smaller than usual and I can feel terrified sweat prickling down my back, even with the air-conditioning blasting out.

So I think it's safe to assume the answer to that question is *NO LET ME OUT LET ME OUT LET ME OUT LET ME OUT...*

"Mm-hmm," I say, squeaking as a scooter with a ten-foot metal spike tied to the back dives around us, missing my window and face by two centimetres.

"We'll be fine," she says reassuringly. "This driver knows *exactly* what he's doing."

As if in response, he beeps six times at a lorry loaded with mattresses and yells something aggressive in Indian through the window.

"Mm-hmmm!" I manage.

Then I try to focus on the scenery instead.

As we leave the outskirts of Delhi and head for the countryside, the buildings are becoming increasingly sporadic and ramshackle: slanted and pale, with mismatched floors stuck to the sides and tops like dolls' house extensions.

Corrugated iron and cardboard are propped everywhere, bright-coloured clothes hang from lines across the front of houses, and people sit on little boxes and benches, eating their lunches.

And as these buildings start to thin out, fields start to appear: long and flat, gold and brown. Rubbish and rubble pile up in heaps at the side of the road.

Camels wander in long lines, smoke drifts.

An enormous truck blasts its horn, telling us to get out of the way immediately or it will crush us to death and this whole plan will have been my fatal undoing.

My ears have gone completely numb.

You know what?

I think maybe I'll do my sightseeing when we get to our destination.

"E to the power of K equals half M V squared," I whisper quickly, closing my eyes again. "V equals I R. F equals M V squared over R. P V equals n RT. S equals D over T."

Speed equals distance over time.

That last one is important: the faster we go, the quicker this is all over.

"Physics formulas," Deepika says approvingly. "That's a new one. We're going to have to go a little faster, I'm afraid, or we're going to miss it. Keep doing your homework and I'll let you know when we get there."

So I slump even further down and put my fingers in my ears.

And I revise as hard as I can.

77

The good news is: I'm alive.

The even *better* news is that by the time the car finally stops and I fall out of the back-seat door, sweating profusely and breathing through my mouth, I've done all my physics revision for the next two weeks.

And a tiny bit of biology.

Plus a few particularly difficult maths problems and a little of Jasper's A-level history project about the Cold War, just for the fun of it.

It was a *very* productive three and a half hours.

And also by far the most terrifying of my entire life.

"See?" Deepika says as I collapse on the kerb with wobbly legs and wait for my adrenalin levels to return to normal again. "All in one piece."

She obviously can't see the contents of my stomach or head. Or the bad dreams about five-thousand-kilo trucks I'll be having for the next five years.

350

"I'm afraid we've got to get moving," she says smoothly, bending down to help me up. "I don't want to sound heartless, but we have –" she looks at her watch again – "twenty-three minutes before this shoot starts."

Blimey. Even Yuka wasn't *this* punctual.

My hands are still shaking, my head is still spinning, but *I am a professional I am a professional I am a professional*...

"Of course," I say, standing up with a slight totter and smoothing my decidedly sweaty and sticky black Lycra clothes out. "Please lead the way."

We walk down a tiny back street.

It's a lot quieter here: ornate, mismatched, slightly dishevelled, but with noble and intricate buildings in pinks and pale greens and oranges that lean against each other on a dusty, pale grey road.

It looks ancient but incredibly charming.

OK, India: I think we got off on the wrong foot.

Let's start again.

"So where exactly are we?" I ask as I'm led through tiny, winding streets: the air warm and thick with the smell of flowers and incense and spices and – I'm just going to say it – cow poop. "What is this place?"

"This is Mathura," Deepika says, gliding half a step

in front of me. "It's the birthplace of *Krishna* and one of India's seven holy cities."

"Krishna? As in, the eighth incarnation of the Hindu god Vishnu, usually portrayed as a blue-skinned child with a flute?"

Deepika glances over her shoulder at me.

"I did a project on him for religious education in Year Three," I explain quickly. "We had to pick a deity to write about."

Actually, that sounds kind of disrespectful, doesn't it? Your deeply held beliefs neatly summarised and written down in my folder? TICK.

"That's the one." She takes a smooth turn into an even smaller back alley and we have to wedge our way past an enormous cow, placidly blocking the path. "In that case, you must know what day it is today."

I really, really don't. Curse you, Year Three project.

Despite your A+ grade, you've totally let me down.

Sadly I've got way too much pride to ask so I nod earnestly as if I do and hope somebody drops a more specific hint later.

With an abrupt twist, Deepika draws to a stop, knocks on a small green door and pushes it open.

It's a packed restaurant, full of intense spicy smells, of bright clothes, of loud noise, of warm smiles.

"*Namaste!*" somebody shouts, followed by a chorus of "*Aapka swagat hai!*" "*Kya chal rahaa hai?*" "*Aap kaise hain?*"

"No time," Deepika says firmly, politely pushing through the room and glancing at her watch. "Sorry, guys. Later."

"Awwww," a young man says cheerfully, as I smile shyly at everyone. "Deeps, you're no fun now you're important."

Deepika flicks an unimpressed hand at him.

Then she speeds up: leading me into a tiny, turquoise-painted and peeling room in the back into which they've somehow managed to stuff six people.

"You must be Harriet!" a woman says, taking my satchel off me. "Just in time!"

"You cut that a bit fine, Deepika," another lady says, holding a foundation pallet up against my face. "We thought you were going to miss it."

"This is going to be the fastest styling *ever.*"

I blink at them, then at Peter Trout: leaning against a wall in a totally different but really very similar denim jacket to the one I saw him in last, holding a plain can of drink.

He nods at me, then leaves the room.

I'm starting to wonder if he really took in any of my

Fizzy Drink project: it's very hot, and sugar and caffeine can actually dehydrate you further.

"Right," Deepika says, glancing at the clock on the wall and gently pushing me into a chair, "we have thirteen minutes. Let's go."

78

I'm not a very big fan of surprises.

As a small child, I did my homework four times: once to work out what I was going to say, another time to decide how to spell it, and a third time in pencil to make sure I didn't accidentally end up halfway through a word at the end of a line, thereby ruining everything.

And only *then* did I go over it in pen.

When I already knew how the whole thing would go and how it was going to end.

If you plan it out, you're always prepared.

Nothing can destabilise you.

So as I sit in the chair in that tiny turquoise room and watch the women scurry frantically around me, I've already projected a fair idea of what's going to happen next.

It's laid out neatly in pencil in my head.

First, I'll get dressed in a beautiful silk *sari*: purples and peaches, or maybe reds and oranges to go with my hair.

Then I'll be led outside where I'll stand in front of some impressive, three-thousand-year-old building with my cheeks sucked firmly in and my shoulders back.

So far, so perfectly ready.

Which is why when they pull out a pair of pale denim shorts and a plain vest something in my head wobbles slightly.

And when they paint on almost no make-up – just enough to cover my spots and make my eyes more visible – and ruffle my hair up so it's wavy and scruffy, my brain rocks a bit more.

What's going on?

"Hurry hurry hurry," Deepika mutters as I'm given a pair of comfy white trainers. "Guys, come *on.*"

She's not very cat-like any more.

Or if she is, her tail is definitely starting to twitch.

The stylist brandishing a hairbrush but not actually using it takes a few steps back and surveys me with her head cocked to one side. "Done," she says happily. "Luckily you're only a *tiny* bit shorter than…"

She clears her throat.

They're obviously on strict instruction to pretend I'm not second choice.

"*Finally,*" Deepika sighs. "How long does it take to put a bit of mascara on?" Then she grabs my hand and starts pulling me out of the room again.

The restaurant is now empty.

A small TV is still blaring in the background, but there's nobody else around: not a waiter, not a smiling face, not a single cheerful comment.

Just a few bowls of *dhal* lying half eaten and abandoned on tables and a couple of prowling cats.

I have no idea what's going on, but I'm starting to worry I've been brought here for the end of the world.

Skipping between the empty seats, Deepika drags me outside. We jog back through the tiny streets: running round cows and hopping over cracked pavements.

"Anish, Harriet," Deepika says quickly to a man standing on the corner with an enormous camera and a clear plastic raincoat over his head. "Harriet, Anish."

The photographer grins, reaches out from under the coat and grabs my hand. "*Namaste.*"

"*Namaste,*" I say uncertainly, glancing into the bright blue sky. "Is it about to rain? Because it looks pretty hot to m—"

An enormous shout suddenly fills the air.

"*Bees! Unnis! Attharah!*"

Still beaming, Anish pulls me towards the end of the path. "*Satrah!*" The yelling is getting louder. "*Solah! Pandrah!*"

"Good luck, Harriet!" Deepika shouts after us.

"What's going on?" I don't speak Indian, but I don't need to: a countdown sounds like a countdown in any language. "What's about to happen?"

"*Chaudah! Tayrah! Baarah!*"

The shouting is so loud it's almost painful: ripping through the sky like thunder.

"*Gyaarah! Das!*"

"You'll see!" Anish shouts. "Just go with it!"

And – with a huge grin of excitement – he tugs me into a wide road filled with the biggest crowd I have ever seen in my life. Tens of thousands of people: shoved tightly together without a single space between them.

Yelling, cheering, holding their hands in the air, beaming from ear to ear.

"*Nau! Aath!*" they scream at the top of their voices. "*Saat! Che! Paanch!*"

"I don't understand," I shout, grabbing Anish's arm as he pulls the transparent raincoat tightly over both his head and the camera. ("*Chaar! Teen!*") "What do you want me to do?"

"Enjoy it!" he yells back.

"*Do! Ek! SHUNYAAAAAAA!*"

With a piercing scream of excitement, there's an enormous bang.

And the air is filled with colour.

79

I was wrong.

No amount of pencil or draft outlines could *ever* have prepared me for this.

Hundreds of neon powder explosions are exploding in every possible direction: vivid reds, neon blues, fluorescent yellows, luminous pinks. They puff into the air in brilliant clouds and rain down: covering everyone in colours.

With shouts of joy, people grab handfuls of orange and purple paint and throw them at each other: smearing them jubilantly across noses and foreheads, rubbing them into necks and along arms.

Shining spurts of brightly coloured water shoot overhead; greens and pinks shower from above us; indigo and cobalt smoke drifts to my left; lavender and magenta waft from the right.

There are pale blues and baby pinks, limes and mints, burgundies and navies.

Golds and yellows and silvers.

359

Jasper was right: I can see so many more colours than I ever thought existed.

And I know it's not physically or scientifically possible, but I think I just found the end of the rainbow.

"Harriet!" Anish shouts, still pointing the enormous camera at me from under his now very appropriate raincoat. "Do something!"

Quickly, I try and pull myself together.

I'm here to model: not stare at the rainbow-coloured sky and wonder how I could possibly have forgotten about *Holi*, the ancient Hindu Festival of Colour.

Except I realise that I've got nothing to model *with*. Where's my product? What fizzy drink am I supposed to be trying to sell? How am I supposed to know what to channel – or who – without being told or shown?

Why has nobody briefed me?

I slip into the first position I can think of: chin up, neck extended, body turned slightly to the side. Focusing, I put my hand on my hip and lower my eyes at the camera.

I try desperately to pose as the crowd jostles around me, singing and shouting.

"No!" Anish yells, holding a hand up to his mouth.

I can barely hear him over the crowd. "No?"

"No! This isn't fashion, Harriet! We don't want posing! No pouting! No attitude! Just relax and have fun!"

I swallow anxiously. No posing? No pouting? No attitude?

Relax and have fun?

Are they kidding me? They want me to throw everything I've learnt over the last fifteen months straight out of the window?

As the crowd screams in delight around me, I do my best to loosen my shoulders, spin towards the camera again and try to give it my most enigmatic expression.

"No!" Anish yells again.

I turn head on and try to smile widely.

"No!"

A stranger covered in pinks and yellows with green hair throws his arm abruptly around me. "WE CELEBRATE LOVE AND LIFE TODAY!" he yells in my ear. "NOW WE ARE ALL THE COLOURS!"

I blink as another technicoloured explosion of powder goes off next to me.

"*Dekho*!" somebody else screams happily.

"This is for you!" a girl yells with a grin, grabbing a handful of paint and smearing it on my cheek. "I give you the gift of yellow!"

"And blue!" a young boy yells, lobbing at me.

"Orange!" It gets smeared across my forehead.

"Green and red!" They go in my hair.

I'm being swiftly covered in thick, colourful powder and paint; I've never been messier or less in control in my entire life; never been more out of my comfort zone or less like a model.

I've never been brighter.

Blinking, I start to laugh.

"Yes, Harriet!" Anish yells as pinks and yellows explode into the air like flowers. "Enjoy it! Just *let go*!"

Let go. Let go. *Let go, Harriet.*

I don't know how... I can't afford... What's going to happen if I... What about my plans, my lists and outlines, the box in my...

Sugar cookies to it.

With a shout, I throw my head back and fling my arms out wide. I open my eyes and gaze up at all the colours, shooting over my head like fireworks.

Let go, Harriet.

And finally, I do.

80

I don't know how long we shoot for.

With colours exploding in every direction and music pumping, I laugh and dance, spin and throw paints around: singing incoherently with strangers and hugging people at random until Anish grabs my arm.

"*We've got to go!*" he yells in my ear. "That was *brilliant!*"

Honestly, I'd forgotten he was even there: all concept of a camera or a modelling job or the fact that I've been flown thousands of miles for thousands of pounds totally melted away.

I wasn't trying, and it was the best shoot I've ever done.

"That was amazing!" I yell, following him out of the crowd, breathing heavily and – judging by the bright orange and green strands of hair stuck to my face – looking kind of like an overgrown Oompa Loompa.

"Sorry we didn't have time to brief you," he smiles

over his shoulder, removing the raincoat. "We needed to hurry or…"

He gestures at the crowd behind us.

There are still enthusiastic puffs of bright smoke and powder, but the paints are starting to sludge together into browns and khakis and everyone is beginning to look a bit straggly and unkempt.

As much fun as they're all still having, the photogenic window of opportunity was clearly narrow.

"If you don't mind me asking," I say politely, wiping a yellow hand across my forehead and watching as it comes away bright pink, "what has any of this got to do with fizzy drinks?"

"No idea," Anish laughs. "My brief was to photograph the model having fun at Holi and make it as colourful as possible. I'm afraid the top creatives have yet to share their genius vision with us."

According to the project I gave the agency, there are sixteen packs of sugar in one regular bottle of soda. I don't see how that has anything to do with this.

Unless…

"May I ask you a favour?" I say as I follow him back down the narrow streets, leaving a trail of bright purple footsteps behind me. "Do you think you could send a couple of those photos to my phone? Just ones you're not going to use – ones with my eyes closed or something. I promise I won't share them publicly."

Yes, that's right: I've had another idea.

It's completely ridiculous, but I suddenly feel like there's nothing to lose.

"Sure," Anish says as the shouts begin receding into the air behind us. "Do you need a break, or can we keep shooting? I'd really like to keep the positive energy up."

I nod, although I'm not sure I can get any happier.

When enormous stars explode they release more energy in a few seconds than our sun will in ten billion years, and they're still *nothing* in comparison to how much brightness I'm giving off right now.

"Let's keep going," I say firmly. "Do I need to get cleaned up first?"

Anish starts laughing.

He laughs and laughs, then turns a narrow corner into a winding street and just keeps laughing.

"Oh no," he chortles as we round the final corner. "I think we've got that covered."

And that's when I go very still.

Because in front of us is a pretty courtyard and a large group of people. Deepika and the stylists are on one side, busying themselves with towels and wipes and hairbrushes. Peter Trout is on the other, staring at his phone.

And in the middle – right where you can't miss it – is the best, most magical thing I've ever seen.

Better than a unicorn. Better than a rainbow. Better than a million shooting stars.

It's an enormous elephant.

81

I was wrong: I could get happier.

Also, I *knew* something like this would eventually happen.

First it was Gary the tiny white kitten. Then Charlie the irritated octopus, Francis the miniature pig, and a plethora of snakes (I feel bad about not giving them names).

Richard the monkey and Zahara the camel.

Every single time I work with an animal, it's just been getting bigger and bigger. For my next photo shoot, they're going to put me in a wetsuit and ask me to ride home on the back of a blue whale.

"We heard you have an affinity with animals," Peter Trout says sharply. "Is *affinity* the right word?"

I stare at the elephant.

It's painted all over: covered with bright patterns in paint – pink and yellow flowers, green swirls, intricate

367

blue borders and orange spots – but it doesn't look silly or clown-like.

Instead, the elephant gazes at me steadily from underneath its make-up with the wise, kind, infinitely knowing eyes of a huge grey wizard and flicks its enormous ears.

Elephants have the largest brain of any land animal. They understand human body language and can identify between different languages; they can even mimic human voices (one could actually speak five words in Korean).

They're famous for their empathy: for comforting one another when stressed by stroking each other's trunks and remembering things for up to eighty years.

They have been known to *paint flowers*.

And they grieve.

When the elephants they love die, they cry and stand around them for hours, mourning and trying to bury the remains. One was even photographed by *National Geographic*, slowly wrapping its trunk around the passed-away elephant's trunk and standing in that position for a full day, saying goodbye.

Basically, elephants have three times as many neurons in their brains as humans, and considerably more compassion and kindness than quite a few people too.

They are the number one best animals in the world.

And I think I'm about to burst into emotional tears on a job yet again.

"Is it…" I take a few steps forward and swallow. "Has it… How is it…"

I can feel myself being drawn towards the elephant on an invisible wire. Everyone around me is slowly disappearing: it's just the two of us.

"Her name is Manisha," Deepika says from somewhere behind me. "It means *wisdom* in Sanskrit. She's from an elephant wildlife sanctuary near Mathura, and she's painted for Holi every year. Not just for this photo shoot. It doesn't upset her."

All of the tension in my stomach abruptly flows away.

She's from a sanctuary.

They've rescued her already and she's not unhappy or stressed and I don't have to feel guilty or maybe arrange some kind of escape plan for both of us so I can go and live with her forever on the plains of India.

Although it's kind of tempting.

"So you don't have to purchase this one," Peter Trout adds. "To clarify."

I flush pink. Wilbur must have told them about Richard the macaque and the four snakes.

"Go for it," Deepika says warmly, and I realise I've

been standing with my hand stretched out for the last few minutes.

Slowly, I inch forward.

Not because I'm scared – I've never been less so – but because, just as Elizabeth the First was the queen of all queens, this is the noble leader of all animals. She deserves my respect and my humility.

Manisha gives a little huffing sound and calmly watches me approach.

Taking a deep breath, I move even nearer.

I close my eyes, unable to believe this is about to happen.

Then I hold my hand out and touch her side.

Her skin is warm and dry, wrinkled and slightly hairy, and I suddenly want to rest my cheek on it and wrap my arms round her tightly.

So I do.

Without hesitation, I start cuddling an elephant.

Manisha gives another little huff and shifts her weight slightly as I open my eyes. Then she reaches out, grabs the bottom of my vest in her trunk and starts trying to put it into her mouth.

I shout with laughter as my tummy is abruptly exposed. "Hey!"

Gently pulling my T-shirt back out again, I pat her face

while her trunk searches the rest of me for something else to eat.

"You've got 100,000 muscles in that, you know," I tell her as it feels its way gently up to my shoulder and starts tickling my neck. "Although as you're an Asian elephant rather than an African elephant you have to wrap your trunk around objects to pick them up rather than pinching them with the end."

With a little puff, Manisha flicks her ears again.

Then somebody says something in Indian from behind me and she reaches down towards the water in a large bucket behind us I hadn't noticed.

"What are you—"

With another little huff, Manisha slowly pulls her trunk out again.

"Oh," I say as she holds it up high above us and I finally understand why Anish was laughing. "*Oh.*"

And she starts spraying.

82

In a single day, we each shower for an average of nine and a half minutes.

Statistically, we do this eight times a week, which is 65.9 hours, or approximately three days in the shower every year.

This means in the average lifetime, we spend six months in the shower.

I could live a million lives and never beat this one.

As Manisha flings clean water high into the air and it starts shattering down on top of my head so I can't breathe, can't talk, can't see, I start to giggle. And as she dips her trunk for a second go, and a third, and a fourth, my laughter gets louder and louder.

There's water and colour streaming everywhere.

Dripping from my hair into my eyes and pouring down my face: running down my neck and legs. All the paint and powder that settled and dried over the last hour is pouring off me: cascading in a swirling torrent of reds and greens and purples and pinks and yellows and browns.

And my new best friend is dripping in them too.

Still laughing, I bend down and cup water in my hands. Then I energetically fling it over both of us again and again.

Finally, when the water is running clear, I stop.

The entire team is still stood exactly where they were to start with: watching me in total silence.

I clear my throat awkwardly.

I've done it again, haven't I?

Will I ever be able to model without getting distracted?

"Umm," I say quickly to Anish, standing patiently under his raincoat, already holding his camera. The poor man has obviously been waiting for me to finish. "I'm so sorry. Where would you like me to stand?"

Deepika starts laughing and Peter Trout puts one hand over his face.

"We're finished," Anish grins. "That was spot-on, Harriet."

And that's when I realise the final two things I didn't see coming:

a) *That wasn't elephant-playtime*

and

b) *they've been shooting the whole way through.*

83

The job's completely over.

Apparently they only needed two different shots for the advert and they've already got them both.

Which means that within six hours of landing in India, I've done exactly what I was flown out here for.

Without breaking anything, ruining anything, falling over, getting fired or accidentally destroying the campaign by leaking it to a national newspaper.

This is turning out to be a *day* of firsts.

Emotionally, I say goodbye to Manisha.

I kiss her gently on the nose and promise to visit again. There's no way I'm not coming back here to see this place properly.

Then I'm taken back to another room of the restaurant, where I'm hosed down unceremoniously with cold water that hasn't just been up an elephant's trunk.

Suffice to say, it's a lot less entertaining.

374

"Here," Deepika says when I'm finally clean and dry, wrapped in a fluffy towel and reaching for my black Lycra clothes. "These are a little gift from us, to say thank you for doing such an amazing job."

She hands me a pile of new clothes, still warm from the sunshine.

A bright orange pair of loose, baggy trousers with a crotch right by the knees, covered in crazy yellow and pink patterns, and a long, cotton red tunic with tiny orange embroidered elephants along the hem.

Gratitude suddenly pulses through me.

Thank *goodness* I don't have to put those boring, sweaty black Lycra clothes on: they're just not... right for me.

I'm not sure they ever were.

Plus, I've worn them four times in a row and I think they're starting to smell.

Happily, I tug on the comfortable, bright colours and then stand in front of the mirror. That's better. So much breezier. So much lighter. So much more *me*.

I look like a multicoloured flying squirrel.

"Are you ready for the drive back to Delhi?" Deepika asks gently. "I promise it'll be *slightly* slower this time. Although not a lot, admittedly, or we'll get rammed off the road."

My phone beeps and I grab it out of my satchel.

Then I click on an attachment from an unknown number.

It's a photo of me.

My hands are held high over my head with my palms outstretched, my eyes are shut and my face is shining with the widest, most genuine smile I've ever seen on myself.

Around me, people are jumping into the air and silently shouting, and there are colours everywhere: dripping down my face, puffed into the air, flicked through my hair and across my top.

It's nothing like my other fashion photos: it's not like modelling at all.

This is something else entirely.

A temporary moment in time, captured forever.

"Actually," I say, holding tightly on to my phone, "how many cars are heading back to Delhi?"

"Two," Deepika says with a quick nod across the road. "Ours, and *that* one."

Parked on the other side is an enormous jeep.

Silver, big wheels, high seats, thick windows, the kind of bumper that actually allows bumps. Not the biggest thing on the road by any means, but also definitely not the smallest.

And in the back is Peter Trout: reading a newspaper and ignoring us all completely.

"Do you mind if I travel in that one?" I say as politely as possible. "For a change of... scenery?"

And maybe a somewhat less friendly companion.

"I don't see why not," Deepika nods. "There's plenty of space in either."

I beam, give her a quick hug and thank her profusely for all of her help. Then – phone still clutched tightly in hand and my steps bouncing with a confidence I never knew I had – I head straight towards the jeep.

There's almost no chance whatsoever that this is going to work, but I'm going to give it a shot anyway.

Let the next Harriet's Epic Happiness Plan begin.

84

Scientists believe that – contrary to traditional popular opinion – humans don't have six basic facial expressions, we have *twenty-one*.

There's the basic happy and sad.

Fearful, surprised, appalled and full of hatred.

Then it gets a little more complicated and nuanced: sadly fearful, happily disgusted, disgustedly surprised, angrily surprised, angrily disgusted and so on.

As I click open the back seat of the jeep and slide in next to Peter Trout with a bright smile, it's hard to tell *exactly* what his face is doing.

But it's probably some of those last options.

And definitely not the first one.

"*You*," he sighs as I close the door behind me and place my satchel firmly in my lap.

"Me," I agree, clicking my seat belt securely. "Hello, again."

He groans. "What do you want?"

378

I'm not under any grand illusions about how this is going to go, by the way. I already know that in advertising the client *always* gets the final say, and that I'm only here because I looked enough like Hannah to be chosen as her last-minute replacement; regardless of what Peter Trout wanted or did not want.

I was definitely not this man's first choice.

Or second, third, fourth, fifth or six.

The fact that I'm even allowed within a hundred-mile radius of him is quite surprising.

But today is all about surprises.

"I just wanted to have a quick *chat*," I say as breezily as I can muster. The ignition turns on and the driver starts steering the enormous SUV away from the kerb. "Is that OK?"

"Something tells me you're going to talk at me even if it's not."

I beam at him. *Oh, I most certainly am*.

"Did you *know*," I say as the jeep heads towards the main road, "that full-fat sugary fizzy drinks are as bad for your health as *tobacco*?"

Peter Trout scowls. "Of course I do. My client is a fizzy-drink company."

"And those who binge on *diet* soft drinks have been proven to have seventy per cent bigger waists after a single decade?"

"Yes." Trout looks like he's considering the repercussions of opening the jeep door and throwing me bodily out. "Believe it or not, you're not the only person with access to statistics, Snowflake."

"Of course," I say a lot more humbly. *Don't blow this, Harriet.* "But did you *also* know that forty-one per cent of children under eleven drink more than one can a day?"

"Oh, for the love of..." he growls. "There you go again. This oh-so-cute, know-it-all routine doesn't work on me, you know. You might charm others with this wide-eyed, quirky act, but I find it terribly tedious. Save it for someone who cares."

I look up and smile brightly.

I heard the words but I didn't really take any of that in: I was sending a text message under my satchel.

"And that three cans a day has so much sugar it can *triple* the risk of heart disease?" I continue, as my phone vibrates. "Isn't that shocking?"

Then I glance down.

Yup: got an immediate reply, as I suspected I would.

"For your *information*," Peter Trout snaps, "you're way off. We're advertising a brand-new soft drink, and it doesn't have any sugar in it at *all.*"

"Oh *really*?" I say, typing under my satchel. "But you know what they say about artificial sweeteners like aspartame, saccharin, sucralose..."

"It doesn't have any of those *either.*"

There's a quick vibration and I glance down and write another message.

"Ah. But what about other additives? If you look in the project I gave you, I think you'll find that there are health risks involving diabetes, even cancer..."

"Don't you get it?" Peter Trout looks about ready to throttle me. "That's the *point* of this drink. It has no additives, no sugars, nothing. It's one hundred per cent natural, full of vitamins and minerals, and therefore *good* for you."

He leans back in his seat. "So if we could enjoy the rest of this journey in peace, I'd be *incredibly* grateful."

I grin and send another text under my satchel.

Then I stare out of the window with my heart pounding and watch the scenery race past. The roads are still chaotic, we're still going too fast, but this time I'm kind of putting my trust in the driver.

Maybe I'm actually learning to let go after all.

An hour later – as we whizz past another long line of camels – my lap vibrates once more and I pick up my phone.

The photo of me has been skilfully edited: the colours intensified, the focus zoomed in and re-cropped so I'm slightly on the side of the picture.

And in the space under one of my arms – in perfectly Photoshopped lettering – it says:

NO ADDED COLOURINGS

I laugh and hold my phone out.

"What about that for a strapline?" I say innocently, heart thumping again. "It's cute, don't you think?"

Peter Trout stares at it in silence.

"Hmm," he says after an agonisingly long pause. "That's good."

My phone beeps again.

It's the same photo but edited differently: a closer version of my face. Underneath it says:

KEEP YOUR COLOURS ON THE OUTSIDE

"That's even better," he begrudgingly says. "Better than what we have right now, anyway."

"Which is?"

"Feel Brighter, All Day, Every Day. It's OK, but it's not quite right." Then he frowns. "Where did you say these are coming from?"

"My dad," I tell him with a triumphant smile. "Richard Manners."

85

Yes, I know.

You can say what you like about my father – I frequently do – but in his defence, he's kind of a secret creative genius.

Just never, ever tell him I told you that or he'll put it on a T-shirt and wear it forever.

"Richard Manners wrote these?" Peter Trout exclaims. Then he folds his arms crossly. "Oh. *I get it.* You just tricked me, didn't you?"

Yup. I really did.

"Please, Mr Trout," I say, leaning forward earnestly. "My dad's really good at what he does. I know he can be a bit of an –" *idiot* – "imaginative and free-spirited maverick sometimes, but he's changed a lot since then."

And I suddenly realise how true that is.

Coming to Russia with me, getting Annabel back, Tabby being born, moving the family to New York, giving up his dream job, taking over the childcare at home so that Annabel could go back to work without a single murmur.

Writing adverts in the shed and running backwards and forwards to job interview after job interview; and looking after the whole family at the same time.

All for us.

And now he's at home: taking care of a baby, a Japanese teenager and two extremely rambunctious pets so that his wife and mother-in-law can drink green things in a sunny climate and his eldest child can play with an elephant.

I know he's a bit of a plonker sometimes.

But in all the ways that truly matter, my dad is the *best.*

"Please," I say desperately, crossing my fingers. "Just meet with him and you'll see a difference. I know I screwed up at my audition, but please don't blame him for my mistakes too."

Peter Trout rolls his eyes, then looks at the photos once more. "These *are* excellent," he admits reluctantly. "We definitely could do with a bit more of his... *pizzazz.*"

And that one would go on a baseball cap.

"So if he comes into the office next week, you'll give him another chance?"

There's a silence. *Please please please please please please...*

"Yes," he says at last. "OK. Especially if it means we can use these slogans. The client is going to *love* them."

A whoosh of happiness floods through me.

And sixteen months after this journey began, we've come full circle.

I just got my dad his job back.

86

Now I have a few more texts to send.

These take a little longer: mainly because we're driving back to Delhi so fast I'm being flung around the back seat of the jeep like a marble in a pinball machine.

Trying not to be sick, I type:

Logging on: how goes the Top Secret Plan? Hxx

Then I press SEND and wait.

The response arrives with impressive speed.

QHFGRQ. TEVYYRQ OL GUR FPNEL ZBYY, NYY ORNAF. UBG GB GEBG! GBOL CVYTEVZ

Frowning, I grab a pen and decode this.

Dusted. Grilled by the scary moll, all beans. Hot to trot! Toby Pilgrim

I can't believe Toby used *two* codes.

This might be Top Secret, but it's not as if we're trying to blow up parliament.

Does that mean ready? H

It means something unexpected happened to the folder and I've had to improvise but don't fret, it's all in hand. Toby Pilgrim

Oh God. *What* happened to my folder?

More importantly, yes, I'm going to fret: what on earth is Toby going to *do*?

Hmm. Maybe he needs a bit of back-up after all.

Quickly, I type:

Team JINTH! Help needed! Meet me at library at 7pm tomorrow! Hxx

I send the final message:

W, target achieved, your unicorn is now a PEGASUS. ;) Hxx

Then I slot my phone into my pocket, look out of the

window and watch as the roads get crazier and the buildings grow larger and the sky smokier and hazier and deeper blue.

And we're back in Delhi again.

I spend the rest of the night experiencing everything the capital of India has to offer.

In wonder and amazement, I watch the huge sound and light show held every evening at the Red Fort; wander around Humayun's Tomb and surrounding gardens; visit the Lotus Temple and the Akshardham Temple and the Kalkaji Mandir Hindu temple.

I take a metro train to India Gate and look at the 200,000 individual pieces of art in the National Museum; explore the biggest spice market in the whole of Asia.

I eat every Indian dish I can get my hands on: ploughing through crispy *samosas* and *panipuri*, gobbling down *dhokla* and *mawa kachori, aloo gobi* and *chapathi* and *madras*.

At least, that's what I *want* to do.

But I don't do any of it.

Because the second the taxi drops me off at my hotel, I have just about enough energy left to thank Peter Trout for everything, pick up my keys from the reception desk and crawl upstairs to my room.

Stuff a tuna sandwich from the mini fridge into my face, empty a tube of Pringles; drink a can of Coke (I know: the irony).

Set my alarm for tomorrow and snuggle into my pillows with visions of elephants and colours whirling round my head.

And fall deeply and blissfully asleep.

87

By the time I arrive back in England at six pm the next day, I'm so happy, floaty and disorientated by my amazing adventures, I almost forget that according to Annabel I'm not supposed to have been anywhere at all.

I freeze, one hand rummaging in my satchel for my keys.

There's a note stuck to the glass.

Dear burglars, have gone for a walk with my baby daughter and dog. Please come in and steal things but also feel free to give the kitchen a quick wipe-down while you're in there.

Yours Sincerely,

Richard Manners

Haha. My father is hilarious.

390

Bunty and Annabel must still be on their way home from Turkey – they're due back in about an hour – so I quickly wheel my suitcase in.

The house is empty: everything is going perfectly to plan.

I glance at my watch.

Right about now, Rin will just be arriving at the library. Jasper should already be there, and Nat and India will be hiding behind a bookshelf, ready for the conclusion of the Top Secret Plan.

A thrill runs through my whole body.

I don't want to sound too vain or arrogant, but there's a realistic chance that I'm a teenage prodigy and I've put every bit of brain power I have into this one: I have truly outdone myself this time.

Swiftly, I dump everything out of my suitcase and ram it back under my bed.

Then I grab the duplicate Top Secret folder I oh-so-cleverly made before I left the country, tuck it under one arm and the bunch of flowers I had delivered specially this morning under the other, and run out of the front door, thumbing at my phone.

Be there in ten minutes! Start 1.a and maybe 3.c! Just make sure they don't see you! Hxx

I can't think of a more beautiful setting for an epic, final love scene than a library. Books, words, poetry: all the stories that have gone before us.

Even the *smell* of old paper is romantic.

Nothing says *be still my beating heart* like a heady scientific mix of acetic acid, benzaldehyde, butanol, furfural, octanal and methoxyphenyl oxime.

Shoving my phone into my pocket, I start racing down the road.

Past the park and postbox; across the pavement.

Turning just before I reach the train station.

And I'm scurrying through the centre of town when a bright spark of colour flashes in the corner of my vision.

I slow down a fraction.

There's a chance it's just a little leftover elephant paint: I may never be completely clean again.

Blinking, I glance around and there it is again: a bright flash.

Except this time I'm close enough to see that it's deep, dark, shiny purple hair. And there's only one person I know with the courage to dye a part of themselves that colour all year round.

"India?" I say as she spins to face me.

"Oh God," India says slowly. "Harriet."

88

Now, *Oh God, Harriet* can mean many things.

Put an exclamation mark on the end, and it's excitement and happiness: *Oh God, Harriet!*

A question mark makes it sympathetic and concerned: *Oh God, Harriet?*

A full stop in the middle could mean fear for my wellbeing or maybe I've broken something important and expensive. *Oh God. Harriet!*

And obviously it goes without saying that it could just mean that I've inadvertently become some kind of deity.

But this has none of those inflexions.

It's a flat *Oh God… Harriet.*

And I'm trying to repunctuate it as hard as I can, but it still just sounds tired.

I swallow. *Don't be neurotic, Harriet.*

"Hi!" I say awkwardly, bouncing towards her. "India! Are you on your way? I'm running late too! Why don't we walk together?"

India blinks a few times. "On my way where?"

"To the… library. I sent a message to everyone in Team JINTH, remember?"

"Right," she says vaguely. "Yeah, there's something wrong with my phone. I don't think I'm getting those texts any more."

The relief is almost overwhelming. No *wonder* she hasn't been answering: you can't reply to messages you haven't read.

"So how are you?" I say a lot more chirpily. "Are you still in trouble? How's the Head Girl Emergency?"

"The…" India frowns, "…what?"

"Your Head Girl Emergency. And Nat told us *all* about how you were suddenly grounded at my house and dragged home. You *poor* thing."

India looks around us.

"Umm, yeah. It's been hard. Crazy busy. Go go go."

Then there's a brief silence.

It's a silence so long and cold you could skate on it and do a little twirl, should you be interested in skating and twirling on silences.

India's always been a little intimidating – even from the start – but I don't remember it ever being *this* awkward between us.

Not even after my In Your Face dance last year when I

won Miss Hammond's riddles quiz.

And that was pretty bad.

"So… umm," I say, glancing at the shopping bags in one of her hands and the coffee in the other, "what're you up to?"

Weird that she didn't pick *our* coffee shop: this is from the one on the other side of town.

"Errands." She looks down at her Topshop bag. "You?"

"I'm off to the library," I explain, then brighten. "Oh my gosh, you should come, India! You've missed *all* the drama. My friend Rin turned up from Japan and she's really hitting it off with Jasper, but they're both too shy to do anything about it, so I've arranged this big, surprise, romantic date for them and now I'm off to make sure it all goes perfectly!"

Then I stop and take a deep breath.

Huh. That was easier to sum up than I thought it would be.

"Right," she says after a few more beats. "That sounds… fun. Anyway, nice running into you, Harriet. See you again soon."

Then India takes a sip from her wrong-brand coffee, gives me a mini finger-wave with the tips of her purple gloves and starts walking the other way.

I blink at her retreating purple back.

"But…" That's the direction she just came from. "Don't you want to come too? You haven't seen any of us for ages."

"No thanks," she says without turning round. "But have a good time."

I can feel my stomach starting to twist.

Now I *know*.

I'm not being neurotic.

My initial instincts were right. I just managed to convince myself I was being oversensitive because it was easier than facing the alternative.

That India was separating herself from the group.

Head Girl Emergencies? What would they even *be* anyway? The wrong photo on the cover of the Year 11 yearbook?

"India," I say, taking a few steps towards her, "have I done something wrong? Are you angry with me?"

"Don't worry about it, Harriet."

I blink in confusion as she carries on walking. She didn't say *no*. "But… when will I see you again?" I call after her miserably. "How about tomorrow? The day after? Next weekend?"

And then – just as I'm drowning in a big pit of confusion – she says the one, single thing she can't take back: three little words that will never be *unsaid.*

With a quick glance over her shoulder, India looks me straight in the eye without a flicker.

"I'll call you."

89

Yup: India is going to call me.

At some undefined, vague point in the distant future, one of my best friends in the world will pick up the phone without urgency or intention or forethought and ring it for no particular reason.

Not: she'll call me tomorrow.

Not: I'll text you the day after or see you at school.

Not: she'll call me on the way to the cafe at the weekend.

She'll just call me. Whenever.

Maybe.

I blink in shock at her still-retreating purple head as the pieces start fitting together with an unpleasant crunch.

India's *dumping me*.

Actually, no, she's not: India has already *dumped* me, past tense. She left weeks ago, abandoning that purple folder on my doorstep and disappearing without even saying goodbye.

And – inexplicably – I didn't even *notice*: that's how terrible I am at reading the subtleties of human behaviour.

I'm even worse than *Toby*.

And just like that, another piece slams into place. Nat must have made up the grounding story and the Head-Girl excuse to stop me panicking just before my big day of castings, and I actually bought it. I must be the most naïve, most easily convinced idiot on the planet.

But I still don't understand *why* this is happening.

And I can't bear not to know.

"India!" I shout after a long startled pause, running down the street after her. "What did I do? Maybe we can sit down, talk about it, go through it point by point, write a list of ways to strengthen our relationship…"

And India cracks.

"*NO*," she says sharply, spinning on her heel with a purple swoosh. "No lists, Harriet. No going through it, point by point. No itineraries, no schedules, no plans, no talking about it, over and over again. No more constant, demanding group text messages. Please, *stop trying to control me.*"

Hamsters blink one eye at a time. I'm so surprised, I do too.

"What?"

"You micromanage *everything*, Harriet. You have to be in charge, *all the time*. Everything has to be as *you* want it. *Your* launderette, *your* sleepover, *your* picnic, *your* drink choice, *your* music, *your* idea, *your* plans."

I open my mouth and then shut it again.

"No, I don't," I manage in a tiny voice. "No, it doesn't."

"It's true, Harriet! You even try and steer *the conversation*. We can't even talk about a single *date* without you changing it back again."

I swallow. "But that's not why I—"

"We can't speak while you're out of the room in case you feel like you're missing something. *We're expected to sit in a cold dark park without eating all evening because you're not there.*"

My stomach's starting to hurt.

"But…" It was a *picnic*. We had *bunting*. It was *fun*. "India, don't say that! We had a good time."

"*Did* we?" She throws her arms up in the air. "Because all *I* remember is us asking you for some space and then being dragged about and told what to do and eat and say without you stopping to ask anyone else what *they* wanted first."

I *did* ask what they wanted. I totally *did*.

I did give them space, didn't I?

"And then you gave us those dumb-ass folders and I

couldn't handle it any more."

Excuse me: *dumb-ass folders?*

"*India*," I say, now wounded beyond measure, "you don't understand. I was trying to *help* you. I rescheduled your revision timetable so it wouldn't be so hard on you any more. I did it to make you happier."

"I don't *want* you to reschedule my timetable!" she almost shouts. "I *want* to live my life according to *my plans.* Not *yours.*"

"But that's what friends are for!"

"It isn't, Harriet! We're not here to be tugged around like puppets on strings, acting the carefully planned-out performance that is your life!"

A typical adult human has 206 bones in their body, and it suddenly feels like every one of mine is breaking.

"That's not... I don't..."

"And now, what?" India runs a hand through her shiny purple hair in irritation. "You're arranging Jasper's *love life* for him? Rin's having her feelings meddled with because she's too sweet and easily overpowered by the bulldozer that is Harriet Manners to say no?"

She has got this *so* wrong.

Jasper and Rin are *meant* for each other: I'm just nudging them in the right direction, that's all.

"I'm trying to *help*," I say in a suddenly croaky voice.

"I want everyone to be happy."

"You know what would make everyone happier? If you just stopped *suffocating them*."

The word *tear* has two very different meanings in English: to cry and to rip apart. But I don't have to choose between them right now, because I'm about to do both.

"I don't suffocate anyone," I whisper, but judging by the strangled sound of my own voice that's not quite true.

India blinks a few times with her dark, close-set eyes fierce, breathing hard.

Then she pinches her nose and exhales.

"Look," she says. "I'm being unfair. You're a sweet girl, Harriet, and your heart is in the right place. But I… I don't think I can do this any more. It's just not working for me."

Then India reaches into her purple handbag.

With a tiny grimace, she pulls out her JINTH badge and holds it out. "I'm sorry," she says gently, pressing it into my hand. "I really am, Harriet. This isn't how I wanted things to end."

But, as she slowly turns and walks away and my phone buzzes one last time:

India Perez has left group: Team JINTH

I realise that in spite of all my plans, all my efforts and all my good intentions, it looks like things have ended anyway.

Or maybe *because* of them.

90

You know what?

The fairy godmother never gets shouted at for meddling. Cupid doesn't get an earful for trying to encourage a romantic match; Puck isn't vilified for trying to keep everybody entertained.

I don't want to sound petulant, because obviously I'm too old for hissy fits and hysteria.

But this is *so* unfair.

Angry and hurt, with my shoulders rigid, I start stomping towards the library.

India's wrong.

OK, it may have *sounded* like she had some valid points – to an unobservant passer-by – but everyone sounds like they're telling the truth if they say it loudly and with a lot of vigour.

I am *not* suffocating.

I *don't need* to control everything around me, and

I *don't* force other people to act my already pencil-mapped-out story.

My friendships are *not* a performance.

This argument with India is just part of being mates, isn't it?

We squabble and shout and get irritated and pretend we didn't see an incoming text message when we actually did. I mean, Nat and I lock horns all the *time*, don't we? And we still manage to come out the other side: bruised and bloodied but strengthened by the battle.

It's just what happens when you love someone: now and then, you wear each other out.

Except...

I walk a bit faster towards the redbrick building, hands still shaking.

Except this time it feels different.

This doesn't feel like an argument. It feels as if I should have wrapped my trunk around India's so I could say goodbye properly.

Because there was something in her face just now that I think I've seen lurking there for months, even if I didn't recognise what it was at the time.

And it's risen to the surface at last.

India has really gone.

With a lump in my throat, I start walking up the

familiar stairs towards a big glass entrance. I'm trying to block out sentences, starting to shatter through my head like bricks.

It's all I can do to keep my epic new social life in some kind of order.

Please don't do anything interesting without me.

So now I've got two diaries: one to make sure I'm in the right place at the right time, the other for making sure everyone else is.

Don't worry: everything is under control.

No.

This is ridiculous. I've taken those lines completely out of context: that's not how I meant them.

I mean, it's not like I try to arrange people's lives for them. Or get them to fly to other countries for me. Or write them endless lists. Or tell them where to be and how to behave and what to eat and…

Oh my God.

I blink. But surely if there was a problem, my other friends would have *said*? Nat would definitely have mentioned it.

I know you've arranged… everything.

Or Jasper and Toby would have…

You don't do things by halves, do you?

OK, so Rin would…

I love how Harry-chan is always saying the things.

No.

Shaking my head, I push through the glass doors of the library. If I had become *that* unbearable, surely the whole of Team JINTH would have disappeared by now?

Trembling, I beep my battered library card on the scanner, wave at Sally the librarian and head straight to the back of the library to find my friends.

Jasper's meant to be at the table by the window, reading a book about Salvador Dali. Rin should be in the Chemistry section, casually skimming through *Modern Quantum Chemistry – Introduction to Advanced Electronic Structure Theory* as suggested.

And Toby and Nat should be hiding in aisle D, tucked behind *On the Origin of Species* so they can make sure the surprise romantic date unfolds properly, as specified by the map I drew.

But they're not: there's nobody here at all.

And that's when it finally hits me.

As I walk faster and faster around the little library, spinning in increasingly frantic circles – as my hands get sweatier and my stomach gets sicker and my cheeks get hotter – I suddenly realise…

My best friends didn't tell me my obsessive planning and calculating and itinerating and pushing was driving them insane.

They didn't ask me to stop arranging their lives and managing everything in minute detail: didn't tell me to stop meddling and forcing my ideas on them, every minute of every day.

Didn't want to, didn't know how to.

Didn't actually have to.

Nope.

Instead, they just left.

91

Neutron stars can rotate at a rate of 600 times a second, but that's nothing compared to how fast my brain is spinning right now.

All my lists. All my schedules.

All my coloured-in charts and calendars and diaries and socialising folders: my picnics, my sleepovers, my attempted zoo visits.

There's no nice way of putting it: I'm a control freak.

"Hi, Harriet!" Sally says as I drop my carefully replicated Top Secret: R+J BIG DATE folder hard on to the desk and start heading towards the exit. "So good to see you again! Have you come to take out *How to Match People by the Matchmaking Institute*? I got your emails and texts and that fax and it's finally been returned!"

Oh my God. I am *awful*.

"No, thank you," I say, impulsively handing the flowers intended for Rin to her. "These are for you, Sally. For all the times I rearranged the biology section into

alphabetical and not binary code order without asking you first."

She blinks at them. "You did what?"

"I'm sorry," I mumble over my shoulder as I pick up my pace. Because it can't be too late to put this right: to unmuddle the mess I've made.

I can only hope I know where everyone has gone.

It's dark by the time I reach the cafe, and there's an eerie, flickering orange glow coming from the windows.

I glance at my watch.

The cafe doesn't normally shut until seven thirty, and it's only seven thirteen: so why is the CLOSED sign hanging up at the front door? And why is it so dark inside?

I tentatively creep closer and peek through the window.

Then I draw an abrupt inward breath.

The cafe is unrecognisable.

The lights are all off, and pink candles are twinkling on every table and counter: sitting on top of the coffee machine, perched where the sandwiches are supposed to go, taking up every spare saucer.

Pink tablecloths have been thrown over every flat surface and pink ribbons are tied around things that have absolutely no need to be tied with pink ribbons: cups, bowls of sugar, the door handle to the toilet.

Hearts – in pink – have been cut out of tissue paper and stuck all over the walls, pink butterflies are plastered to the picture frames and pink streamers are hanging from the wall lights.

And on every (now pink) chair is a cuddly toy.

Every single stuffed cartoon animal you can think of – Mickey, Minnie, Winnie, Paddington, Elmo, Little Miss Sunshine, Snowman, Miffy, Pikachu, Totoro – and many less distinguished ones too: teddies and frogs and sheep and cows and rabbits and cats, all sitting neatly, one per chair.

Like the world's fluffiest charity fundraiser.

I peer a bit closer: there's a little owl in my seat, wearing round glasses. A fuzzy tiger in Nat's, wearing a dress, a purple bear with its feet up on India's and the meerkat from the insurance advert sitting in Toby's.

What the *sugar cookies* is going on?

It looks like a Tenderheart Care Bear exploded in here and then Hello Kitty came in and tidied up the mess.

"Down!" somebody hisses, and before I have a chance to see who, I've been tackled to the floor with an *oomph*.

Awkwardly, I blink upwards.

Toby's crouched over me with enormous diamante

sunglasses on and his bright green bobble hat, pulled down ridiculously low.

"Mission saved," he whispers at me urgently. "Secrecy levels high, proceed with caution."

I think I'm just going to make a sign that says WHAT for whenever I'm around Toby so I never have to say it again.

"What?"

"All is advancing. The marks are in place."

"Toby," I blink. "Firstly, why are you wearing Nat's diamante sunglasses? And secondly, what *is* this? What's going on?"

"I think they make me look suitably mysterious and enigmatic," he explains. "And this is the Top Secret Romantic Date Plan. As requested."

"But this isn't The Plan," I whisper, kneeling up so I can peek through the window again. "This is... Well, I don't know *what* this is."

"It's the *other* plan," Toby explains, kneeling up so he can look through too. "I went over to Nat's and asked her to help, but she was busy. Then I explained what was going on and she dropped the folder in the bath. Which was weird, because she had to go and run a bath first."

I open my mouth and then shut it again. "*What?*"

I *knew* I should have laminated it.

"Then she told me as the plan was ruined I should probably just do whatever I thought was best and use my imagination. So I did. Look."

Side by side, we inch up a little more.

And I see what I didn't see before.

In the corner, under an enormous bunch of pink flowers, is a little round table. It has pink cupcakes on it, pink ice cream and pink biscuits. Pink rose petals and a scattering of pink glitter.

Pink teacups and pink plates.

Inexplicably pink sugar cubes in a pink bowl.

And in the middle of all this hideous pinkness are two people, sitting very close together.

Jasper and Rin.

92

I've probably made this quite clear by now, but I really hate the colour pink.

Shakespeare only used the word 'pink' in two plays – *Romeo and Juliet* and *Anthony and Cleopatra*. Flamingos are pink because of all the canthaxanthin they consume (the natural dye in shrimp) and pink is actually the colour of a Gentoo penguin's poop.

As far as I'm concerned, pink is humiliation and sugar mice and candyfloss and that one ballet lesson I did before they not-so-subtly suggested tap or maybe maths.

It's not a romantic colour at all.

But as I stare through the window, I realise – in a sudden wave of shame – that nobody gives a rat's bottom if I don't like it because this isn't *my* big romance.

It's supposed to be Rin's.

And she loves pink more than anything else in the world, apart from Hello Kitty: who is sitting at the table next to her.

414

I glance sideways at Toby.

In the chronology of the world, there was a bigger gap between the stegosaurus and the T-rex than there is between the T-rex and us, and that's basically how far off I was with the library scene I thought was adorable.

But what Toby's done is nothing short of magic. It's absolutely, incandescently perfect.

Curiously, I press my face against the glass. The window's a tiny bit open, and I might just be able to hear what they're saying.

"It's going remarkably well," Toby whispers at me proudly. "Apparently the word *love* comes from the Sanskrit *lubhayati* which means *desire*. Did they tell you that in India?"

"*Sssshhhh*, Toby," I snap. "I'm trying to hear what's going on."

Which is quite hard, because after thirty seconds it becomes increasingly clear that the answer to that is *nothing*.

Literally nothing is going on.

Jasper's got his hands folded on the tablecloth and is staring around him with a shell-shocked expression, while Rin focuses intently on her lap.

"She is five apples tall," she says eventually, as if in answer to a question asked quite some time ago, "and her pet cat is Charmmy Kitty."

"Wait," Jasper says, frowning, "they measure height in *fruit*? And Hello Kitty is a cat. How can she have a pet cat?"

"No no," Rin says in alarm. "Kitty is not *full* cat. Only half cat, half girl. Her cat is *full* cat."

"But… Can she speak like a cat? How do they communicate? Do they meow at each other?"

"It is very difficult to explain." Rin's cheeks are starting to match her environment. "I am not saying it properly."

"She *is* saying it properly," Toby whispers to me. "Sanrio explain in detail that Kitty is a *human* cartoon character. Just like the Simpsons are human, but also have four fingers and blue hair."

"*Shhhhh*, Toby," I hiss. "I'm *listening*."

There's another long silence.

"This is *kawaii*, *ne*?" Rin says after another few minutes, pointing around her. "*Kawaii* mean cute in Japanese, because is also the colour of blush."

The significance of pink to Rin is starting to make sense now: love, cuteness and beauty are one and the same for her.

"Mmm," Jasper says awkwardly. "Ah. I don't suppose you know when the rest of Team JINTH is turning up, do you?"

There's another silence.

"Do you like watermelon?" Rin says eventually.

Oh my God. Deathwatch beetles attract mates by repeatedly banging their heads on the floor. It looks exactly like that's what's happening here.

This has to be stopped immediately.

On Tuesday 29th October 1929 the Wall Street Crash became the greatest stock market disaster in the history of the United States: it was so bad that prices didn't return to normal again until 1954.

This is basically the date version of that.

It's suddenly abundantly clear that Jasper and Rin *don't* have a crush on each other at all.

In fact, I'm not even sure they ever did.

I just got the idea in my brain that it would make them both happier and forced it on them like I force everything else: like a bonkers juggernaut with a binding machine.

"Toby," I say, turning quickly to the side. "I think we need to go and save them right n…"

I stop in amazement.

What's up with Toby's face? He's grinning from ear to ear, leaning far too close to the window, and every time Rin says something he laughs into his hand: just like he always…

Oh. My. God. *And there it is.*

Final, conclusive evidence that no matter how much studying I do or how smart I – and my exam results – think I am, I am never, ever going to understand people.

Or words or gestures or facial expressions or pretty much anything else of vital importance.

How did I not see it before you? They're perfect together.

When Nat and I first spotted a chance for romance, we were both looking in the same direction, except I was seeing Jasper and Rin, and she was seeing Rin and *Toby.*

After marooning herself in my bedroom for days, Rin's face lit up when she saw *Toby* again; she came out because of *him.*

The bounce in her step was because *he* was walking next to her; she was trying to impress *him* with her key rings.

You know what, judging by how closely she remembered what shoes he was wearing last summer, she may have even liked him in Tokyo too.

And Toby…

I look more closely at his face.

It's rosy and bright and totally focused. He's clearly *besotted*. Enough to try to make Rin comfortable by recalling every fact he knew about Japan; to show her his *kawaii* socks; to pay close attention to what she likes and then give it to her, without a single thought for himself.

And the second Nat saw my stupid Top Secret: R + J BIG DATE folder, she realised I was barking up the wrong tree and threw it in the bath so Toby could take the reins.

But why didn't they just *tell me*?

Because – I realise with the umpteenth wave of shame – India was right. Rin is too gentle to resist my bulldozing.

And Toby hasn't actually realised he likes her yet. He's just as clueless about people as I am.

That's what Nat wanted: for Toby and Rin to slowly realise they liked each other on their own.

Without plans, itineraries or schedules forced upon them.

She is a wise and very knowing soul, my Best Friend.

We have *really* got to communicate better.

Obviously, though, I have learnt my lesson.

I now know not to try to control, or manipulate, or make things happen. I will not pull strings, or force people, or intervene with nature, or fiddle with chemistry. I am a much wiser, less bossy and demanding person than I was a few minutes ago.

I will not be meddling any more. No more meddling for me. Nope. None.

Don't meddle, Harriet.

Do not meddle. No meddling. No Harriet. Meddling, no. Nope to the meddling; meddling nope. Do not under any circumstances…

OK: just *one more tiny meddle.*

"Toby," I burst, grabbing his arm impulsively, "oh my gosh. I think that tablecloth is on fire!"

"I doubt it," he says, wrinkling his nose. "They're flame-retardant, Harriet. With so many candles in there, I double-checked."

"Then I guess there must be a faulty one! Oh no! Go and check, Tobes! In person! Then you can write a letter of complaint to the manufacturers! Go! Go go! GO!"

Toby blinks. "But what about the Top Secret plan?" he says in confusion. "Harriet, you made a plan. And I made a plan. We need to follow the plans."

"Oh, screw the plans!" I cry, dragging him to his feet and ripping the diamante sunglasses off his face. "Screw them all up and throw them in the bin! Go go!"

Toby cautiously straightens his Spider-Man cardigan and then knocks on the cafe door.

I tap on the window. "*Psssssst.* Jasper! *Get out here.*"

He doesn't need telling twice.

Visibly relieved, Jasper stands up, gives Toby an encouraging pat on the shoulder and bolts out of the front door.

Then he crouches down next to me.

"Bloody hell, Harriet," he says. "That took you long enough."

93

I'm not going to go into detail.

I think we should respect Toby and Rin's privacy enough to let them have their special romantic moment in the cafe alone without spoiling it by telling you everything.

I'm sure you can imagine it.

Suffice to say, Rin's face has never lit up harder and Toby has never been more awkward, more charming or more completely random.

There's a quick discussion about where Paddington got his hat from (his uncle Pastuzo).

Then one about how Care Bears are having a resurgence in Japan despite becoming less cool here twenty years ago.

It takes Toby a *really* long time to remember that one of the tables is supposed to be on fire.

And by the time he tentatively says "I'm going to hold your hand now, Rin; it's only fair I warn you," and Rin responds with a delighted "Thank you very much, Toby, I

will be super chuffed," I think we're all done here.

It's over to them.

Triumphantly, Jasper and I flop back on the pavement and lean against the wall.

I don't know how Jane Austen's Emma did it: I am completely *exhausted*.

"Well," I laugh, rubbing my eyes, "who saw *that* coming?"

"Everyone," Jasper says lightly. "Literally everyone. There are people living on the outer reaches of this Universe who saw that coming, Harriet."

Oh. Guess it was just me, then.

"MACS0647-JD, by the way," I sigh. "That's the furthest galaxy they've found from us."

"Indeed," Jasper says, leaning his head back. "And on MACS0647-JD they're all holding banners that say *Work It Out Already, Harriet.*"

"You didn't exactly help, King," I chide him. "Why couldn't you have just told me?"

"And watch you do to *them* what you tried to do to *me* and Rin?" he laughs. "No, thanks. I decided to take the fall on that one so you wouldn't scare them both off."

"Huh. OK, that's quite smart actually." I think about it. "But that still doesn't explain why Rin was being kind of weird to me about *you*."

"You know what?" he says after a short pause. "I'm going to let you work that one out for yourself, Harriet."

We sit in silence for a few seconds.

"Is… she scared of me?" I say uncertainly.

"Nobody's scared of you, Harriet-uccino. You drink hot chocolate and pretend it's coffee. You eat the biscuits sane people throw away. You try to pet an octopus and get covered in blue ink. You're literally the most unscary and colourful person I know."

Huh. What is that supposed to m—

I feel myself suddenly blush bright red.

Hang on. Did Rin think Jasper was meant for *me*?

But why would she possibly…

And – out of nowhere – recent memories suddenly start flashing in front of me in sharp, vivid flashes: except now they look a little different.

Jasper searched for hours for Dunky because I told him it was lost. He took me to the gallery and helped me to believe in myself through the power of pictures. He gave me the confidence I needed, after India refused to. He looked after Rin, because he knew it would make me happy.

The biscuits… He burns biscuits on purpose because he knows they're my favourite. (Nobody on the planet is that bad at baking.)

He defends me if anybody makes me cry.

He never, ever cancels on me until he knows the plan's already over.

And suddenly it's as if there's a rainbow of new memories, flashing in front of my eyes.

Jasper once told me that people with tetrachromacy can see a hundred million different shades, and that all it takes is one extra cell to see the world differently: in all its colours.

I think that one cell is what he is for me.

"*There* you go," Jasper says finally, watching my face light up with his bright blue and brown eyes. "Crikey, it's like watching paint dry."

I stare in wonder at this whole other Jasper: who I've never seen before but who's been here this whole time.

"But... but I irritate you," I say blankly, brain still whizzing and spinning. "I'm controlling and supercilious and demanding and bossy and I never listen to what other people want. I-I annoy the hell out of you, don't I?"

"Totally," Jasper says. "Because you never, ever see what's directly in front of your face, Harriet. And that includes me."

94

In 1977, Earth received a signal from deep space that lasted 72 seconds. We still don't know what or where it came from.

That's exactly how I feel.

As if something really big has just happened and I had no idea it was coming and I have no clue what to do now it's here.

I'm just staring into dark, infinite space studded with untold galaxies as if I'm seeing it all for the first time.

With my eyes wide open.

"You don't need to say anything," Jasper says, clearing his throat. "We can still be friends, either way."

I blink at him.

His eyes are as bright as ever, and the little freckles scattered across his cheek look like stars. His blue hoody is pulled up, a tiny muscle is jumping at the base of his jaw and under the glow of the candlelit cafe his hair is

a mixture of golds: of bronze, of mahogany and copper and rust.

My stomach's starting to flip, and – if I'm truthful – it's not for the first time. I think maybe the cafe is my new happy place because it always has Jasper in it.

But –

"I can't…" I say slowly. "I don't…" Panic's rising and there's a loud rattling inside my head. "Please, it's not that I…"

"Look." Jasper scratches his head. "I get it. Nat explained it to me. And I get that you had your heart broken badly and all this obsession with control is just a way of making sure it doesn't happen again."

I blink at him in amazement.

Firstly, has Nat also guessed Jasper likes me? What other wise knowledge has my best friend been hiding? Is she turning into Gandalf as well?

And secondly: Jasper's kind of right, it is.

But that's not *all* of it.

Because it's not the walking away from love that's the hard part: it's the falling in.

It's losing yourself to it and not knowing who you are without it. It's needing somebody else more than you need yourself. It's being happier with them than you are on your own.

And I've only just got to a point where I can stand completely alone again.

Where I'm master of *myself*.

"I..." The panic's still rising and the box is shaking harder. "Jasper, I'm sorry, I don't think I..."

Something else is hitting me now too.

This is the first time in my entire life that I've ever had more than one friend; the first time it wasn't just Nat, who's basically my spirit-twin. And I think I got overexcited and this is how I've tried to hold on to my friends: with lists and charts and schedules.

I'm so desperate to make sure things don't go wrong – that I don't screw it up and end up without anyone – I don't know how to just let things *be.*

I'm so scared of being on the outside again that I force myself into the middle, at any cost.

And that's why I lost India.

The box is rattling so hard I'm worried Jasper can physically hear it too. I'm leaning all the weight I have on it: desperately trying to keep it shut.

"Harriet," Jasper says as I start anxiously ripping my fingernails apart with my teeth, "you don't need to make a decision now. I didn't even know you back when it all happened and I never met..."

For the first time in six months, I don't need to change

the subject or pretend I can't hear my friends talking.

He stops himself for me.

"...But I *do* know that life isn't tidy. You can't just neatly lock your heart away so it never gets ripped or crumpled again. Sometimes you need to let yourself get a bit... messy."

I swallow and squeeze my eyes tightly shut.

The big box rattles again.

And again.

And suddenly I can't hold on any more: I don't want to.

It rattles one more time, and – with an enormous bang – there's an explosion of colour: of bright, beautiful reds and blues and greens and yellows and pinks, purples and oranges and golds, until it feels like this time I'm coated in them from the inside out.

I don't want to live without colour.

I don't want to live without love, without joy, without adventure, without excitement, without surprises.

Without everything that makes life *bright*.

I don't want to lock it all away inside me; to control everything so it's all in order. I don't want the people around me to do what I say, when I say it: to always be and feel what I'm expecting them to.

I don't want to keep pencilling in the lines of my life

before it's even happened.

To give it an outline to follow.

I want to colour it in with mess, with beauty, with brightness. With a hundred million shades that exist if I can just relax enough to see them.

If I can just finally let go.

With my eyes still closed, I take a deep breath.

Gently, I touch the box in my head: the box stuffed full of everything that has ever hurt me.

Of everything that might.

The box that isn't actually real, and can't open or shut or explode or rattle or lock or *do* anything other than sit there inanimately in my head, like the extended metaphor it is.

But that I keep relying on so heavily anyway.

And I make my final decision.

Swallowing, I wait patiently until it stops shaking.

I say thank you for being there when I was so sad and lonely.

For giving me the strength I needed.

Then I pick the box up with both hands.

And push it out of my head forever.

"So…" I say, finally opening my eyes again. "Jasper

King." I can feel myself starting to glow. "Are you saying that you are or could be one of the *many* boys who may have recently smacked their head on the floor next to my cloak?"

His nose twitches. "Harriet…"

"Are you saying – I don't know – that you think I'm actually *hilarious* and adorable as a can of tomato soup?"

"Of course not," he says with questionable conviction.

"And I just want to check: can I confirm that you have been totally and utterly overwhelmed by my seductive strategies?"

He smiles. "Shut up, Harriet."

"OK," I agree, laughing. "I'm shutting up now."

And I lean forward and kiss him.

95

Here's a list of Things I Was Not Expecting Today:

- I was not expecting to keep kissing Jasper until my lips start tingling and my head starts spinning and my ears start going numb.

- I was not expecting to want to do it again, and again, and then maybe a fourth time.

- I did not expect to find myself walking down the road towards home, publicly holding Jasper King's hand.

- And I definitely did not expect to love every single second of it.

But you know what?

It feels kind of nice, not knowing what's going to happen for once. Not being in control. Not feeling so sure

how the story is going to end.

In fact, I think I'm really going to embrace this spontaneity thing. From now on, I am a chilled-out creature of impulse; an airy nomad of spur-of-the-moment decision-making.

Floating like a feather, drifting like a bird.

Maintaining flight without flapping my wings: using hot-air currents with my specially locked tendons, like an albatross, or a pelican, or the red-billed…

"Do you think Rin and Toby are going to be all right?" I blurt, stopping on the pavement. "What if something goes wrong? What if they don't blow all the candles out? What if they lock themselves in? Or out? Maybe we should go back and…"

Jasper lifts his eyebrows at me.

"…is something somebody *else* might say," I finish smoothly. "Not me. I, the new improved anti-control-freak Harriet Manners, would say hey, why don't they just spontaneously melt the whole place to the ground? Just for fun?"

Maybe I'll send Toby a text.

"Speaking of melting," Jasper says as we carry on walking towards my house, hand in hand, "what happened to that Icarus statue I made you last year? I don't think I ever saw it again."

Fudge nuggets. I was really hoping he'd forgotten about that.

"It's in the shed," I admit with an ashamed face. "With a blanket over its head. To –" *stop it freaking out my dad* – "keep it warm and protected from the elements."

"Under a *blanket*?" Jasper winces. "Ouch. Ancient Greek burn. Maybe I'll just take it back."

"Please don't," I grin. "I really love it. Although in fairness, there was nowhere else to put it. That thing is *enormous.*"

"Next time I'll make you a tealight holder."

I laugh and we turn the corner into my road, still holding hands. This is going to *really* shock my parents. I told them I was never, ever dating again as long as I lived and I'm pretty sure they believed me.

At least, they definitely said they did.

"You know," I say as we reach our gate, "the Ancient Greeks wouldn't eat beans because they thought they had the souls of the dead inside th—"

There's a pink VW Beetle parked in the driveway, which means Annabel and Bunty must have returned while I was out.

But that's not why I've stopped talking.

On the middle of the doorstep right outside our front door is a very large pair of sparkly orange, yellow and blue striped shoes.

"What…" I say in confusion. "Whose are those? I don't know anyone who would wear these, apart from…"

The air suddenly shoots out of me.

In 2011, Shogun Rua registered the hardest punch ever recorded with a right fist acceleration of 25mph and 1169lbs of force, and it feels like he just took a shot at my windpipe.

…Apart from *Wilbur.*

Why would he be here? Unless…

No.

No. No no no no no no no no no no.

No no no no no no NONONONO NO NO NO NO.

"What's going on?" Jasper says as I drop his hand and race towards the house.

There isn't time to explain.

Because I knew it was all going to come out eventually: that at some point – after the hundreds of lies I've told in the last few weeks – I'd get my comeuppance.

I just didn't realise it would be *now.*

96

I know I tend to read quite a lot into every situation, and look for a deep, hidden meaning that isn't always there.

But the front door's already open.

I am in *so* much trouble.

"Stop!" I shout, bursting into the kitchen without even pausing to take off my shoes. "Whatever anyone is saying or revealing or about to say or reveal, please just stop!"

Then I pause and frown.

Wilbur's seated at the kitchen table, wearing a vivid yellow leather jacket, an orange shirt, pink trousers and some kind of red PVC cowboy hat.

Bunty's sat opposite him, decked out in a faded pink waistcoat covered in bells and a long violet dress with mirrors all over it. Annabel's between them, looking tanned and much less tired in a black pinstripe suit, and Dad's opposite her: in a Batman T-shirt and jeans.

Tabby's squidged on Dad's lap in the carrot onesie Rin

bought her (it's orange and has little green spikes coming out of the hood).

This is like the weirdest Fellowship of the Rings *ever*.

"Hello, Harriet," Annabel says calmly, gesturing at the portentously empty seat next to her. "Why don't you sit down? And hello to you too, Jasper. Please feel free to join us."

"Plop yourselves down," Dad confirms.

"Plant your *derrieres*," Wilbur says cheerfully.

"I *love* your flying squirrel trousers, darling," Bunty adds warmly. "I have a pair in blue *just* like them."

Why are they being so nice?

What kind of horror are they planning for me that requires easing in?

"I think I'll stand," I say carefully. They're not going to catch me *that* easily. "There are some things I need to tell you first."

And then I will prepare to run.

I glance quickly down at my feet. Nat's wrong: there *is* a time and a place for rubber shoes, and it's right *now*.

"Take a seat, Harriet," Annabel says again more firmly. "That is not a question."

Flushing, I give Jasper a quick glance that says *I'm sorry you had to see this, please don't think less of me.*

He gives a warm one back that says *I've got your back.*

Then I perch awkwardly on the edge of my seat.

"Right," I say, taking an enormous breath. "So here's what happened…"

"You forged a legal contract, faked a sick note, skipped school yet again, took your infant sister on a shoot for *Vogue* then ran away to India on another one while pretending to be in Norfolk," Annabel says without batting an eyelid. "Yes, I've just heard."

Sugar cookies.

They've obviously sat here, piecing together my horrendous litany of untruths between them.

"Well," I say, picking at a biscuit, "it doesn't sound *so* bad when you put it like that."

There's a silence.

A silence so long you could put it into a swimming pool and whizz down it, should you be interested in making slides out of silences.

Yup: I'm definitely grounded.

Until I'm seventy, at which point I'll be locked up in a retirement home to keep future generations safe from my meddling too.

"OK," I sigh, closing my eyes. "Please let me know – on a scale of one to ten – roughly how bad my punishment's going to be so I can prepare myself first."

"Have a cookie," Annabel says unexpectedly. "I made them myself, fifteen minutes ago."

I open one eye out of curiosity. Annabel is indeed holding out a plate of somethings that seem to be cookie-*shaped*.

Some of them are a little bit burnt. After last year's dinosaur efforts, clearly horrible biscuit-making runs in the family too.

"*So that's a ten of punishment,*" Dad whispers loudly. "Maybe even an *eleven*."

Annabel play-punches him on the arm.

I blink at the cookies suspiciously. Something very bad is *definitely* about to happen.

That's why they're trying to alter my blood sugar first.

"Wilbur actually just came here to tell us that the bank account details you gave him aren't working," Annabel continues lightly. "Do you happen to know anything about that?"

Oh…

"I won't give bank details over the phone, emu-wombat, so I had to come in person," he explains. "You just *never* know when the FBI are listening."

"Umm," I say, staring at the table, "the bank details I gave you don't work because I gave you the wrong numbers."

"You silly baby-koala," Wilbur says, patting my hand affectionately. "I can't transfer the money you've made over to you without them."

"I know," I say, shrugging. "That's kind of the point."

There's another silence.

And when I eventually look up, Wilbur's face has gone bright pink and is wobbling so hard he looks like he's made entirely of jelly.

"Ah," Annabel says with a knowing nod. "*There's* the missing piece. I knew we'd find it somewhere."

Dad puts a gentle hand on top of my head.

"How did you…" Wilbur says after a few seconds of even wobblier facial expressions. "What did you… Who told you that… No. I can't take your money, muffin. I *won't* take it."

"Yes," Annabel says firmly. "You will."

Wilbur glances at her in confusion, then at Dad – who nods as well – then at Bunty.

"Take the money, darling," she says serenely. "Harriet made it for you. Karmically, it's yours."

For a few seconds, Wilbur looks like he's about to either cry or explode with happiness.

Then he sits up straight and grabs both my hands.

"Baby-baby panda, you're the best fairy godmother a fairy godmother could ever have. Thank you."

And I smile, because he didn't need to say it.

The millions of colours that make up Wilbur have started flooding back.

That's all I wanted to see.

97

I guess it just goes to show.

Sometimes a tiny bit of plan-making and scheduling and itinerating and meddling isn't such a bad thing.

Maybe I won't stop *all* of it.

I mean, with my epic organisational skills it would kind of be a waste, wouldn't it?

Exactly.

"So does this mean I'm not in trouble?" I check, standing up again. "I'd just like it confirmed that this time I've absolutely got away with everything."

"Oh, we're going to distribute punishment," Annabel says casually. "Little by little. Here and there. When you least expect it. Make no mistake about that, Harriet."

"Maybe one morning you'll wake up," Dad agrees, narrowing his eyes, "and BANG. No cornflakes."

Annabel nods. "Maybe one day I'll take the lid off your favourite marker pen and just… I don't know.

440

Leave it off."

"We might arrange some kind of family day out,"
Dad says flippantly. "Walking. Really far. For no reason.
Up mountains. With no mobile reception."

"You may come home and find that your books are
no longer alphabetised or even genre-ised."

"It's going to be a long-drawn-out torture, darling
girl." Dad high-fives Annabel. "We can't *wait.*"

Noooooooooooooooooooooooooo.

"Now remain seated," Annabel smiles, tapping the
chair. "We have something else to talk to you about."

Bat poop.

I really thought I was out of the woods there.

I give Jasper and Tabitha a terrified glance and slide
back into the chair again.

"I actually came for two reasons, baby-baby
kookaburra," Wilbur says, leaning forward. "A rather
smashalazing opportunity has just popped up like a mole
in one of those computer games, so I came to run it
by your two unfairly pretty parents first and see if they
wanted to smack it with a hammer."

"In person," Dad says, raising his eyebrows. "In case
you pretended to be us on the phone."

"Or forged our signatures again," Annabel agrees.
"Or maybe tried to steal our baby."

"Or just went ahead and got on the plane anyway."

Yeah: I definitely haven't got away with anything.

"S-smashalazing?" I say, grabbing on to the only bit I can justifiably repeat. "W-what opportunity? Is it another job?"

"It's close but no potato," Wilbur grins. "A foreign agency has asked me to loan your prodigious sparkliness to them for a few weeks, possum. They've been watching your ascent for a while and we think this could be what tips you into Supermodel-land."

"But…" I kind of thought I'd finished ticking off the How to Be a Perfect Model list. "Don't I have school?"

"*Now* she has school," Dad laughs. "The last three days while she was in India and last week, not so much. But *now* she has school."

"It's the Easter Holidays next week, sweetheart," Annabel reminds me. "So you're not going to miss any, as long as you promise to take your revision with you and do it while you're out there."

"And I've said I'll come with you," Bunty says jubilantly. "We're going to get into *all* sorts of mischief and mayhem, darling."

Annabel frowns at her.

"By which I mean *no sorts of trouble at all*," Bunty beams. "Definitely no arrests. The government will not throw us out, I promise."

I turn to look at Jasper.

He's leaning against the kitchen counter: completely unfazed by the showdown that's just happened in front of him. He looks so handsome, with his bronze hair and square jaw and bright eyes.

I was kind of hoping I could spend the holidays hanging out with him.

"I'm not sure…" I say slowly, turning back. "I have quite a few awesome plans here."

I was about to go upstairs and make them into laminated things of permanence. And then not use them, obviously. Just store them in my wardrobe.

Maybe bind them, in case of a planning emergency.

"OK," Annabel says nonchalantly. "So do you want to let Nat know you're not going or shall we?"

I freeze. "Nat? What's Nat got to do with it?"

"We thought she could go with you too. We've already checked it with her mum."

"My treat," Bunty adds. "A little holiday for the two of you."

One in 10,000 people are born with their organs reversed or 'mirrored' from their normal, expected positions.

It suddenly feels like all of mine are suddenly flipping

over too.

My brain included.

A *holiday*? I get to go on holiday with *Nat*?

The best, wisest, coolest person in the entire world, and my non-kissing soulmate? The girl who has been so busy with college that I've barely seen her for the past month?

With a squeak, I jump out of my seat. "*Really*?"

"And Rin is going to extend her stay in England – she's just landed a big modelling contract in London so we're going to look after her a little longer while she shoots it," Annabel adds. "She can stay in your room and, erm... *look after* Victor."

Annabel makes quotation marks with her fingers again.

I blink at them. Rin landed the *Vogue* jeans editorial for Wilbur?

So my epic plan actually *worked*?

Also, that means she gets to spend a little longer with Toby?

I couldn't have arranged this better myself.

I know because I definitely tried.

"Plus, I won't be around quite so much," Dad adds with a little twinkle. "You'll never believe it, but my old advertising agency have offered me a freelance contract, with a view to a permanent one. They said something about not being able to live without my killer slogans. I'm going to be *very* busy being an uncontrollable creative genius again."

We beam at each other. Dad Happiness Goal: TICK.

My head is starting to whirl.

A brand-new modelling agency. A new country. An all-expenses-paid holiday with my best friend and awesome grandmother.

But –

"Go," Jasper says firmly from the corner as I spin round to look at him. "It's only two weeks, Harriet. You shouldn't even be deliberating. I'll be here when you get back, with an extra helping of specially burnt biscuits."

I grin gratefully. I like him *so* much.

My phone beeps.

ARE WE GOING ARE WE GOING ARE WE GOING ARE WE GOING ARE WE GOING ARE WE

I laugh and it beeps again.

ARE WE GOING ARE WE GOING ARE WE GOING ARE WE GOING SAY WE'RE GOING SAY WE'RE

Then a third time.

ARE WE GOING ARE WE GOING ARE WE GOING ARE WE

And I can feel the colours inside me: exploding like a rainbow.

The truth is, some people may see a million shades, others may see one hundred million, but we're all wrong. There are actually an *infinite* number of colours in the Universe, and there is no limit to what we are capable of seeing if we are brave enough to open our eyes.

The colours are there in front of us, and we can shade our lives as brightly as we like.

Smiling, I send Nat this:

WE'RE GOING x

Then I look up.

"OK," I say, ready to burst with happiness. "So where are we off to?"

Bunty smiles. "Australia."

I guess this story isn't quite over yet after all.

Acknowledgements

Thanks first to my wonderful agent, Kate Shaw. You have stuck by both Harriet and me with unwavering dedication and affection from the start, and this series wouldn't exist without you. I will always be grateful.

Thanks to my editor Lizzie Clifford: the genius wizard behind the curtain that my readers can't see, but who is so essential to the magic in my books. I am a better writer (and more of a geek) because of you.

Thanks to Ruth Alltimes, an integral and beloved part of the Geek Girl universe, to Lily Morgan for her eagle-like copy-editing eye, and to Kate Clarke, Elisabetta Barbazza and Mary Kate McDevitt for their wonderful and frankly iconic front covers. Thanks, as always, to the whole of Team Geek at HarperCollins: to Rachel, Hannah, Nicola, Paul, Simon, Sam, Carla, Alison, Geraldine, Sonia, Catherine, Mary, Camilla and Jo. I remain in awe of how tirelessly and creatively you work to bring Harriet to the world.

Finally, thanks to my amazing family: Mum, Dad, Tara, Dan, Grandad, Grandma, Lesley, Judith, Robin, Lorraine, Veronique, Caroline, Louise, Adrien, Vincent, Freya, Ellen, Mayne, Dixie, Buddy, Handsome and Ghost.

You are the rock this castle is built on.

Thank you. x

DON'T MISS THE FINAL

GEEK GIRL

COMING SOON!

And read on for a sneak peek of

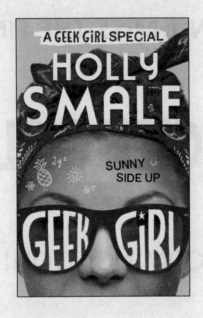

1

My name is Harriet Manners and I am hyper.

Genki is a Japanese word that means *high energy, full of beans* or *peppy*, and I know it fits me perfectly because I haven't slept properly in six whole days.

Frankly, I haven't *needed* to.

I'm so super-charged, I'm basically a worker ant: grabbing hundreds of tiny minute-long power naps just to keep me performing as normal.

Trust me: I've got the data.

Thanks to the awesome new Sleep App on my phone, I've been able to track my nocturnal activities in detail. Statistically the average teenager needs 8.5 hours of decent rest per night, but – according to my sleep graphs – my deep sleep states have been dropping steadily for the last 144.3 hours.

Last night, in fact, I officially got no hours of proper sleep at all.

Not a single wink, let alone forty.

So it's pretty lucky that today I am firing on *all cylinders.* Giraffes can go weeks without napping, and I can only assume that I must be able to do the same now too.

Seriously: I am *buzzing.*

"*And,*" I continue, stabbing a finger at the magazine in front of me, "it says here that the tunnel includes six thousand tonnes of railway tracks, which is the same weight as two thousand elephants! Isn't that cool?"

I blink at buildings rushing past the window.

"At its deepest point, it runs seventy-five metres below sea level, which is the same as 107 baguettes on top of each other! Crazy, huh?"

Frowning, I click my biro rapidly in and out again with tiny *snaps* and make a little note next to this fact. "How many fish could you get into that space, do you think? Should I try and calculate it?"

"Oooh!" I add before anyone can answer, pointing

at a squat bird on a wire. "French pigeon!"

It's been a pretty exciting journey already.

Eleven in the morning, having departed London just two hours ago, and I've already completed three Sudoku puzzles, learnt three new foreign phrases and filled out my entire crossword book in pen. I didn't even bother pencilling it in first: that's how fired-up I'm feeling.

"*Plus*," I say, my jiggling leg bumping up and down repeatedly, "did you know that the Channel Tunnel is the longest under-sea tunnel *in the world*? Doesn't that just completely blow your—"

"Harriet?" a loud voice says from some way behind me. "Treacle-top, who the fiddlesticks are you talking to?"

I blink a few times.

Then – with a lurch of surprise – I spin round.

My modelling agent Wilbur is standing at the other end of the packed Eurostar train carriage wearing a fluffy green jumper covered in sequins, a pale lilac scarf covered with pink rabbits and neon-yellow trousers.

In one hand is a tray with two hot drinks on it and in the other is an enormous golden croissant.

Blankly, I turn to the seat next to me.

There's a large purple suitcase with a bright blue fake-fur coat draped over it and a wide-brimmed, orange-feathered hat perched on top.

Oh my God: you have *got* to be kidding me.

At what precise point in this conversation did Wilbur get up and go to the buffet car without me?

Exactly how long have I been publicly monologuing at a pile of accessories?

Ugh. Up to now, the jellyfish was the largest animal on the planet without a brain.

I think we have a new winner.

"Umm," I stammer as the young French couple behind me start quietly giggling. *Cover your tracks, Harriet.* "Hey there, Wilbur. I was just reading this magazine to the… uh… pigeon outside. He looked… lonely."

"Well of course he does, darling," Wilbur agrees chirpily, swinging into the spare seat opposite. "They're the rats of the sky, and who wants to date that?"

Then he holds out one of the coffees from the tray, pauses slightly and swings it back again. "On second thoughts, poodle, I think you've had *quite* enough caffeine for one morning. You're starting to look like the victim at the start of a horror movie."

Typical. First you're given caffeine for the second time in your entire life, and then you're suddenly being cut off at the source with no explanation at all.

I might be shaking and sweating slightly from the end of my nose, but I am *fine.*

Wilbur puts a gentle hand on my still-kicking foot until it stops, calmly takes my still-clicking pen off me and puts the Eurostar magazine away, from where I'm now folding and unfolding the corners repeatedly.

"*Breathe,* possum," Wilbur smiles, patting my hand and proffering the golden croissant instead. "You've got this, munchkin, and you're not a baby mouse: there's no need to take in oxygen that fast."

I swallow and stare out of the train window as we rush past another French station and one more surge of adrenaline, fear, apprehension and excitement blasts through me. I never said what *kind* of energy I've been packed to the brim with all week, did I?

Nervous, mainly.

Include the significant quantities of central nervous system stimulating methylxanthine alkaloid I've imbibed this morning (caffeine), and I'm basically powering off raw natural chemicals like a sleep-deprived rocket.

I'm fine I'm fine I'm fine I'm—

"*Mesdames et messieurs*," a calm female voice says as the Eurostar begins to pull into the enormous, cathedral-like Gard du Nord. "*Je l'espère vous avez eu un voyage agréable. S'il vous plaît que vous prenez vos bagages avec vous. Bienvenue a Paris.*"

And that's the *main* reason I haven't been able to sleep solidly for over a hundred and forty hours.

Why I've been lying on my back, staring at the glow-in-the-dark galaxy on my ceiling while my brain spins in tight little circles, like a dying neutron star.

Three little words, three long days, one huge city.

Yup.

I'm doing *Paris Fashion Week*.

To be continued . . .

See how it all began...

Harriet Manners knows a lot of things.

* Cats have 32 muscles in each ear
* Bluebirds can't see the colour blue
* The average person laughs 15 times per day
* Peanuts are an ingredient in dynamite

But she doesn't know why nobody at school seems to like her. So when she's offered the chance to reinvent herself, Harriet grabs it. Can she transform from geek to chic?

The geek is back!

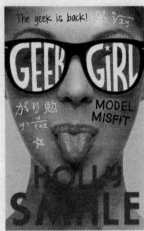

Harriet Manners also knows:

* Humans have 70,000 thoughts per day
* Caterpillars have four thousand muscles
* The average person eats a ton of food a year
* Being a Geek + Model = a whole new set of
graffiti on your belongings

But clearly she knows nothing about boys. And on a
whirlwind modelling trip to Tokyo, Harriet would
trade in everything she's ever learnt for just the
faintest idea of what she's supposed to do next…

Geek girl goes Stateside...

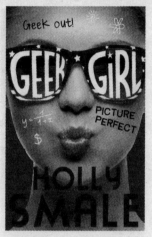

Harriet Manners knows a lot of facts:

* New York is the most populous city
in the United States
* its official motto is 'Ever Upward'
* 27% of Americans believe we never
landed on the moon

But she has no idea about modelling Stateside. Or,
even more importantly, what to do when the big
romantic gestures aren't coming from her boyfriend...

The original geek returns...

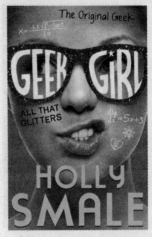

Harriet Manners has high hopes for the new school year: she's a Sixth Former now, and things are going to be different. But with Nat busy falling in love at college and Toby preoccupied with a Top Secret project, Harriet soon discovers that's not necessarily a good thing. . .

A romantic festive GEEK GIRL special!

Harriet Manners knows a lot about winter.

* She knows that every Christmas Santa
climbs down 91.8 million chimneys
* She knows that snow isn't white,
it just looks that way
* She knows that Rudolph the red-nosed
reindeer was almost definitely a girl

But Harriet's favourite season is extra special this year
because four days ago she had her First Ever Kiss.

Now she just needs to work out what's supposed to
happen next...

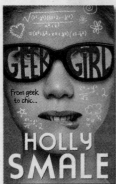